THE
INQUISITOR'S
APPRENTICE

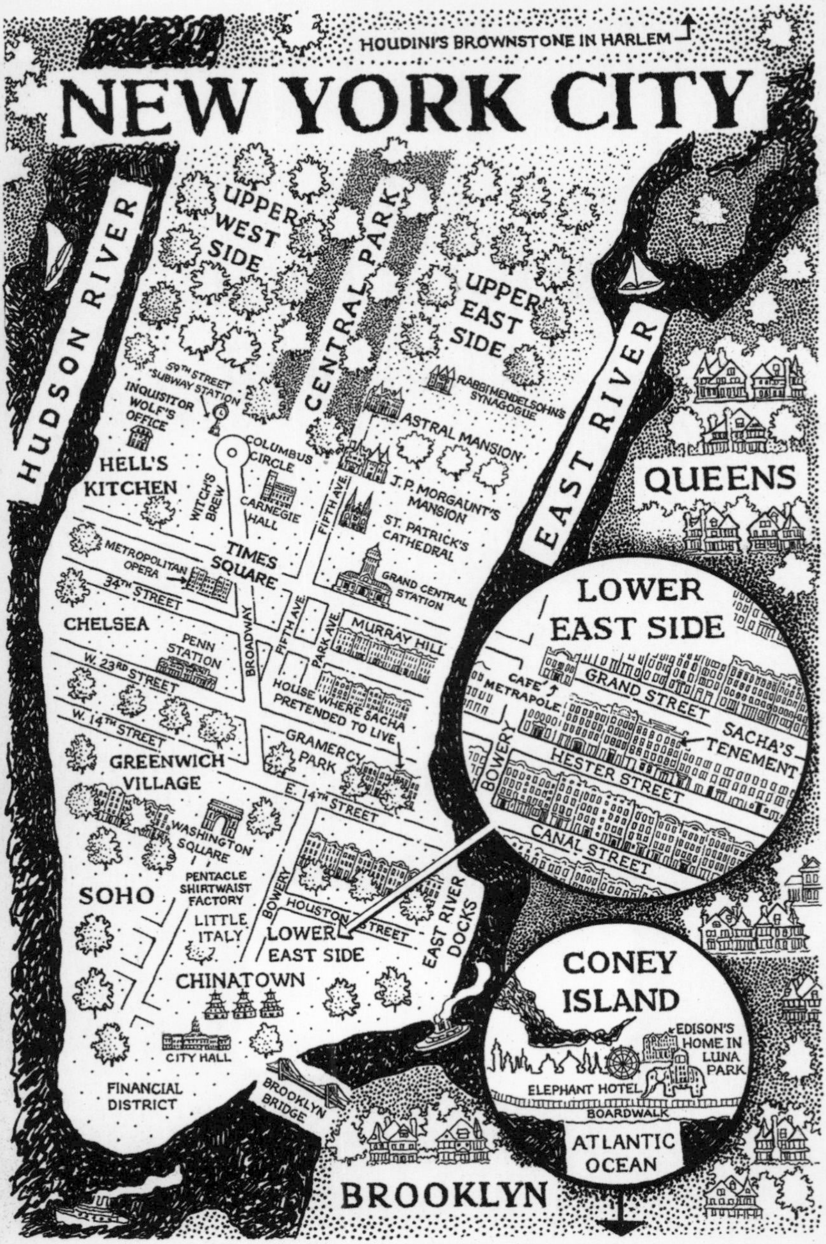
HOUDINI'S BROWNSTONE IN HARLEM
NEW YORK CITY
HUDSON RIVER
UPPER WEST SIDE
CENTRAL PARK
UPPER EAST SIDE
EAST RIVER
59TH STREET SUBWAY STATION
INQUISITOR WOLF'S OFFICE
RABBI MENDELSOHN'S SYNAGOGUE
ASTRAL MANSION
COLUMBUS CIRCLE
HELL'S KITCHEN
WITCH'S BREW
CARNEGIE HALL
FIFTH AVE
J.P. MORGAUNT'S MANSION
ST. PATRICK'S CATHEDRAL
QUEENS
METROPOLITAN OPERA
TIMES SQUARE
GRAND CENTRAL STATION
34TH STREET
CHELSEA
BROADWAY
FIFTH AVE
PARK AVE
MURRAY HILL
PENN STATION
W. 23RD STREET
HOUSE WHERE SACHA PRETENDED TO LIVE
W. 14TH STREET
GRAMERCY PARK
GREENWICH VILLAGE
E. 14TH STREET
WASHINGTON SQUARE
PENTACLE SHIRTWAIST FACTORY
SOHO
LITTLE ITALY
BOWERY
HOUSTON STREET
LOWER EAST SIDE
EAST RIVER DOCKS
CHINATOWN
CITY HALL
FINANCIAL DISTRICT
BROOKLYN BRIDGE
BROOKLYN
LOWER EAST SIDE
CAFE' METRAPOLE
GRAND STREET
BOWERY
SACHA'S TENEMENT
HESTER STREET
CANAL STREET
CONEY ISLAND
EDISON'S HOME IN LUNA PARK
ELEPHANT HOTEL
BOARDWALK
ATLANTIC OCEAN

THE INQUISITOR'S APPRENTICE

CHRIS MORIARTY

ILLUSTRATIONS BY

MARK EDWARD GEYER

sandpiper

HOUGHTON MIFFLIN HARCOURT
Boston   New York

The text of this book is set in 13-point Mrs. Eaves.

The Library of Congress has cataloged the hardcover edition as follows:
Moriarty, Chris, 1968–.
The inquistor's apprentice / Chris Moriarty ; illustrations by Mark
Edward Geyer.
p. cm.
Summary: In early twentieth-century New York, Sacha Kessler's ability
to see witches earns him an apprenticeship to the police department's
star Inquisitor, Maximillian Wolf, to help stop magical crime, and with
fellow apprentice Lily Astral, Sacha investigates who is trying to kill
Thomas Edison, whose mechanical witch detector could unleash the
worst witch-hunt in American history.
[1. Magic—Fiction. 2. Witches—Fiction. 3. Apprentices—Fiction.
4. Gangs—Fiction. 5. Jews—New York (State)—New York—Fiction.
6. Edison, Thomas A. (Thomas Alva), 1847–1931—Fiction.
7. New York (N.Y.)—History—20th century—Fiction.
8. Mystery and detective stories.] I. Geyer, Mark, ill. II. Title.
PZ7.M
[Fic]—dc22
2011009596

ISBN: 978-0-547-58135-4 hardcover
ISBN: 978-0-547-85084-9 paperback

Manufactured in the United States of America
DOC 10 9 8 7 6 5 4 3 2 1
4590305163

To Grandma and Grandpa—
and all the friends and family
who made sitting around their kitchen table
so special

CHAPTER ONE

The Boy Who Could See Witches

THE DAY SACHA found out he could see witches was the worst day of his life.

It started out as a perfectly ordinary Friday afternoon—if you could ever call Friday afternoons on Hester Street ordinary.

People said there were more human beings per square mile on New York's Lower East Side than in the Black Hole of Calcutta, and Sacha thought it must be true. The roar of all those people was like the surf of a mighty ocean. You could hear them working and eating, talking and praying, running the sewing machines that clattered away from dawn to dusk in the windows of every tenement building. You could feel their dreams crackling along the cobblestones like the electricity in the big transformers down at Thomas Edison's Pearl Street power station. And you could feel the shivery static charge of their magic—both the legal and the illegal kind.

Not that anyone was worried about illegal magic at half

past four on a Friday afternoon. Fridays on Hester Street were only about one thing: shopping.

Pushcarts packed every inch of pavement from the East River Docks to the Bowery. Mobs of housewives jostled and hollered, desperate to get their *Shabbes* shopping done before sunset. Salesmen cut through the crowd like sharks, hunting for customers to cajole, bully, or physically drag into their basement storefronts. Pack peddlers and day-old-bread sellers battled for space in the gutter, each one bellowing at the top of his lungs that his wares were cheaper, better tasting, and better for you than anyone else's.

Every piece of food had to be sold now, before the whole Lower East Side shut down for *Shabbes*. After that the city closed all the stores on Sunday to make sure the *goyim* stayed sober for church. And after that . . . well, if you had anything left to sell on Monday, you might as well just throw it out. Because no Jewish housewife was ever in a million years going to feed *her* family three-day-old anything.

Most Fridays, Sacha's mother got off work at the Pentacle Shirtwaist Factory just in time to race home, grab the week's savings out of the pickle jar behind the stove, and dash back outside half an hour before sunset.

That was when the real craziness began.

You'd think a woman with only half an hour to do three days' worth of grocery shopping wouldn't have time to haggle. But if you thought that, you didn't know Ruthie Kessler. Sacha's mother went shopping like a general goes to war. Her weapons were a battered shopping basket, a blistering tongue, and a fistful of pennies. And her children were her foot soldiers.

Sacha and his older sister, Bekah, would sprint up and down Hester Street, ducking around knees and elbows and dodging within a hair's breadth of oncoming traffic. They'd visit every shop, every pushcart, every pack peddler. They'd race back to their mother to report on the state of the enemy's battle lines. And then Mrs. Kessler would issue her orders and dole out her pennies:

"Three cents for an onion? That's *meshuga*! Tell Mr. Kaufmann no one else is charging more than two!"

"What do you mean you're not sure how fresh Mrs. Lieberman's tomatoes are? Are you my son, or aren't you? Go back and *squeeze* them!"

"All right, all right! Tell Mr. Rabinowitz you'll take the herring. But if he chops the head off like he did last week, I'm sending it back. I never buy a fish until I see the whites of its eyes!"

This Friday the shopping seemed like it would never end. But at last the sun sank toward the Bowery. The shouting faded, and the crowds began to break up and drift away. Mrs. Kessler looked upon her purchases and found them good—or at least as good as a hardworking Jewish mother was willing to admit that anything in this wicked world could be.

"We've got a few minutes," she told her children as they hefted their overflowing baskets and began to stagger home. "Let's stop off at Mrs. Lassky's bakery for some *rugelach*."

"No thanks," Bekah said. "I'm not hungry. And anyway I have homework."

Mrs. Kessler watched her daughter go with narrowed eyes, fingering the little silver locket she always wore around her neck. "So secretive," she murmured. "You'd almost think . . . well, never mind. It's a mystery what girls want these days."

It might be a mystery what Bekah wanted, but there was no mistaking what the girls lining up outside Mrs. Lassky's bakery were after. The big English sign over the door said LASSKY & DAUGHTERS KOSHER BAKED GOODS. But that sign was only there to fool the cops. And since there was no such thing as a Jewish Inquisitor in the New York City Police Department, the handwritten Hebrew signs taped to the shop window made no bones about what was really for sale inside:

NOSH ON THIS!
OUR
DELICIOUSLY EFFICACIOUS
KNISHES
ARE GUARANTEED TO
GET ANY GIRL MARRIED WITHIN THE YEAR
(MULTIPLE DOSES MAY BE REQUIRED
IN SPECIAL CASES)

STOP SAYING "OY VEY!"
START SAYING "OYTZER!"
ONE BITE OF OUR
MYSTERIOUSLY MONOGAMOUS
MARZIPAN
WILL MAKE HIM YOURS FOREVER!

TIRED OF WAITING FOR HER
TO MAKE UP HER MIND?

HAVE A MOTHER-IN-LATKE
YOU PICK THE PERFECT SON-IN-LAW,
WE DO THE REST!

Sacha had never quite understood *why* magic was illegal in America. He just knew that it was. And that his mother and practically every other housewife on Hester Street cheerfully ignored the law whenever disapproving husbands and fathers—not to mention the NYPD Inquisitors—were safely elsewhere.

Luckily, though, Sacha didn't have to worry about that. He'd made it all the way through his *bar mitzvah* without showing an ounce of magical talent—and he couldn't have been happier about it.

Inside Mrs. Lassky's tiny shop, the air was thick with magic. Customers packed every nook and cranny like pickled herring. Half of them were shouting out orders, the other half were trying to pay, and they were all yammering away at each other like gossip was about to be outlawed tomorrow. Behind the counter, the Lassky twins scurried back and forth under drifting clouds of pastry flour. Mrs. Lassky sat at the ornate cash register accepting cash, compliments—and, yes, even the occasional complaint.

"Do you see anything on that sign about a perfect *husband?*" she was saying as Sacha and his mother finally reached the front of the line. "A perfect son-in-law I can deliver. But a perfect husband? There is no such thing!"

The other women waiting in line at the counter began chiming in one after another.

"She's right, *bubeleh*! Show me a woman with a perfect husband, and I'll show you a widow!"

"Perfect, shmerfect! Take it from me, sweetie. If it's after ten in the morning and he's not drunk, he's perfect!"

When Mrs. Lassky caught sight of Sacha, she leaned over the counter and pinched him on both cheeks. "So handsome you're getting, just like your Uncle Mordechai! But skinny! We need to fatten you up a little. How about a nice hot Make-Her-Challah-for-You? Not that you need any luck with the ladies." She pinched his cheeks again for good measure. "Sooo adorable!"

"No thanks," Sacha said, blushing furiously and wiping flour off his face. "Just a *rugelach*. And plain's fine."

"Well, if you change your mind, remember I've got two lovely daughters."

"Speaking of daughters," Sacha's mother said ominously, "I'll have a Mother-in-Latke."

"Oh, Ruthie, you've got nothing to worry about. Your Bekah's the prettiest girl on Hester Street."

"Kayn aynhoreh!" Mrs. Kessler muttered, making the sign to ward off the evil eye. "And anyway she's as stubborn as a mule. You should hear the wild ideas she's picking up at night school." Mrs. Kessler made it sound as if you could catch ideas like you caught head lice. "Do you know what she told

me the other day? That marriage is just a bourgeois convention. I could've *schreied*!"

"Well," Mrs. Lassky said, "I don't know anything about bourgeois convection. But I *do* know about son-in-laws. Come here, girls! And bring the latkes so I can make one up special for Mrs. Kessler!"

Sacha's mother squinted at the tray of steaming hot latkes. "Hmm. I could do with a little less handsome. Handsome is as handsome does—and it doesn't do much after the wedding night. And while you're at it, why don't you add a dash of frugality and another shake or two of work ethic?"

"Your mother," Mrs. Lassky told Sacha, "is a wise woman."

And then she did it.

Whatever *it* was.

Something flimmered over her head, like the hazy halo that blossomed around street lamps on foggy nights. Sacha guessed it must be what people called an aura. Except that the word *aura* sounded all mysterious and scientific. And the flimmery light around Mrs. Lassky and her latkes just looked grandmotherly and frazzled, and a little silly and, well . . . a lot like Mrs. Lassky herself.

"What did you just do?" he asked her.

"Nothing, sweetie. Don't worry your curly head about it."

"But you *did* something. Something magi—*ow!*"

Sacha's mother had just kicked him hard in the shin.

"Why'd you kick me?" he yelped, hopping up and down on one foot.

"Don't fib," his mother snapped. "Nobody likes a liar!"

Later Sacha would wonder how he could have been so stupid. But at the time, he was too outraged to hear the bell tinkling over the bakery's front door. Or to see Mrs. Lassky's mouth falling open in horror. Or to notice the crowd behind him parting like the Red Sea for Moses.

"I am not a liar!" he insisted. "I *saw* it!"

But just as he was about to say what he'd seen, a heavy hand clapped him on the shoulder and spun him around—and he was face-to-face with a New York City Police Department Inquisitor in full uniform.

Sacha's head was about level with the man's belt buckle, so it took what seemed like an eternity for his eyes to travel up the vast expanse of navy blue uniform to the silver badge with the dread word INQUISITOR stamped boldly across it. Above the badge the man's eyes were the crisp blue of a cloudless sky.

"Well now, boyo," the Inquisitor said, taking out his black leather ticket book and checking off the box for MAGIC, ILLEGAL USE OF. "Why don't you tell me just exactly what you saw. And make sure you get it right, 'cause you're going to have to repeat it all to the judge come Monday morning."

CHAPTER TWO

Whose Pig Are You?

THE DISASTER AT Mrs. Lassky's bakery turned Sacha's life completely upside down. Before the month was up, he was yanked out of school, dragged away from all his friends, and subjected to every standardized aptitude test the New York City Police Department could throw at him.

Most of the tests were strange. And some of them were downright pointless—like the one where they had him just sit in a dark room and read spells out loud while some machine whirred away in the background, doubtless recording for posterity his total inability to do magic of any kind.

But the worst was the Inquisitorial Quotient (IQ) test: a five-hour multiple-choice ordeal held in an unheated basement and proctored by a bored-looking Irish girl who made it quite clear that this wasn't her idea of a fun way to spend the weekend. Sacha filled out his answer sheet in a fog of confusion, mostly guessing. In fact, the only thing he really remembered about the test was the pig.

It was a large pig—a Gloucestershire Old Spot, according to the student sitting next to Sacha. And someone turned it loose in the exam room with a sign tied to its back that read

I'm Paddy Doyle's Pig Whose Pig are You?

The sign didn't seem to be strictly necessary, since someone had put a hex on the pig that made it squeal, "Wh-wh-whose pig are you? Wh-wh-whose pig are you?"

The poor animal looked completely bewildered by the situation. Sacha couldn't help laughing along with everyone else, but he was secretly relieved when the bored Irish girl grabbed the sign off its back and broke it in two over one knee. After that the pig just ran around squealing and farting like a normal pig until she chased it out. When she came back, she announced that no extra time would be given—and anyone who failed could go right ahead and blame Paddy Doyle.

Sacha was pretty sure he *had* failed, though he doubted it was the pig's fault. But just when it looked like life on Hester Street was finally getting back to normal, an alarmingly official letter arrived in the mail. It announced that Sacha had been accepted as an Apprentice Inquisitor to the New York City Police Department—and ordered him to report for duty by eight a.m. next Monday morning at the offices of Inquisitor Maximillian Wolf.

"What an honor to have an Inquisitor in the family!" Mo Lehrer told Sacha's mother when she'd read the letter to him for the fortieth time or so. "It's almost as good as a doctor!"

"It's a *mazel*," Mrs. Kessler agreed from her place at one end of the rickety table that filled up half of the Kesslers' kitchen. "A real blessing."

"That's the great thing about America, right? Anything can happen here!" Mo was leaning through the tenement window between the kitchen and the back room. It wasn't a real window, of course—just a hole in the wall. But when the city had passed a law saying that every room in the tenements had to have a window, the landlord had come around and knocked a bunch of holes in the walls and called them windows. Just like the Kesslers called their home a two-room apartment, even though they could only afford to live there by renting out the back room to the Lehrers.

Sacha's mother, who believed in making the best of things, liked to say the Lehrers were just like family. In a way they were, since Mo Lehrer was the *shammes* who swept Grandpa Kessler's little storefront synagogue on Canal Street. Actually, in some ways they were even closer than family. The tenement window between the two rooms had to stay open all the time for the Lehrers to get any fresh air at all, and the Lehrers needed a lot of fresh air because they ran a sweatshop. Day and night Mrs. Lehrer bent over her sewing machine and Mo Lehrer wielded his twenty-pound flatirons as they worked frantically to transform piles of cloth into finished clothing for the uptown department stores. But they always had time to talk to Bekah and Sacha—and to slip them enough candy to set their father muttering about how the Lehrers were spoiling them rotten.

"Isn't that right, Rabbi?" Mo asked Sacha's grandfather. But Grandpa Kessler was snoring happily in the big feather bed that filled up the rest of the Kesslers' kitchen. So Mo turned to Sacha's father instead. "Isn't that right, Danny?"

"Sure," Mr. Kessler agreed without looking up from his copy of Andrew Carbuncle's best-selling memoir, *Wealth Without Magic*. "Only in America."

"You got that right," Sacha's Uncle Mordechai mocked from behind the ink-splotched pages of the *Yiddish Daily Magic-Worker*. "Only in America can Jewish boys grow up to become cogs in the anti-Wiccan machine just like gentiles!"

Uncle Mordechai had been kicked out of Russia for being a Blavatskyan Occulto-Syndicalist—which he considered to be piling insult on top of injury, since he was actually a Trotskyite Anarcho-Wiccanist. Still, the change of continent hadn't altered Mordechai's politics. He devoted his days in New York to writing for a series of bankrupt revolutionary newspapers, acting in the Yiddish People's Theater, and planning the revolution over endless tiny glasses of Russian tea at the Café Metropole.

Mordechai looked like a revolutionary hero too—or at least like the kind of actor who would play one in a Sunday matinee. He was what Sacha's mother called "dashingly handsome." He had long legs and an aristocratic profile and glossy black curls that flopped into his eyes all the time just like

Sacha's did. But while Mordechai's curls looked debonair and sophisticated, Sacha's curls just looked messy. Sacha had tried to figure out what the difference was. He'd even secretly borrowed a little of the Thousand Tigers Pungent Hair Potion that Mordechai got from his favorite Chinatown wizard. But it hadn't helped. Whatever Uncle Mordechai had, you couldn't buy it in a spell bottle.

"At least being an Inquisitor is a job," Sacha's father pointed out, still without looking up from *Wealth Without Magic*. "That's more than some people in this family have. And stop tipping your chair back, Mordechai. We only own three chairs, and you've already broken two of them."

Uncle Mordechai tipped his chair back even farther and crossed his pointy-toed shoes on the kitchen table in a flamboyant manner calculated to convey his unconcern with such mundane matters as chairs. "I have two careers," he proclaimed, tottering on the brink of disaster. "The pen and the stage. And if neither of them is financially remunerative at the moment, I regard this as the fault of an insufficiently artistic world!"

"Never mind that, Mordechai." Sacha's mother leaned over to stir the fragrant pot of matzo ball soup simmering on the stove top and to adjust Grandpa Kessler's cane, which was holding the oven door closed while her bread baked. "The point is, our Sacha's going to be an Inquisitor."

Mrs. Kessler's opinion of Inquisitors had changed completely in the last month. When the Inquisitors had simply been the division of the New York City Police Department responsible for solving magical crimes, she'd thought they were drunken Irish hooligans just like the regular cops. But now that *her* son was going to be an Inquisitor, she wouldn't hear a bad word about them.

"I still don't get it, though," Bekah said skeptically. "Who ever heard of a Jew being an Inquisitor? And why Sacha?"

"Because he's *special!* They said so with their fancy test."

Bekah rolled her eyes. Bekah was sixteen and rolled her eyes often. At the moment she was wedged between Sacha and their grandfather on the feather bed, trying to do her night school homework. As far as Sacha could see, she wasn't making much progress. She'd written out *America is founded upon the principle of the right of the common man to life, liberty, and the pursuit of happiness without interference by magical powers* three times— only to rip it up and start over when their grandfather jostled her elbow and ruined her careful penmanship.

"I'll say he's special!" Grandpa Kessler snorted. The sound of arguing voices had woken him up, and he wasn't about to miss out on an argument, even if it was one the family had already had many times in the last few weeks. "He's the grandson and great-grandson of famous Kabbalists, and what do his magical talents amount to? *Bubkes!*"

"Unless being able to memorize the batting averages of the entire Yankees starting lineup counts as a magical talent," Bekah quipped.

Sacha sighed. He would have liked to argue with Bekah, but she was completely right. If only he could have learned his Torah lines as easily as he learned baseball statistics, his *bar mitzvah* wouldn't have been a public humiliation.

"Never mind that." Mrs. Kessler checked the bread and loaded a little more coal into the stove. As she bent over the stove, her little silver locket swung toward the fire, and she absentmindedly tucked it back into the collar of her worn-out dress. "The main point is that this apprenticeship is a great opportunity for Sacha. Isn't it, Sacha?"

"Uh . . . yeah . . . sure," Sacha mumbled.

But actually he wasn't sure at all. On the one hand, there was the money. It was exciting to imagine himself all grown up and making enough money to move his family out of the tenements and into the wide-open green spaces of Brooklyn. It was nice to picture his mother and sister quitting their jobs at the Pentacle Shirtwaist Factory. Or his father studying all day like the learned man he was instead of wrecking his back hauling slimy barrels of fish at the East River Docks. But on the other hand . . . well . . . did Sacha really want to spend his life writing out Illegal Use of Magic citations and dragging people like Mrs. Lassky off to jail?

He still felt awful about Mrs. Lassky. He'd had no idea she'd get into so much trouble. After all, lots of people used magic—at least when the cops weren't looking. New spells traveled up and down Hester Street as fast as gossip. There were spells to make bread rise and spells to make matzo not rise. Spells to catch husbands and spells to get rid of them. Spells to make your kids listen to your good advice and stay home and study instead of loitering on street corners like gangsters. Even Sacha's mother used magic whenever she was sure her father-in-law wasn't looking. So what had Mrs. Lassky done that was so terrible?

"Sacha?" his father asked. "Are you all right?"

He realized everyone was staring at him. "I . . . I feel kind of bad about Mrs. Lassky."

"Don't worry," his mother said airily. "She just paid a fine."

"And she should have paid a bigger one!" Grandpa Kessler said. "This back-alley witchery is a public disgrace—a *shande far di goyim*! And it's against religion too. As the learned Rabbi Ovadia of Bertinoro said, 'God weeps when women work magic.'"

"Well, maybe God wouldn't have to weep if the men would let women into *shul* to study real Kabbalah," Bekah said tartly.

"Don't talk back to your grandfather, young lady!" Mrs. Kessler snapped.

"What? I'm only saying what you've said a hundred times before—"

"And don't talk back to me either!"

Bekah waited until their mother had turned back to her soup and then looked at Sacha and rolled her eyes again.

"I see you rolling your eyes," their mother told Bekah without even bothering to turn around. "I guess that means you don't want any blintzes this Sunday morning?"

"No! No!" Bekah cried. "I take it back! I unroll my eyes!"

Everyone laughed. Whatever else people said about

Ruthie Kessler—and they said plenty—no one could deny that she made the best blintzes west of Bialystok.

"That's funny," Mrs. Kessler said while everyone else was still laughing. "I thought I had enough water, but I don't. Now where's that bucket got to?"

Sacha sighed and got up to look for the water bucket. But his mother found it first. "I'll go," she told him. "You rest up. You have a big day tomorrow."

"You shouldn't be out alone after dark," Mr. Kessler objected. "If you don't want Sacha to go, then I will."

"You most certainly won't! You've got no business being outside in the rain with that cough of yours!"

"What cough?" Sacha's father snapped as if the mere suggestion that he was sick were a mortal insult. But then he promptly proved her point by coughing.

Mrs. Kessler snorted and stalked out the door, muttering that she'd made it all the way from Russia to the Lower East Side and wasn't about to start being afraid of the dark now.

"Be careful, Ruthie!" Mrs. Lehrer called after her. "I *saw* someone down there the other night!"

No one listened. Mrs. Lehrer was nice—but crazy. Not that anyone ever actually came out and said she was crazy. They just shook their heads sadly and said things like "She came out of the pogroms, poor woman. What can you expect after what she's been through?"

Sacha had worried about this when he was younger. After all, his own parents had survived the pogroms. Did that mean they might go crazy too? But finally he'd decided that Mrs. Lehrer's craziness didn't seem to be catching. Mostly it just amounted to pinching pennies so she could buy her sisters tickets to America and sewing all her savings into an old coat that she never took off because—as she told Sacha and Bekah at every possible opportunity—*you never knew*.

Mrs. Lehrer's habit of seeing thieves in every shadow was understandable given the amount of cash she had sewn into her money coat. But everyone knew better than to pay any attention to it. So before the door had even closed behind Sacha's mother, they'd all gone back to arguing about his apprenticeship.

"Don't pay any attention to your Uncle Mordechai," Mo told Sacha. "Being an Inquisitor is a good, honest profession. Why, Inquisitors have become mayors, senators . . . even president!"

"Right," Bekah snorted. "And everyone knows how honest politicians are."

Now it was Mr. Kessler's turn to roll his eyes. "And you think Mordechai's Wiccanist friends wouldn't be just as bad the minute they got into power?"

"Well, they certainly couldn't be any worse, could they?" Bekah crossed her arms defiantly. "Benjamin Franklin founded the Inquisitors to protect ordinary people from magical crime, and what do they do instead? Run around giving tickets to poor Mrs. Lassky while J. P. Morgaunt and the rest of those Wall Street Wizards get away with murder!"

"Bilking widows out of their life savings in the stock market might not be nice," Mr. Kessler pointed out, "but it's not exactly murder."

"Besides," Mo added, "the Inquisitors *do* catch rich men. They caught Meyer Minsky—"

"And he was out on parole six months later and running Magic, Inc., just like always. Besides, he's a gangster. A *Jewish* gangster. When was the last time you saw an Astral or a Morgaunt or a Vanderbilt in prison?"

"Fine," Sacha's father teased. "Run upstairs and join the Wobblies. I've seen you talking to that skinny redhead up there. In my day if a boy and a girl liked each other, they did something about it, end of story. But if you'd rather run all over town making speeches about magic-workers' rights, be my guest."

Bekah tried to look outraged, but her face was so red that Sacha had to smother a laugh. He glanced at his father in amazement. Mr. Kessler worked such long hours that he was barely ever home except to eat and sleep—but judging by Bekah's blushes, he'd spotted something that even their mother's sharp eyes had missed. Sacha knew who the Wobblies were, of course: the Industrial Witches of the World, whose makeshift headquarters were located in a cheap rear flat on the top floor of the Kesslers' own building. But obviously he was going to have to take a closer look at the idealistic young Wobblies who traipsed up and down the stairs past their apartment every day. Especially the redheads.

"I don't even think about boys that way," Bekah protested, still blushing furiously. "Especially not—I mean, I have no idea who you're talking about!"

"Good," their father said mildly. "Then I guess I don't need to meet him."

Bekah bit her lip. "And—and Mama doesn't need to hear about him?"

"I'm sorry. Are you saying you *do* know who I'm talking about?"

"Gee, Daddy, maybe you ought to join the Inquisitors instead of Sacha."

Meanwhile, Uncle Mordechai had finished with the *Yiddish Daily Magic-Worker* and picked up the *Alphabet City Alchemist*. The main headline screamed "The Robber Barons Are Stealing Our Magic!" in letters Sacha could read all the way across the table.

"Of course Bekah's completely right about the Inquisitors," Mordechai announced, as if the conversation had never strayed from politics in the first place. "Asking them to catch magical criminals is like setting a fox to guard the henhouse. Which just goes to prove my original point: America is a myth founded on a fable founded on a—"

But instead of finishing his speech Mordechai grabbed his pocket watch, read the time, and clapped a hand to his handsome head. "My God!" he cried. "I'm late for rehearsal! Again!"

He leaped from his chair, knocking over a pile of IWW newsletters, which knocked over Grandpa Kessler's *Collected Works of Maimonides* in fourteen volumes, which toppled Bekah's teetering stack of schoolbooks—and sent her civics essay slithering into the soup.

"Farewell and adieu!" Mordechai cried, ducking out on a fresh family debate—this one about how to get the soup stains out of Bekah's homework and the taste of civics homework out of the soup. "I'd love to stay and help clean up, but we're opening Sunday, and the show must go on!"

The rest of them spent the next several minutes blotting soup off of Bekah's essay and hanging the damp pages out on the fire escape to dry. Then they listened to Mo Lehrer and Grandpa Kessler argue about whether Pentacle Stationery Supplies Indelible Ink was kosher or not—a thorny question because of the appalling rumors about what really went into it.

It was only when the soup boiled over that Sacha's father looked up with a worried frown and asked, "Where's your mother?"

CHAPTER THREE

Watcher in the Shadows

MR. KESSLER SLAMMED his book down, jumped to his feet, and was gone before Sacha even knew he was leaving.

Cough or no cough, Sacha's father took the steep stairs two at a time. Sacha stumbled headlong behind him, keeping one hand on the wall to steady himself in case he tripped over something in the pitch-black stairwell. He could hear Mo behind him, wheezing like a steam locomotive but still keeping up with them all the way down the stairs and across the garbage-strewn back lot.

By the time they made it past the privies and caught a glimpse of the water pump, Mr. Kessler was already walking back toward them. One look at his face told Sacha that something was very wrong.

"What is it?" he asked.

His father pointed to a splintered board leaning against

the wall beside the pump. Two words had been chalked onto it in crooked capital letters that were already beginning to wash away in the rain:

PUMP BROKE

"She must have gone to get water somewhere else," Mr. Kessler said disgustedly. "Without taking us with her like any sensible woman would. We'd better split up or we'll never find her." He frowned at Sacha. "And you'd better go home."

"I'm not a child!" Sacha protested. "I'm coming with you!"

His father gave him a put-upon look. But then he shrugged his shoulders. "Fine. But stick with Mo. I don't want *you* getting lost too. You can check the Canal Street pump. I'll cover the rest of the neighborhood."

Canal Street glistened black and silver under the moonlight. The rain was falling in earnest now, and a rich, loamy smell wafted up from the sidewalks—a reminder that there was still living earth somewhere deep beneath the city.

Half the streetlights were broken, as usual, so the only-in-New-York mishmash of Jewish, Chinese, and Italian storefronts seemed to belong to a world of ghosts and shadows. Bloomingdale Brothers was closed. The Napoli Café and the perpetually busy Lucky Laundry (CHANGE YOUR SOCKS, CHANGE YOUR FORTUNE!) were both locked and shuttered. Even Rabbi Kessler's little storefront synagogue was deserted, though his students often lingered on the front stoop talking Kabbalah long after Mo Lehrer had locked up for the night.

Sacha honestly *tried* to wait for Mo like his father told him to. But after about half a block, he couldn't stand it anymore. He veered into the middle of the empty street—always the safest route at night, since you never knew who was hiding behind the heaps of garbage on the sidewalks—and took off running.

As he stepped off the curb, he heard glass shatter under his feet and saw the shards of a broken spell bottle skittering away across the cobblestones. He could just make out the five-cornered symbol of Pentacle Industries on the label. And he could practically hear his mother kvetching about J. P. Morgaunt's monopolies and asking why people thought they could find happiness at the bottom of a spell bottle—and was it her imagination, or was the neighborhood getting worse lately?

Oh God, what if something had happened to her?

He pushed the thought out of his mind and kept running.

Soon Canal Street opened out into the Bowery. Rain-slicked cobblestones rolled away like waves on a storm-tossed ocean. Open construction pits gaped like scars. Arc lamps buzzed and flickered high overhead, casting a sickly glow that only made the shadows under the Elevated Railway tracks look blacker and more dangerous. The pump was under those tracks—and Sacha didn't even want to think about what else might be lurking under there at this time of night.

Sacha had never seen the Bowery so deserted. There was no one on the street at all, not even the usual collection of drunks and spellfiends. The only sign of humanity was the demonic grin on the twenty-foot-high billboard of Harry Houdini that soared above the marquee of the Thalia Theatre.

Sacha crossed the street, squared his shoulders, and stepped into the darkness under the tracks.

As soon as his eyes adjusted to the shadows, he saw the bucket, right by the pump where his mother must have dropped it. And a few feet beyond, his mother lay senseless on the cobblestones. He knelt and touched her face.

"Mama," he asked when her eyes finally opened, "what happened?"

She looked at him as if she'd never seen him before. Then she passed a hand over her forehead and shuddered. "I . . . I don't know."

He helped her to her feet and turned back to get the bucket.

"Leave it!" she gasped. And then, in a quieter, more controlled voice: "Your father and Mordechai can come back for it later."

Sacha obeyed. Or at least he started to. But when he looked toward the street, he saw a dark figure standing between them and the light, blocking their escape. At first he thought it was Uncle Mordechai. But it was too short to be Mordechai. And there was something about the shadowy figure that made the hair on the back of Sacha's neck stand up like a dog's hackles.

"Who's there!" he called, trying to make it sound like a challenge and not a question.

The shadow didn't answer, but a ripple shivered through the air around them. And not just the air. Sacha could have sworn the ground moved too. It felt as if the whole city had just shuddered underfoot like a horse twitching off a fly.

Then Sacha heard the silvery tinkle of bells.

He knew right away that they were *streganonna* bells: the little silver chimes the Italians sewed onto their horses' bridles to ward off the evil eye. A moment later a rickety cart turned onto the Bowery from the direction of Mulberry Street and Little Italy. Sacha's knees went weak with relief. It was an Italian greengrocer, heading out to the East River Docks for an early morning pickup. And since he'd be running empty in this direction, they could catch a ride home with him—far safer than walking.

But when the cart rumbled into sight, Sacha caught his breath in fear. It was a wreck, held together with rusty nails and baling twine. The ancient nag in the traces seemed barely strong enough to walk, let alone haul a full load. Yet the cart was heaped almost to overflowing with bones and rags and all the dusty odds and ends of people's lives that get put to the curb when no one can figure out how to fix them or remember why they were worth keeping in the first place. This was no simple greengrocer. It was the Rag and Bone Man.

The Rag and Bone Man was a legendary figure that mothers all over New York used to scare naughty children into behaving. He had a different name in every neighborhood, but he was feared everywhere. He collected scrap metal and worn-out clothes and gnawed bones for the ragpickers and the glue factories. But people said he traded in dreams too. They said he bought nightmares and lifted curses. And some people claimed he wasn't above selling them on for future use by third parties. The rabbis scoffed at such old wives' tales, but every woman on Hester Street still made the sign of the evil eye when the Rag and Bone Man passed by. Even Sacha's normally sensible mother had sent him running downstairs with a bone last week, saying, "Quick, Sacha! Throw it on the cart! I dreamed someone died last night!"

The Rag and Bone Man reined in his horse and peered toward the Elevated tracks. He glanced at Sacha and then turned a hard stare on the shadowy watcher. Some silent challenge seemed to pass between them. Then the watcher turned away and slipped into the shadows.

For a moment Sacha struggled to make sense of this silent confrontation. Then he put it out of his mind. It didn't matter, he told himself. Right now the only thing that mattered was getting his mother home safely.

He heard someone calling his name. It was Mo Lehrer, hurrying across the Bowery toward them, waving frantically. The Rag and Bone Man looked at Mo, nodded to Sacha, and then flipped the reins on his horse's skeletal back and shambled off into the night.

"Did you see that?" Sacha asked when Mo reached them.

"See what?"

"Nothing. Let's go."

As they turned the corner onto Hester Street, Mr. Kessler caught sight of them and came running from halfway down the block.

"*Danken Got* you're safe!" he cried. Then he got close enough to see his wife's face. "What happened? Were you attacked?"

"I don't know." Mrs. Kessler still sounded dazed and weak. "I think there was someone there, but I . . ."

"Did they *hurt* you?"

"I don't think so."

"Did they rob you?"

Sacha's mother looked momentarily confused. She dug around in her pockets and extracted a pitiful handful of coins that could only have tempted the most desperate thief. "Maybe Sacha interrupted them."

"Oh, well," Mo said comfortingly. "All's well that ends well."

Only when they reached their apartment did they realize that something had indeed been stolen. After a few cups of strong tea, Mrs. Kessler began to seem more like herself again. She rubbed at the back of her neck as if it hurt—and then she let out a moan of grief and horror. "My locket!"

It was gone. Above the collar of her dress where the locket's silver chain usually rested, there was only a bright red welt where the thief had torn it from her neck.

She wanted to go straight out and look for it, but Sacha's father wouldn't let her. Instead he and Sacha went. By the time they came back an hour later, covered in soot and grime, they had crawled over every inch of ground under the Elevated tracks. But it wouldn't have mattered how long they searched. There was nothing to find. The locket was gone.

"There there, Ruthie," Mr. Kessler said, patting her shoulder awkwardly.

Sacha didn't know what to say. That locket was his

mother's most treasured possession. It held three silky curls of baby hair: one from Bekah, one from Sacha, and one from their baby brother who had died on the boat from Russia. His mother never talked about that baby. No one on Hester Street talked about the past much—not unless they wanted to end up as crazy as poor Mrs. Lehrer. But once Sacha had come home early from school and found his mother sitting alone at the kitchen table looking at the locket and weeping as if the baby had died yesterday instead of years ago.

"I'm sorry," he told her now. It wasn't enough, but he couldn't think of anything else to say.

"It's nothing." His mother wiped her eyes on her apron and tried to smile. "Just a silly piece of jewelry."

Then she started fussing over Sacha and his father, scolding them to take off their wet shoes and socks, and forcing hot tea down their throats as if the worst thing that had ever threatened her family was a head cold.

Sacha relaxed under her fussing—once she started fussing over you, there wasn't much you could do except sit back and enjoy it. But his mind kept turning to that dark shadow under the Elevated tracks.

Had the watcher been a mere bystander, or the thief himself? And what kind of thief would walk past all the jewelry stores and rich tourists and drunken sailors on the Bowery only to steal a cheap locket from a woman who was far too poor for any self-respecting criminal to bother with?

CHAPTER FOUR

Sacha Makes a Promise

WHEN SACHA WOKE the next morning, his mother and father were already up and dressed.

He slipped out of bed, steeling himself for the long, cold trip to the water pump. Then he saw that his mother had put out a fresh towel and was filling a brimming basin with hot water for him. And that wasn't all: She'd set a second plate at the table next to his father's and loaded it with a thick wedge of noodle kugel and a towering portion of chopped herring with eggs and onions.

"Sit!" she said, carving a massive slice of black bread off the loaf for him. "Eat! You need your strength today!"

Sacha stared, overwhelmed. Yesterday he'd been a kid. Today his mother was taking care of him just like she took care of his father—as if he were a grown man going off to work.

And she was right, crazy as it sounded. Even a lowly Apprentice Inquisitor made more money than Sacha's father earned working twelve-hour shifts at the docks. Sacha hadn't been able to look his father in the eye for days after he'd found that out. But what could you do about it? America was a new world, where none of the old rules applied.

Only when he was already at the table eating did he realize the other amazing thing: that his mother was doing any of this at all a few short hours after she'd been knocked unconscious and robbed in the street.

"How are you feeling?" he asked her.

"How should I be feeling?"

"Well—I mean—after last night—"

His mother made a disdainful spitting sound that seemed to dismiss the violent theft of her most treasured possession as a mere triviality. "Be quiet and eat your breakfast!"

Sacha obeyed—as if he had any choice in the matter. But he couldn't help shaking his head in wonder. He'd read enough adventure stories in *Boys Weekly* to be pretty sure that any normal American mother would still be lying around fainting and crying into her handkerchief after such a shock. Sacha wasn't sure how to feel about this. Because the truth was that he often wished his family would act more normal and less . . . well . . . foreign. But on the other hand, normal parents would probably have never managed to get him and Bekah to America in the first place.

Either way, he could see that his mother had put the loss behind her and didn't intend to talk about it again. And he knew she'd only get angry with anyone who tried to offer sympathy—almost as angry as Mr. Kessler would get if Sacha ever dared to suggest that his cough was getting worse every winter and he might want to think about taking it a little easier now that Sacha was old enough to earn a paycheck.

The early morning symphony of ash bins and trash cans had just begun when the three of them left for work together. Uncle Mordechai had come in late again and was sleeping against the door on a pile of Mrs. Lehrer's unfinished sewing. They clambered over him, Sacha's father muttering all the while that any grown man who slept this late deserved to get stepped on. They crept through the back room, trying not to wake the Lehrers. Then they slipped out the door and felt their way down the unlit stairs into the pale gray light of a New York dawn.

They stood on the front stoop to say their goodbyes. From here Sacha's father would go east to the docks while his mother went west to the Pentacle Shirtwaist Factory. And Sacha would head north to Astral Place to catch the subway.

But Sacha's mother didn't seem ready to leave quite yet. She glanced at him as if she wanted to say something but couldn't find the right words. Then she turned away to watch the garbage men, as if they were the most interesting thing she'd seen in weeks. Then she sniffled and dug through her purse to find a nickel for his subway fare.

She pushed the coin into his hand.

"Thanks," Sacha mumbled.

"I don't want them to think I sent you to work with dirty shoes your first day," she said. Then she pulled out a handkerchief, blew her nose—and surreptitiously dabbed at her eyes a few times.

Sacha gave her a hug. He tried to give her a kiss too, but she pushed him away. "Enough mooning around. Do you want to be late for your first day of work?"

"Go figure," Sacha's father said as they watched her hurry away. "The woman watches Cossacks burn her house down, walks halfway across Europe, and gets mugged on the Bowery without shedding a tear, but she can't put her son on the subway without getting all *verklempt*." He shrugged eloquently. "As the great Rabbi Salomon Ben Gabirol said, 'When God created woman, he made a mystery beyond all mysteries.' Hey, listen! We have a few minutes before I have to put you on the subway. What do you say we stop off at the Metropole for a cup of coffee?"

Sacha stared at his father in amazement. The Café Metropole was Uncle Mordechai's territory. It was a place for fun and frivolity, where young men wasted time and money that they should be spending to support their families. If his father was willing to buy two whole coffees at the Metropole—and to stand at the bar for the precious minutes it took to drink them—then he must think Sacha's first day of work was a truly momentous occasion.

Sacha nodded, not trusting himself to speak, and they set off for the Bowery.

The turn north from Hester Street onto the Bowery always amazed Sacha, no matter how many times he made it. It was like crossing an ocean in a single step. Hester Street was a piece of the Old Country, where laundry hung from every fire escape and familiar faces smiled at you from every doorway. But the Bowery . . . well, the way neighborhood women talked about the Bowery said it all. If they ran errands to the cluttered little shops on Hester Street, they'd say they'd been out to fetch bread or eggs or milk or buttons. But if they went to the Bowery they'd say, "I went to America today."

And they were right. It *was* America. Plate-glass windows displayed everything from diamonds to cash registers. Horns blared as horse-drawn omnibuses battled with motorcars for control of the thronging avenue. Iron trestles marched overhead like monsters from a Jules Verne novel. And every twelve minutes—you could set your watch by it—the Elevated roared overhead, belching coal smoke and shaking the nearby buildings until their very foundations rattled.

People were different on the Bowery too. They moved differently: with the purpose and efficiency of workers who had stripped off all their old habits in order to survive in a new country and a new century. Polish tailors mingled with the children of freed slaves and Italian stonemasons and Irish ditchdiggers, shuttling back and forth every rush hour like cogs in a vast machine. Looking up the Bowery was like looking into the future. And at seven thirty on a Monday morning, the future looked like it was in a hurry.

Sacha and his father struggled through the tide of commuters until they reached the corner of Grand Street. Then they dove out of the current and staggered through the polished mahogany doors of the Café Metropole.

The Café Metropole was the spiritual home of every exiled European intellectual in the city. Your rude waiter (and the waiters at the Metropole proudly bore the title of rudest in

New York) might have a master's degree in Theoretical Magery from Budapest or a doctorate in necronomics from Heidelberg. The shabby fellow drinking coffee at the next table could be a distinguished Kabbalist, or a radical Wiccanist philosopher, or an exiled aristocrat from one of the great magical dynasties of Europe.

Of course, no one actually *did* magic at the Metropole; it was just about the most obvious place in New York for the Inquisitors to run one of their infamous undercover stings. Still, the Metropole's regulars included witches and wizards educated in the top European universities. And—according to rumor—even a Mage or two. There was no doubt about it: when you drank at the Metropole, you weren't just drinking coffee. You were drinking in a thousand-year-old tradition of Old World magic.

At this hour the Metropole was full of humble working men grabbing a morning cup of coffee on their way to the docks or factories. They all seemed to know it was the first day of Sacha's apprenticeship. *Mazel tovs* rained down from every side. Even the pale and preoccupied Theoretical Magicians huddled in the back corner looked up from their geomantical proofs and smiled vaguely in Sacha's direction.

Mr. Kessler ordered two of the Metropole's famous Viennese coffees, cocked an elbow against the counter, set one foot on the brass bar rail, and began talking. Seeing his father here, Sacha could imagine him as a student in Moscow. He could imagine how much he must have enjoyed debating politics and philosophy—and how good he must have been at it.

After all, Mr. Kessler was just as smart as Uncle Mordechai. The only difference between the two brothers was that Sacha's father had given up his own dreams to take care of his family.

Their coffees arrived, strong and sweet, in little glasses with filigreed silver handles. Sacha sipped his coffee and enjoyed the strange feeling of having his father talk to him like a grownup and equal. Finally he worked up the nerve to ask the question that had been preying on his mind all night.

"Who do you think stole Mama's locket?"

"What do you mean? You think it could be someone we know?"

"No! I just meant . . . well . . . why would anyone want it?"

"Who knows? It was probably some hopped-up spell-fiend who wandered over from Chinatown. Those poor wretches will steal anything to get a fix."

"You don't think the thief could have been after the locks of hair?"

His father stared, openmouthed. "What are you talking about? You afraid someone's going to set a dybbuk on you?"

At the word *dybbuk*, a man drinking next to them gasped and made the sign of the evil eye. Mr. Kessler gave him a disdainful look before turning back to his son. "You've been reading too many penny dreadfuls, Sacha. You're getting an overactive imagination."

"Well, but . . . couldn't it have been a hexer or a conjure man?" Sacha didn't know much about hex casters and con men, but he had heard that they sometimes used locks of hair to bind their victims.

"What could a con man possibly steal from us that would make it worth his while? And anyway, you and Bekah don't need to worry. You have your grandfather looking out for you."

"Grandpa?" Sacha asked incredulously.

"Sure. What do you think he and Mo are doing at *shul* every night, playing poker? I might not have gone into the family business, but you still come from seven generations of Kabbalists. It'd take more than some cheap conjure man to lay a hex on you or Bekah."

"Oh." Sacha felt bewildered. He'd always known his grandfather was a Kabbalist. But it had never occurred to him that Kabbalah had anything to do with practical magic—or that his grandfather could possibly have anything in common with the hexers and con men the Inquisitors arrested. "Um . . . do you think I should tell Inquisitor Wolf about Grandpa?"

Sacha's father made a wry face. "I wouldn't bring up the topic if you can manage to avoid it."

They drank for a while in silence.

"So," Mr. Kessler said, as cheerfully as if no one ever mentioned dybbuks and conjure men. "The big day's finally here. Excited?"

"Well—I—"

"You're not worried about Inquisitor Wolf, are you? Don't be. Sure, he's got this big reputation. But I know you. You're smart and honest, a hard worker. What could he possibly find to complain about?"

Sacha met his father's gaze—and was shocked to realize that they were looking at each other eye to eye. When had he gotten as tall as his father? And when had his father started stooping like that? Had he always looked so old and tired?

"I just hope I can help out around the house some . . . you know . . . like Bekah does."

He knew he'd made a mistake as soon as he said the words. He'd known his father was ashamed when Bekah had to quit school to work at Pentacle. Now that shame hung in the air between them.

"You mean help out with *money?*" Mr. Kessler asked stiffly. "You think we took you out of school just so you could make *money* for us?

"No, but—"

"We did it for you. We did it for your future."

"I know, but—"

"No buts! You've been handed a chance in life, and I want you to grab it with both hands and not look back. You understand me?"

Sacha nodded, not trusting himself to speak.

"Promise me you'll look out for number one and forget about the rest," said the man who'd been looking out for Sacha all his life.

Sacha hesitated.

"Promise!"

"Okay, okay! I promise."

But in his mind he was promising something very different.

I'll do whatever it takes to keep this job, he swore. *I'll be the best appren-tice anyone's ever seen and the fastest to make Inquisitor. I won't rest until you've quit the docks and Bekah's gone to college and Mama's sewn her last shirtwaist.*

CHAPTER FIVE

Lily Astral

SACHA DASHED through the turnstile of the Astral Place subway station just as the uptown express arrived in a shriek of steel wheels and a cloud of old newspapers.

Astral Place was named after the oldest of the old New York families. The Astrals didn't live on Astral Place anymore, of course. They'd moved uptown to Millionaire's Mile, along with all the other high-society families. But the subway stop still bore their name, and terra cotta beavers adorned its walls in memory of the fur trade that had made the Astrals rich when shamans and medicine men still roamed Manhattan Island.

Someday Sacha would be able to catch the subway right near his house on Canal Street. But for now everything south of Astral Place was a mud-choked construction site. Sacha wondered idly which rich family their station would be named after when it was finally finished. Well, as long as it wasn't

J. P. Morgaunt. Normally Sacha didn't mind politics, but he really was going to scream if he had to hear one more stupid joke about Pentacle's Tentacles.

Sacha elbowed his way through the rush-hour crowd and just managed to claim the last open seat. It was a good seat, too: a smartly dressed banker was reading the morning paper right next to him, which meant that Sacha got to catch up on the latest headlines for free.

Mostly it was the usual bad news. Congress was considering banning all immigration from Russia because of "undesirable magical elements." Another bribery scandal was rocking City Hall. The contractor on the new Harlem subway line had been caught using illegal magical workers to cut costs. Harry Houdini had been called before ACCUSE (the Advisory Committee to Congress on Un-American Sorcery) to prove that he pulled off his miraculous escapes without aid of magic. And Thomas Edison had invented a mechanical witch detector.

Great, Sacha told himself. His first day of work, and Thomas Edison had already invented a machine that made him obsolete. If that wasn't Yiddish luck, he didn't know what was!

He was craning his neck to read about the witch detector when the banker noticed him reading over his shoulder. The man gave an outraged gasp and glared at Sacha as if he'd just caught him trying to pick his pocket. Sacha straightened his neck and stared innocently out the window—straight at an ad for Edison's Portable Home Phonographs.

He'd seen the ad before. Who hadn't? It was plastered on buildings and billboards all over the city. It showed two little girls gathered around a shiny new Edison Portable Home Phonograph. They were listening to music—some kind of uplifting patriotic hymn judging by the expressions on their faces. They both had blue eyes and blond curls and pert little button noses. And the advertising slogan painted in flowing script under the picture read "Edison Portable Home Phonographs—Real *American* Entertainment."

It was a popular ad. Even Sacha had been impressed when he first saw it. But somehow he'd never noticed before now how very blond those two little girls were. Or how the word *American* was painted in ever-so-slightly bolder and brighter letters than all the other words—as if to hint that other kinds of entertainment and the people who enjoyed them weren't quite as American as the people who bought Edison Portable Home Phonographs.

It gave Sacha the creeps. Worse, it reminded him of Bekah's mocking question: Who ever heard of a Jewish Inquisitor?

Sacha was still asking himself that question when he stepped into the booking hall of the Inquisitors Division of the New York City Police Department.

At first glance, the Inquisitors Division looked just like any other police station. High ceilings. Dirty walls painted in an institutional shade of green. Marble floors littered with spittoons, cigarette butts, and tobacco stains. An ornately carved booking counter. On one side of the counter was the waiting area, where victims and criminals were packed elbow to elbow on hard wooden benches. On the other side was the typing pool: two dozen efficient-looking girls in prim and proper shirtwaists pounding away at clattering typewriters.

The Inquisitors stood around the booking counter, gossiping and joking and flirting with the typing pool girls. Some of them were in uniform and some were in plainclothes. Most of them looked Irish. And all of them looked far too intimidating for Sacha to risk more than a quick sidelong glance at them.

It wasn't until Sacha saw the criminals that he truly realized this was no ordinary police station. Scanning the faces of the suspects chained to the long wooden bench was like reading an illustrated catalog of magical crime. There were horse whisperers decked out in soft tweed caps and rumpled corduroys. There were ink-stained hex writers from every corner of Europe. There was even a fresh-faced traveling salesman toting a leather-bound edition of the *Encyclopedia Britannica*. He had a look of long-suffering innocence on his face that seemed to say getting arrested was just a terrible mistake. But the cops all knew him, and this obviously wasn't his first trip to the lockup. He must be a conjure man, Sacha decided. The encyclopedia probably turned into rats (or worse) as soon as he'd pocketed your final payment.

In fact, a lot of the suspects seemed to have been here before. There was something practiced and coordinated about the way they all slid down the bench, with a little clink of their chains, when the desk sergeant finished booking a suspect and called out "next!"

At the moment the sergeant was struggling to keep the

peace between a scrawny little fellow and a shrieking woman who seemed determined to take the law into her own hands. The arresting officer was doing his best to keep the pair apart, but he was no match for the victim's stiletto-sharp umbrella.

"You again, Bob?" the sergeant sighed as the outraged woman swiped at the little man but hit the arresting officer's ear instead. "We oughta start charging you rent."

"I'm innocent this time!" Bob cried. "I swear I was just picking her pocket!"

"Come on, Bob. You think I was born yesterday?"

"It's the truth, Sergeant! I just needed a couple bucks to take a flutter on the ponies."

"I'll give you a flutter!" the fat woman bellowed. "He stole a lock of my hair, officer. Yanked it right out while he was pretending to bump into me. But I'm onto him. I grew up in Chicago, an' I know a conjure man when I see one. One minute it's 'Pardon me, missus,' and the next minute you've been hexed into signing away your life's savings!"

"Don't worry, ma'am, we'll get to the bottom of this. Bob, are you willing to submit to a lie detector test?"

Bob puffed out his scrawny chest and tried to look virtuous and indignant—not so easy when you're being poked in the ribs by an umbrella. "I got nothing to hide."

The sergeant sighed and turned around to scan the desks behind him. "Margie! Lie detector!"

One of the typing pool girls looked up from her machine, squinted at the accused with her hands still poised over the keys, and drawled, "He's lying."

"Aw, come on, Margie!" Bob cried, the picture of outraged innocence. "How can you tell from all the way over there? The least you could do is look a guy in the eye before you call him a liar!"

Margie came over to the booking desk and looked Bob in the eye. Sacha recognized her now as the bored girl who had administered his Inquisitorial Quotient test. He could see magic drifting lazily around her head like smoke rings. He would never have thought that magic could look bored, but there was no mistaking it: This was bored magic.

"Yep," Margie said. "You're lying."

"Margie! I thought we were friends! How can you do me this way?"

But Margie just yawned and walked back to her typewriter.

Sacha was still shaking his head over this when a mountainous Inquisitor in full uniform appeared in front of him. The name on the giant's gleaming Inquisitor's badge was Mahoney.

"And why aren't you in school on this fine Monday morning?" Mahoney asked him.

"I'm not supposed to be in school," Sacha protested. "I work here."

"Are we hiring children now?"

"I'm not a child, I'm thirteen!"

"Well, excuse me," Mahoney said with a good-natured grin. "And who might you be coming here to apprentice for?"

"Inquisitor Wolf."

Mahoney's friendly grin vanished. "You're the boy who can see witches."

"I—I guess so," Sacha stuttered.

"And what might your name be, if you don't mind my asking?"

"K-Kessler?"

"K-Kessler." A smile spread across Mahoney's face. But this time there was nothing good-natured about it. "What kind of name is that?"

"Uh . . . Russian?"

"It don't sound Russian to me."

Sacha was almost whispering now. "Jewish?"

"Well, well." Mahoney called out to the Inquisitors gathered around the booking desk. "Lookee here, fellows! It's Wolf's new apprentice. The freak. And that's not the half of it. Turns out he's one of the Chosen People!"

Someone snickered. Cold, unfriendly eyes turned toward Sacha from every corner of the room. Even the criminals seemed to be looking down their noses at him.

Later, Sacha thought of all sorts of things he could have said to Mahoney. Like that he was as good an American as anyone else. Or that Mahoney could go back to Ireland and eat potatoes if he was smart enough to find any. Or . . . well, none of it was exactly brilliant. But it was all better than what he actually said. Which was nothing at all.

"Run along, then," Mahoney said when he saw that Sacha wasn't going to stand up for himself. "And don't worry. You and Wolf ought to suit each other fine. He's the most un-Christian soul that ever walked the halls of the Inquisitors Division."

Inquisitor Wolf's office was the last door at the end of the
hall. It was a small, dusty room shaped like a shoe box, and its
only window looked out on a blank brick wall covered with a
painted advertisement for Mazik's Corsets and Ladies' Foun-
dation Garments: *"It's not Magic—it's Mazik!"*

Every inch of wall in the office was stacked to the ceiling
with case files. Someone had tried to impose order on the
mess by stuffing the files into cardboard boxes, but most of
the boxes were so full they were practically exploding. Dog-
eared mug shots jockeyed for space with grimy newspaper
clippings, unidentifiable objects taped to index cards, and
handwritten notes scribbled on everything from train tickets
to Chinese laundry receipts.

Amidst the avalanche of paper stood a desk so clean that
it was hard to believe its owner worked in this disaster zone of
an office. Behind the desk sat a young black man wearing a
blue and white striped seersucker suit, a silk tie in a fashionable shade of mauve, and a haughty expression.

At first Sacha mistook him for a grownup, but in fact he
was only sixteen or seventeen. Yet he was so self-assured—and so
impeccably dressed—that he made Sacha feel like a grubby little
boy. What on earth was he doing here? Surely he couldn't be an
Inquisitor? He must be some kind of clerk, Sacha decided.

"Sit," the clerk told him, without even looking up from
the file he was scribbling in.

Sacha looked around for a chair, but the only one he
could see was buried under case files, just like everything else

in the office. Sacha took the files from the chair and tried to decide where to put them. The top one on the stack was labeled CHINATOWN (IMMORTALS OF). Sacha hesitated, wanting to peek inside. But he couldn't be quite sure the clerk wasn't watching him, so he set the files carefully on the floor and sat down to wait.

It was a long wait. As the minutes ticked by, Sacha began to fidget. Did Inquisitor Wolf know he was here? Was he going to be blamed for being late? Was he even in the right office?

He cleared his throat.

"Yes?"

"Um . . . nothing."

"Suit yourself."

Since there didn't seem to be anything else to do, Sacha began looking at the bewildering mass of case files lining the walls.

It was easy to see the magical significance of labels like SHAMANS, BANSHEES, and MAGICAL SUPPLIES (ILLEGAL TRAFFICKING IN). But what did COAT CHECKS and WALKING STICKS have to do with magical crime? Who were TATTERED TOM and THE WOMAN IN WHITE? And what on earth would anyone file under CROSSROADS, ITEMS SOLD AT?

Sacha ran a finger along the spines of the stacked files until he came to a name he knew, a name everyone knew: HOUDINI.

"Why do you have a file on Harry Houdini?" he asked, affecting what he hoped was a casual tone of being in on the big secret. "He's not even a real magician. I went to a performance once. It was all flimflam. No real magic at all."

"And that's your expert opinion, is it?" The clerk sounded amused.

"Sure."

"I suppose all the *other* stage magicians you've seen used real magic?"

"Well . . . um . . ."

"Real illusionists never use real magic in their shows. It's a point of honor. After all, any two-bit backstreet conjure man can *actually* make a rabbit disappear into a hat. It's faking it that takes talent." The boy's mouth twitched. "But naturally you must know that already, since you know so much about magic."

"Uh . . . yeah . . . naturally," Sacha said, retreating back to his corner.

Eventually he got up enough courage to try again. "Excuse me," he said. "I just realized that . . . well . . . we haven't been introduced."

"No, we haven't."

"I'm Sacha Kessler."

"I'm Philip Payton." Payton smiled—a rather nice smile, actually—and Sacha told himself he'd been silly to feel so intimidated.

"And . . . uh . . . what are you doing here?"

The smile went out like a blown fuse. "What's that supposed to mean?"

"Nothing! I just . . . um . . . well . . . I mean, do you work for Inquisitor Wolf?"

"Brilliant deduction. I can tell you'll make a star Inquisitor. And now if you'll excuse me, I need to finish this report before lunch."

"But does Inquisitor Wolf know I'm here?"

Payton heaved a long-suffering sigh, walked over to the closed door behind his desk, and opened it just wide enough to stick his head into the next room. "Excuse me for interrupting, but Sacha Kessler wants me to tell you that he's arrived. He seems to think apprentices get extra credit for being on time."

Sacha heard an indistinct murmur from inside the office.

"Not yet," Payton replied.

Another murmur.

"*I* know. But he kept pestering me."

Sacha cringed.

Finally Payton closed the door and turned back to Sacha. "Inquisitor Wolf told me to tell you that if it's *quite* all right with you, he would prefer to see you when the other apprentice arrives."

The *other* apprentice? It had never occurred to Sacha that there would be another apprentice. He wasn't at all sure he liked the idea. He was still getting used to it when the door opened and a *girl* walked in.

And not just any girl. A rich girl. Everything about her said Old Money, from the hand-embroidered lace on her dress to the haughty look on her aristocratic face.

Her cool blue eyes surveyed the room, dismissed Sacha as beneath notice, and settled on Payton. "Sorry I'm late," she said. "The traffic was so ridiculous that Mother's motorcar overheated and we had to sit in the middle of Fifty-ninth Street until it cooled down enough to start again."

"Don't worry about it," Payton told her—and Sacha noted bitterly that *she* rated his nicest smile. "Inquisitor Wolf's been busy with cases all morning and wasn't ready to talk to you anyway. Have a seat."

The girl cleared her throat delicately and looked at the only chair in the room—the one Sacha was sitting in. Sacha leaped to his feet as if someone had lit a fire under him.

"Thank you," the girl said. But she didn't sound thankful. She sounded like she thought giving up his chair for a lady was the rock-bottom least a civilized male could do—but still probably more than you could expect from someone like Sacha.

To his surprise she shook his hand before sitting down. "I'm Lily Astral."

Lily *Astral?* Sacha's chin almost hit the floor.

Her pale eyebrows rose in amusement. "According to the rules of polite society, I think you're supposed to tell me *your* name now."

"Uh . . . Sacha Kessler?"

She peered at him curiously. "The walking witch detector?"

"I guess." Why did everyone here seem to know all about

him? And why did they all give him the same look he was see-ing in Lily Astral's big blue eyes? The one that made him feel like he belonged in a Coney Island freak show.

"You guess?" Lily Astral asked. "Don't you know? And how *do* you see witches, anyway?"

"I just do. I can't describe it. People look different when they're doing magic."

The blue eyes narrowed. "But only when they're *do-ing* magic?"

"Well . . . yeah."

"And the rest of the time they just look normal?"

He nodded reluctantly.

"Then you can't really see witches at all, can you? You can only see magic." She sat down, crossing her prim little white-stockinged ankles. "That doesn't sound nearly as im-pressive."

Right then and there, Sacha decided that he hated Lily Astral.

But just as he was beginning to list to himself all the reasons why, the door to the inner office burst open and Inquisitor Wolf appeared.

CHAPTER SIX

Inquisitor Wolf

THE FIRST THING Sacha noticed about Maximillian Wolf was the first thing everyone noticed: nothing.

In a city like New York, charm was cheap. Any shopgirl or salesman could buy a little glamour to help win the next sale or just get that extra edge it took to get ahead, and most did. It wasn't exactly legal, but it worked. And New Yorkers were too ambitious to turn down anything that worked.

But Inquisitor Wolf didn't seem to think he needed that kind of help. In fact, he seemed to go to great lengths to be as unglamorous and unmagical as possible. His long, lanky legs were encased in baggy trousers that had never seen the inside of a tailor's shop, let alone a fitting spell. His jacket hung off his bony shoulders like a scarecrow's sack. His hair looked like it hadn't been brushed for weeks. His spectacles were covered with smudges and fingerprints. And his dishwater-gray eyes wore a sleepy, absentminded look that seemed to say he was still waiting for the day to bring him something worth waking up for.

As far as Sacha could tell, the only remotely interesting thing about Maximillian Wolf was the extraordinary collection of food stains on his tie.

"Er . . . hmmm," Wolf said, looking at Sacha and Lily as if he was trying to find a polite way of asking them what they were doing there.

"Your new apprentices," Payton prompted.

"I thought they were supposed to start next week."

"This *is* next week."

"Did I miss another weekend? What was I *doing?*"

"Working. What else?"

"I don't even know why I ask anymore," Wolf sighed. He thumbed through the case files on Payton's desk, slid one out of the middle of the pile, and drifted back into his office looking like he was well on his way to forgetting about his new apprentices all over again.

"Don't just stand there!" Payton urged, shooing them across the room and through Wolf's door. "Go in!"

Wolf looked surprised to see them, but he waved vaguely toward the two straight-backed wooden chairs in front of his desk. Then he wiped his glasses on his tie, opened the case file, and settled in to read it as serenely as if the two of them weren't going through agonies waiting for him to say something.

Sacha and Lily stared at each other. Lily gave a little shrug as if to say she didn't know what was going on either.

Then they waited.

And waited.

Sacha didn't dare watch Wolf, so he examined the office instead. It wasn't much bigger than the front room where Payton sat—and it was even messier. Every flat surface was covered with papers, books, and food. The papers were piled so high that they spilled over onto the floor in shaggy white drifts. The food looked like it must have been inedible (at least by Sacha's mother's standards) even when it was still fresh. And most of the books looked like they'd been read in the bathtub.

But the strangest thing in the room was a muddy heap of black wool on the floor next to Wolf's desk. At first Sacha thought it was a dog. Then he realized it was just Wolf's overcoat. He must have shucked it off onto the floor, mud and all, when he got to work that morning.

"So," Wolf asked, his eyes still on his file, "do you two have names?"

Sacha and Lily stared at each other again, neither one wanting to speak first.

"I'm Lily Astral," Lily said finally.

Now Wolf did look up, blinking in astonishment. "Good heavens, a girl," he murmured. "And Maleficia Astral's daughter too. What on earth am I supposed to do with you?"

Lily blushed furiously and muttered something about just wanting a fair chance, no matter who her mother was.

"Fair?" Wolf asked, still in the same tone of mild amusement. "If you don't mind my saying so, Miss Astral, you appear to be under a serious misapprehension about the nature of

the Inquisitors Division. Not to mention life in general. I fear that severe disappointment lurks in your future."

By this time Lily's face was so red that Sacha almost felt sorry for her.

But then Wolf turned his attention to Sacha, and he forgot all about Lily's problems.

"And I suppose you would be . . . um . . ." Wolf glanced back at the file on his desk. Whatever he was looking for, he didn't seem to find it there.

"Sacha Kessler."

"Right. Kessler." Wolf's oddly colorless eyes settled on Sacha. "Why do I think I know that name? You don't have any relatives who would have come to the attention of the police before? No wonderworking rabbis or practical Kabbalists or revolutionary rabble-rousers?"

"Oh, no! Nothing like that! We're complete and utter nobodies!"

That was Sacha's first lie. He regretted it bitterly the minute the words were out of his mouth. And he would have regretted it even more if he'd known how many other lies he'd end up piling on top of it.

He had the oddest feeling that Wolf knew it was a lie, too. Not that he said so. He just went all bland and mild and absentminded. But as the seconds ticked by, Sacha's skin began to itch and he had to bite his tongue to keep from blurting out a confession just to fill the awkward silence.

Just when Sacha was sure he couldn't stand it anymore, Wolf turned back to Lily Astral. "There are two sorts of girls in this world," he told her. "Girls who like to stare at omnibus accidents, and girls who don't. Which kind are you?"

Lily blinked in surprise. "I—I suppose I'm the staring kind."

"I'm sorry to hear it," Wolf said cheerfully. "Ghoulish curiosity is a dreadful character flaw in a young lady. But quite promising from a professional standpoint. You're hired. And only mostly because your father would have me fired if I didn't hire you."

While Lily was still choking on that, Wolf turned back to Sacha. "And what about you? You don't have any rich relatives. Why should I hire you?"

"Well," Sacha stammered, "I can . . . you know . . . see witches?"

Wolf leaned back in his chair and crossed his arms over his chest. His face still looked bland and expressionless, but Sacha got the distinct impression that he was laughing at them.

"It seems to me that between the two of you, you have the makings of exactly one decent apprentice," he said. "Miss Astral here has a burning ambition to be an Inquisitor, but"—he leaned forward again to check her file—"no magical abilities whatsoever. Or none that she'll admit to, anyway. You, on the other hand, are overflowing with talent but don't seem to have a clue why you want the job. Or am I missing something?"

Wolf took off his spectacles and held them up to the light as if he were trying to formulate a plan of attack against the smudges and fingerprints. He took his already untucked shirt-tail and began using that to clean the glasses—or more likely just rearrange the smudges, considering that the shirt looked like Wolf had been sleeping in it for a week.

The silence thickened. Sacha could feel Lily staring at him out of the corners of her eyes like a spooked horse. "I, um," he stammered, "I want to fight magical crime? And, uh, protect and defend the innocent?"

Wolf looked up—and Sacha felt a quiver of shock run down his spine.

Judging by the thickness of Wolf's glasses, he had expected to see the vague, myopic gaze of a nearsighted man. But Wolf's eyes were as bright as fresh-fallen snow on a sunny day. In fact, Sacha would have bet good money that Wolf didn't need glasses at all.

Then the moment passed. Wolf put his glasses back on—no cleaner than before—and was once more average and forgettable. He was also clearly disappointed with Sacha's answer.

Sacha felt a hot wave of shame sweep over him. Who was Wolf to judge him? Who was Lily Astral? What did they know about his life and his reasons for being here?

"My family needs the money!" he blurted out before he could stop himself. "Is there something wrong with that?"

Wolf lowered his eyes to the files on his desk so that Sacha couldn't read their expression. "There's not a thing in the world wrong with that," he said softly. "And what's more, it's the first true thing you've said to me."

Then, Wolf smiled at Sacha. It was a clean, clear, honest smile. There was humor in it. And intelligence. And not even the faintest hint of meanness. People would follow a man who smiled like that, Sacha caught himself thinking. They'd follow him just about anywhere.

"Message from Commissioner Keegan," Payton called, sticking his head around the door. "You're supposed to be at J. P. Morgaunt's mansion. The commissioner's already waiting for you there. He seems quite put out about it."

Wolf raised an eyebrow. "Since when does Mr. Morgaunt rate a house call?"

"Since he got Commissioner Roosevelt run out of town on a rail," Payton drawled.

"Sailing off for an African safari with three French chefs and a string of polo ponies hardly constitutes being run out of town on a rail," Wolf observed mildly. "Most people would consider it a thrilling adventure."

Payton snorted. "Not most New Yorkers!"

Wolf coughed as if he'd gotten something caught in his throat. Then he unfolded his lanky body from behind the desk, slouched over to the muddy heap of coat on the floor, and began shrugging his way into it. "I suppose the commissioner will expect me to bring the apprentices?"

"We might as well keep him happy," Payton agreed smoothly.

Wolf made a face at that—but he nodded at Sacha and Lily to follow him. They had just about made it to the door when Payton put a hand up to stop them.

"Pockets!" he announced in the peremptory tone of a train conductor ordering passengers to produce their tickets.

Without a word of protest, Wolf began emptying out his pockets and placing their contents in Payton's hands.

Suddenly Sacha understood why Wolf's clothes looked so baggy and bulgy. In short order he produced several chewed pencil stubs, a collection of rubber bands worthy of a slingshot champion, and a dozen crumpled scraps of paper entirely covered in tiny, deceptively neat yet completely illegible handwriting. The scraps of paper seemed to come from every corner of New York and every walk of life. There were laundry tickets, lottery tickets, Bowery playbills. Even a greasy wad of old newsprint that looked suspiciously like a used fish wrapper.

Payton collected these items as solemnly as Moses receiving the Ten Commandments. As he followed Wolf out of the office, Sacha looked back and saw Payton frowning over the fish wrapper as if he expected it to reveal all the secrets of the universe.

CHAPTER SEVEN

The House of Morgaunt

SACHA AND LILY followed Wolf downstairs, through the chaos of the booking hall, and out onto the sidewalk. The Inquisitors Division was right on the edge of Hell's Kitchen—a notorious slum where no cabbie would risk picking up a fare. Nonetheless, a shiny black hansom cab jingled around the corner and stopped in front of them before Wolf even had time to put his hand up. Wolf climbed in as calmly as if cabs always appeared out of nowhere for him, and soon they were trotting through Central Park.

As they neared the East Side, the scene grew more fashionable. Society ladies strolled under the towering elms and chestnuts. Nurses pushed wicker prams full of fat babies. Draft horses gave way to thoroughbreds, and there were even a few long black motorcars gliding among the carriages like sharks prowling through schools of lesser fish.

Sacha forced himself not to stare at the motorcars; he

didn't want to give Lily the satisfaction. But when he caught his first glimpse of Millionaire's Mile, he couldn't stop his jaw from dropping.

He felt as if he had fallen out of New York and landed in a book of fairy tales. Roman villas sprawled beside French châteaus and Venetian palazzi. And each mansion was larger and more opulent than the next. New York's Wall Street Wizards and Robber Barons were determined to outshine their neighbors, and they had the money to do it.

Still, everyone who'd ever read a New York newspaper knew that James Pierpont Morgaunt's new mansion would be the greatest of them all. It had been under construction for years, not because the work was going slowly—no one who worked for Morgaunt would dare to dawdle—but because Morgaunt kept updating its design to incorporate the latest scientific advances.

Morgaunt had hired Thomas Edison to install every imaginable modern convenience. The kitchen was equipped with automated ovens and automated dish washers. The books in Morgaunt's vast library were recorded in an automated card catalog. The central heating plant was connected to an exotic-sounding device called a Therm-O-Stat. Even the bathrooms were automated—whatever that meant!

From the outside, the Morgaunt mansion was a crouching Gothic pile that covered a whole city block. But as their cab pulled through the monumental front gate, the illusion of a medieval fortress gave way to the reality of a construction site. The bones and sinews of Edison's modern conveniences sprawled everywhere like broken clockwork. Half of the court-yard was buried under something that looked like a giant bicycle chain. A group of engineers were puzzling over it like paleontologists trying to put together one of the dinosaurs over at the Museum of Natural History.

"What do you think *that* is?" Sacha whispered to Lily.

"It's the automated horseless carriage parking system," she answered promptly. "Morgaunt told us about it last time he came to dinner. You press a button, and the car you want just rolls right off the conveyer belt. He's already assigned number and letter codes to all his motorcars. He's even bought the rights to print special numbered license plates from City Hall. He says it's a growth industry. In five years everyone's going to be building automatic motorcar parks."

"But who'll use them?" Sacha asked doubtfully. "You can't park a horse like that."

"Horses are history," Lily scoffed. "Too much pollution."

Sacha expected a butler to meet them at the door, but instead they were met by a black-eyed, black-haired, olive-skinned woman in a black dress tight enough to make him blush.

"That's Morgaunt's librarian," Lily whispered as they followed her across an echoing marble entrance hall toward a set of double doors that looked as if they were carved out of solid blocks of bronze. "Her name is Bella da Serpa. She says she's Portuguese, but no one knows the first thing about her. Except that she's helped Morgaunt gather the greatest collection of magical manuscripts in the world. Not that he *uses* them, of course. It's all quite respectable; he just collects them for the pictures."

But Sacha hardly heard her, because they had just stepped into the famous room that people were already calling "the" Morgaunt Library.

Sacha's first thought was that it was the library of a madman. Books ranged along the walls in shelves that rose two, three, four stories overhead. Spindly wrought-iron staircases spiraled up to narrow balconies from which rolling ladders rose, row upon row, to ever narrower balconies. Daylight filtered faintly through soaring Gothic windows, and the oak-paneled walls were decorated with the mounted heads of dead animals. There were white rhinos and Kodiak bears, African lions and Bengal tigers. And they all stared down at Morgaunt's visitors with their glassy eyes as if to say, What hope do you have of standing up to the man who killed *us*?

Two figures waited in front of the immense fireplace. Sacha noticed Commissioner Keegan first because he was standing. But from the moment he saw the man slouched in the big leather wing chair next to Keegan, Sacha knew he was the real power in the room.

Presidents trembled before James Pierpont Morgaunt— and as soon as you met him you knew why. Morgaunt was as tall as Inquisitor Wolf but much broader. His steel-gray eyes bored into you like augers. His steel-gray hair looked sharp enough to cut you. His hands were smooth-skinned and immaculately clean: a rich man's hands. But when Sacha took a closer look at them, he saw that they were as sinewy and powerful as the hands

of the roughest laborer. And there was something about the way he used them—the way he held a glass of Scotch or gestured as he spoke or picked an invisible piece of lint off his immaculate trousers—that made Sacha sure he'd be terrified of Morgaunt even if he weren't the richest man in America.

"Ye're late!" Commissioner Keegan snapped before anyone else could get a word in.

"Yes," Wolf said in his blandest voice. "I'm afraid I was unavoidably detained."

Keegan glared. "I should have listened to the people who told me to run you out of town with Teddy Roosevelt. They all warned me about you. They said ye'd be a thorn in my side."

"And have I been?" Wolf asked in the absentminded tones of a man trying to feign polite interest in someone else's problems.

In the shadows of the wing chair Morgaunt snorted in amusement.

"Don't sass me, boyo!" Keegan's Irish brogue got thicker as he got angrier. "I didn't want to call you at all, but Mr. Morgaunt insisted. Said he needed the best Inquisitor on the force to get to the bottom o' this."

"Er . . . the bottom of what?"

Keegan waved impatiently in Morgaunt's direction. "Use your eyes, man!"

For the first time, Sacha noticed the leather-upholstered footstool drawn up in front of Morgaunt's chair—and the silver chafing dish in which Morgaunt was icing his swollen ankle.

"Gout?" Wolf asked in a blandly sympathetic tone.

"No, you prat! He sprained it!"

"Er . . . condolences. But perhaps in that case a doctor might be more helpful than an Inquisitor?"

Morgaunt smiled. Even his smiles were terrifying. His eyes slid across Wolf in a way that could only be considered insulting. "Hello, Miss Astral," he said to Lily. "Your new employer has an unusual sense of humor. Do you think he would find it entertaining to hear that I sprained my ankle foiling an assassination attempt?"

Lily gasped. Sacha managed to stay silent, but he was shocked too. Morgaunt was no stranger to assassination attempts. A few years ago he'd narrowly escaped death at the hands of bomb-throwing Wiccanists. Sacha remembered the joke that had gone around New York at the time: Morgaunt had died and gone to hell, but he'd been sent straight back home again when the Devil himself turned out to be a Pentacle Industries employee. Sacha had never been sure if the point of the joke was that Morgaunt was meaner than the Devil or richer than the Devil. Either way, it was probably true.

"Can you identify the assassin?" Wolf asked.

Instead of answering, Morgaunt planted both feet on the floor and leaned forward with his elbows on his knees in order to stare at Wolf. He examined him like a collector classifying an exotic beetle. "What are you, Wolf?" he asked abruptly. "Irish? German? What?"

It was a predictable question in a city where most people's jobs and social status were determined by who their parents were. But Wolf's reply surprised Sacha.

"No one knows."

Morgaunt raised one eyebrow in a silent question.

"I was left on the doorstep of the Sisters of Mercy Orphanage."

"In a basket with a note, no doubt," Morgaunt scoffed.

"No note."

"So the nuns named you Maximillian? That's a pretty fancy name for an orphan."

Wolf smiled faintly. "The Sisters of Mercy had high hopes for me."

"And you've lived up to them. You must be a very able man to have risen so fast without money or family to smooth your path."

"I've been lucky in my friends."

"Or maybe not so lucky." Morgaunt leaned back into the shadows of his wing chair and put his foot up again. "Roosevelt didn't take you to Washington with him. Your choice or his?"

"Mine. I don't have the stomach for politics."

Morgaunt chuckled. "What real man does? Politics is just lies, bribes, and flattery. There are better ways for a man of action to make his mark on the world."

"Is that why someone tried to kill you last night? Because they didn't like the mark you've made on the world?"

Instead of answering, Morgaunt signaled to his librarian, who slithered silkily out of the room and came back a moment later with fresh ice for his ankle. When she had tended to him, Morgaunt began speaking in clear, efficient sentences that seemed to Sacha like they could have been stamped out by the hydraulic presses in one of his steel mills.

"The assassin struck here in my house last night, after a private dinner party. But I wasn't the target. The target was Thomas Alva Edison. And the assassin was no ordinary killer. It was a dybbuk."

Sacha's blood ran cold in his veins at the sound of the word *dybbuk*. What madman would set a dybbuk loose in New York? A dybbuk was the most terrifying creature in all of Jewish magic. It was hunger incarnate. It devoured souls and grew fat on shadows. The crowded warrens of New York's tenements harbored more souls—and more shadows—than any place on earth. Worst of all, a dybbuk could only be summoned by a Kabbalist. And that meant that Morgaunt was accusing a rabbi of the crime.

Sacha glanced sideways at Wolf, trying to gauge his reaction. But Wolf seemed more struck by Morgaunt's other piece of news. "Thomas Edison?" he asked. "The inventor? The Wizard of Luna Park?"

Morgaunt snorted. "A silly name for a gullible public. He's no more a wizard than Commissioner Keegan here. He's a man of science. A man for a new country and a new century. A man who puts the spellmongers out of business by turning magic into machinery. That's the way of the future, Wolf. No more of your quaint European superstitions and your mom-and-pop spell shops. The age of magic is over. This is the age of machines. And the future will belong to the men who have the machines."

"And what's your interest in Mr. Edison's machines?"

"Money, Wolf. Money and power."

Wolf gazed impassively at Morgaunt. Since arriving in Morgaunt's house, Wolf had risen to new heights of blandness. Was it possible to be this dull by accident? Or was boring people to death part of Wolf's famous investigative method?

"Oh," Morgaunt said, picking up his glass of Scotch and swirling it so that the golden liquid flashed and glimmered in the firelight. "You think I should beat around the bush a bit more? Spin you some idealistic little fairy tale about how I'm really in it for the good of the common man? Well, I don't beat around the bush, Wolf. And I don't lie either. I can't be bothered to." His steely eyes sparked with amusement. "Sometimes I think I'm the last honest man left in New York."

"You mean, now that you've gotten rid of Roosevelt."

"Yes. I suppose that is what I mean. But you're still here, aren't you, Wolf? And I'm starting to think you might be an honest man too. That would be a pity. Honesty isn't a very healthy hobby for a policeman." He smiled his terrifying smile. "Not in New York, anyway."

"Thanks for the warning," Wolf said, as calmly as if they were discussing the chances of rain showers that afternoon instead of the chances that he'd get shot in the back if he got in Morgaunt's way. "I'll bear it in mind next time I get the urge to commit a reckless act of honesty while on duty. Meanwhile, do you have any thoughts about who might have wanted to kill Mr. Edison?"

But Morgaunt wasn't ready to tell him that. He turned away from Wolf and shot a canny look at Sacha from under his steel-wool eyebrows. "Is that your new apprentice? The one who sees magic?"

"So they say." Wolf sounded like a reluctant witness repeating inadmissible evidence acquired by hearsay.

Morgaunt looked Sacha up and down. "I'm about to render you obsolete, young man. Edison's just invented a machine for me that will do what you do—and most likely do it better and cheaper. What do you say to that?"

Something curious happened to Wolf as Morgaunt spoke these words. He didn't move a muscle, and yet a sort of current rippled through his body. Not witchcraft, exactly. But some kind of energy that crackled just on the edge of Sacha's second sight. Could Wolf have honed the simple art of paying attention to such a height that it had become its own form of magic?

"Edison's reinvented Benjamin Franklin's etherograph," Wolf murmured in a voice even more expressionless than usual.

"Better than that," Morgaunt said. There was a grim rumble of satisfaction in his voice. You couldn't really call it a purr. It was more like the sound a lion might make when it glimpsed a particularly tender-looking gazelle. Sacha told himself that this was probably as close as the man ever got to sounding happy. "Come take a look."

Morgaunt hobbled over to a tall mahogany cabinet behind his desk. Wolf didn't offer Morgaunt his arm, and Sacha couldn't blame him. The mere thought of touching the man made you feel like you were freezing to death from the inside out.

Morgaunt unlocked the cabinet with a key that he pulled from his own vest pocket, and opened it to reveal row upon row upon row of tightly packed white and gold cylinders. At first Sacha thought they were bobbins of thread. But then he realized that he'd seen these little cylinders before: They were phonograph recordings.

"This is my little library of souls," Morgaunt told them. "It might not look like much, but I daresay there's more information in this little cabinet than in all the rest of my library. Imagine, Wolf. Edison can take everything that's in a man's soul and record it on a few ounces of wax and gold foil and play it back to you as easily as if it were just the latest Bowery-dance-hall song."

"And how will this help you find witches?" Wolf asked.

"Because when you hear a man's soul, you hear everything he is. Magic included. Magic most of all." Morgaunt's eyes glittered like whetted knife blades. "How about it, Wolf? Would you like to sit for the recorder? I'm told it's a remarkable experience. You might learn something. You might surprise yourself."

"I surprise myself plenty already," Wolf said laconically. "I think I'll pass."

Suddenly Morgaunt pulled out one of the cylinders and tossed it to Sacha, who barely managed to avoid dropping it. It was surprisingly light: a delicate confection of wax and gold leaf that felt like it might crumple at the slightest pressure.

Sacha turned it over. He noticed how the gold glinted in the firelight. He felt the odd pattern of grooves and ridges that swirled around it like the whorls of a fingerprint.

"Whose . . . uh . . . soul is this?" he asked.

"I could tell you," Morgaunt said with a mocking grin, "but then I'd have to kill you."

"Can we listen to it?" Lily asked. "I'd like to hear what a soul sounds like."

"What an excellent idea, Miss Astral." The smile that spread over Morgaunt's face as he spoke was even worse than his normal one. It was sly and disdainful. He seemed to be making fun of them to their faces—and enjoying the fact that they were too stupid to see it. "Miss da Serpa, would you do the honors?"

The librarian undulated over to Sacha and took the cylinder from his unresisting hands. She stared hard at Sacha while she did this, and he found it utterly impossible to breathe while her dark eyes were locked on his.

By the time he could move again, Miss da Serpa had loaded the cylinder into a machine that looked for all the world like an Edison Portable Home Phonograph, cranked the machine into life, and stepped back to listen.

What came out was . . . music. But it was like no music Sacha had ever heard. It made him feel naked. Worse than naked. It laid bare every secret shame, fear, and desire he'd ever had. It cut into him like a surgeon's scalpel and yanked his guts out into broad daylight for everyone to see. And short of stopping his ears with his fingers, there was nothing he could do about it.

Finally the music faded. Sacha brushed a hand across his brow and realized he'd broken out in a cold sweat. What a horrible invention! It was indecent. Shameful. Imagine taking a person's deepest feelings and *playing* them as if they were the latest show tune! Even Uncle Mordechai wouldn't expose himself like that. And Sacha didn't have to wonder for a second what his father would think about it.

He glanced furtively at the others to see if they were as shattered by the strange music as he was. But Wolf and Morgaunt both seemed as cool as ever. And Lily seemed to have enjoyed it. In fact she was so enthralled that for a minute Sacha was afraid she was going to ask Miss da Serpa to play the awful thing again.

"That's the most astounding thing I've ever heard!" she gushed. "It makes the best opera ever written sound trite and artificial and . . . and *obvious*. Such passion! I mean, there's no other word for it, is there? And yet, so contained. As if whoever it is has a job to do that's so important he can't afford to think about what he wants—or even who he really is inside— until it's done."

She blinked, obviously struck by a thought that surprised her. "Do all the cylinders sound like that?" she asked Morgaunt. "All those people I pass by in the street without a second glance every day—do they all have *that* going on inside their souls?"

"No." Morgaunt smiled that sly smile that set Sacha's teeth on edge. "This one's rather special."

"Yes, I suppose it must be." Lily sighed a little regretfully. "I'm sure *my* soul wouldn't sound nearly so interesting. I don't think English governesses and Newport beach parties are the sort of life experience that creates passionate intensity."

Wolf coughed politely, as if to suggest that maybe it was time to get back to the main point of their visit. "There are a lot of cylinders in that cabinet," he observed. "Edison's been a busy boy."

"Haven't you been reading the papers? We plan to put a witch detector in every police station in the city by this time next year."

Wolf pushed his glasses up on his nose and peered myopically at Morgaunt through the smudges and fingerprints. "If you do that, you'll unleash a witch-hunt the likes of which this country hasn't seen since the Salem Witch Trials."

"Witch-hunt is such a melodramatic word!" Morgaunt's smile broadened. "I prefer to call it a registry. A magician's etheric emanations are every bit as unique as his fingerprints. Edison's etherograph will generate magical fingerprints of every man, woman, and child in New York. Once we have those on file, we'll be able to identify the author of any magical crime—or, for that matter, any unauthorized use of magic whatsoever. What's more, we'll have a registry of every potential magical criminal in the city. We can make it illegal to employ them. Or rent an apartment to them. Or let their children go to school. We can wash the streets clean of conjure men and soothsayers and fortunetellers. We can clean up this city once and for all and make it safe for respectable nonmagical people."

He grinned. "And, naturally, we can make sure that people do it all with *our* patented etherographs, sold through *our* dealerships, serviced by *our* repairmen, and rendered obsolete by *our* new models."

"Brilliant," Wolf said listlessly.

"No, Wolf. The brilliant part is what happens later, after we've made it impossible for any law-abiding citizen to employ witches or use magic. There'll be no magic left to do all the vital things ordinary Americans depend on witches to do. No magic to wash their dishes. No magic to cook the food in their restaurants. No magic to make their clothes and books and toys and candy"—here his gaze slid toward Sacha and Lily. "In a little while your average American will go from one year to the next without witnessing a single act of real magic. A little longer, and they'll forget whatever magic they used to know. A little longer still, and they'll forget there ever was such a thing as magic."

"And then they'll depend on your machines for everything."

"Precisely."

"And you?" Wolf asked in the dull tones of an accountant trying to make sure he'd gotten his numbers right. "Will people like you and the Astrals and the Vanderbilks stop using magic too?"

"Why should we?" Morgaunt asked boldly. "Magic is only dangerous in the hands of little people. It's perfectly safe in the hands of men with the strength and foresight to guide America into the future."

"That's not what the law says," Wolf pointed out, still in the same dogged monotone.

"Law!" Morgaunt scoffed. "Law is for drunks and weaklings. The only law that applies to superior men is the law of power. You should know that, Wolf. You're no ordinary plodder."

"Oh, I'm quite ordinary," Wolf protested.

"You just pretend to be," Morgaunt snapped, "because of some half-baked romantic notion of democracy and equality. But how deep would I have to scratch before you showed your true colors?"

And then Morgaunt began to work magic.

It was so subtle that at first Sacha didn't even see it. Morgaunt still had that coldly mocking smile on his face. He lounged in his wing chair swirling his Scotch lazily in one hand. But somehow it *felt* like he had reached out and grasped Wolf by the throat and was slowly strangling him.

Before Sacha knew what was happening, the entire room was thick with magic. And this was nothing like the ordinary everyday magic Sacha knew from Hester Street. This magic was larger than mere human beings. It gave him the same unnerving feeling he always got when he looked into the open pits that workmen were digging all over town for the new subway lines. You walked around the city all your life thinking that you were standing on solid ground. But then they brought in the steam shovels and ripped up the cobblestones, and you realized that the earth—the real, living, breathing earth—was still alive down there in the dark beneath the city. And if it ever woke up, it would shake off New York and all its teeming millions like a dog shaking off a flea.

Wolf and Morgaunt stared at each other. The room seemed about to catch fire. The very air crackled with magic. It felt as if all the magic in the world were being sucked in around them like a great whirlpool, spiraling down into the glowing golden liquid in Morgaunt's hand.

Morgaunt raised his glass in an ironic toast. "Here's to you and me, Wolf. The last two honest men in New York."

Wolf didn't answer. A dark flush had spread across his usually pale features. His breath was as ragged as if he'd just run up a flight of stairs. Sacha wanted to rush to help him, and he could see that Lily felt the same. But they were both frozen to the spot.

And then it was over.

Morgaunt tossed back his drink with one sharp flick of his wrist and broke the spell. Wolf staggered, gasping for breath.

"Well, what are you waiting for?" Morgaunt taunted. "Isn't it time to trot off and arrest someone like a good little policeman?"

"I haven't seen the crime scene. I haven't interviewed witnesses. I haven't even spoken to Edison. And you want me to arrest someone? You don't need an Inquisitor on this case, Mr. Morgaunt. You need an errand boy."

Morgaunt grinned. "You wound me. I would never turn

you into an errand boy. By all means, conduct your little investigation. But the end will be the same no matter what you do. It's all just a game of chess, Wolf. Ordinary players take the board as they find it. I set the board up before the game ever starts so that no matter what moves you make, I still win."

"And what opening moves did you have in mind for me?" Wolf asked sullenly.

"You have a bad attitude, Wolf. I like that in a man. I think I'm going to enjoy breaking you even more than I enjoyed breaking Roosevelt. That reminds me, I have a clue for you." Morgaunt leaned over to pluck a letter off his desk. "It arrived in this morning's mail. I've been enjoying our little chat so much that I completely forgot about it."

Wolf scanned the scrawled handwriting that slanted across the page. "A note from the Industrial Witches of the World claiming responsibility for the attack. That's awfully convenient for you. Aren't they trying to organize a strike at the Pentacle Shirtwaist Factory?"

"Oh, yes," Morgaunt murmured. "You're going to be much more fun than Roosevelt."

"I suppose you expect me to go down to IWW Headquarters now and arrest some poor slob for attempted murder?"

"Would I tell you how to do your job?"

"I guess I'll have to talk to them one way or another." Wolf looked at the letter again and sighed. "Why is it that people who confess to crimes by mail never seem to remember to put a return address on their letters?"

"I don't think you'll have any trouble finding them,"

Morgaunt said with a laugh like ball bearings rolling across an iron floor.

And then Sacha's heart clenched in terror, because he knew exactly what Morgaunt would say next.

"IWW Headquarters is at number eighteen Hester Street. Your new apprentice can show you the way."

CHAPTER EIGHT

Industrial Witches of the World Unite!

THE TRIP TO Hester Street took a year off Sacha's life.

First, Lily had to ask him what Morgaunt had meant with his last wisecrack. And Sacha had to say he had no idea. And then there was a traffic jam. And then, as if things weren't already bad enough, Wolf decided that what with all the traffic, they might as well walk the last few blocks.

It was one of those golden fall afternoons when all of New York pours onto the sidewalks—and every out-of-work Yiddish actor and revolutionary on the Lower East Side was basking in the sun at the Café Metropole's outdoor tables.

Sacha skulked past, doing his best to hide in Wolf's long, skinny shadow. Even so, he could hear Uncle Mordechai waxing eloquent about the vital distinction between Hamiltonian Wicco-Federalism and Jeffersonian Popular Wiccanism. He shrank into his coat collar and prayed that his uncle was having too much fun planning the revolution to notice that his favorite nephew was aiding and abetting Big Magic right under his nose.

Wolf took forever to get there—mainly because he didn't seem to be able to pass any beggar by without stopping to talk while he fished around in his pockets for coins to give him. But finally they made it down Hester Street and into Sacha's building without anyone recognizing him.

Their tenement was a good one—anyway, a lot better than some of the places Sacha could remember living in. The Kesslers had a third-floor front apartment, with two windows opening onto Hester Street and a fire escape big enough to sleep the whole family on stifling summer nights. But seeing the building now, with Wolf and Lily beside him, Sacha realized it was desperately shabby. Maybe even worse than shabby.

For the first time in his life, he was glad there were no lights in the stairwell. It was so dark that his own mother could have tripped over him without recognizing him. As long as he kept his mouth shut and the neighbors kept their doors closed, he was safe. All he needed now was for his luck to hold until they made it past the third floor.

Meanwhile, Lily was peering around the windowless entryway. "Does anyone see a light switch?"

"I . . . uh . . . don't think there *are* any—"

"Nonsense!" Lily interrupted. "I know for a fact that Commissioner Roosevelt passed a law requiring landlords to install lights at least two years ago!"

"Well, bully for him!" Sacha muttered.

"You needn't laugh," Lily huffed. "Some of us actually *care* about poor people!"

By the time they made it to the top floor, Wolf had knocked over two ash bins and narrowly missed stepping in a full chamber pot, while Lily had "rescued" a "lost" baby she found playing on the stairs and returned it to its parents—only to be told to mind her own business in language not suitable for a young lady's ears. Finally, they gathered at the top of the stairs. Someone had propped open the door to the roof, so there was a dingy trickle of daylight. While Wolf took off his glasses and wiped his face on his sleeve, Sacha glanced at Lily to see how she was taking her first encounter with the tenements.

There was a large, sooty smear down the front of her white dress, and she was still catching her breath. But she seemed pretty calm, he thought.

Until she opened her mouth.

"How can people *live* like this?" she gasped. "They're no better than animals! And those *poor* children! It's enough to make you think the missionaries are right and they'd be better off in an orphanage!"

Sacha bit his tongue and turned away, thankful that the corridor was too dim for her to see the angry flush spreading across his face. "Let's get this over with and get out of here," he said. "Where are the stupid Wobblies anyway?"

"If you can't figure that out," Wolf drawled, "you might want to consider another line of work."

And indeed, there was a huge banner strung over the last door on the left. The banner had been designed to be carried down the broad avenues of New York by a phalanx of demonstrating workers, not hung in a hallway barely wide enough for two people to squeeze past each other sideways. Bold purple letters marched across its face, spelling out one of Uncle Mordechai's favorite rallying cries:

WITCHES OF THE WORLD UNITE!
YOU HAVE NOTHING TO LOSE BUT YOUR CHAINS!

On the bright side, Sacha told himself as he trailed down the hallway after Wolf and Lily, things couldn't possibly get any more ridiculous than this.

But of course things can always get more ridiculous—and usually do.

The boy who answered Wolf's knock had carrot-colored hair that corkscrewed from his head like rusty springs popping out of a broken mattress. His bony wrists stuck out of his sleeves halfway up to the elbow, and his neck was so skinny that his tie looked like a hangman's noose.

But worst of all was the expression on his face. It was eager, sweet, pathetically earnest. You knew as soon as you laid eyes on him that he was the kind of fellow who could be counted on to finish last every time, like the nice guy he was. Basically, he was the walking definition of a *shlimazel*. Or a *shnook* or a *shmendrick* or . . . well . . . there were a thousand pitying words in Yiddish to describe this kind of boy. And

Sacha's family could happily have spent a thousand years arguing over which word fit him best. But all Sacha cared about right now was getting out of here before this ridiculous boy or any of his crazy Wobbly friends recognized him.

"Greetings, comrades!" the young man cried before any of them had a chance to speak. "Long live the Revolution!"

"Umm . . . yes," Wolf said. "Who's in charge here?"

"I am." He reached out to shake Wolf's hand, and his coat sleeve rode up so far that Sacha could have sworn he saw an elbow. "Moishe Schlosky at your service!"

Sacha squinted at Moishe, trying to remember if he'd seen him before. Could this be the skinny redhead his father had been teasing Bekah about? But no, that was impossible. The very idea of plump, pretty, vivacious Bekah with *this* fellow was ridiculous. There were thousands of skinny redheads on the Lower East Side, and if Bekah was seeing one of them, it definitely wasn't this one!

"Aren't you a little . . . er . . . young?" Wolf asked.

"What's young? I've been a presser at Pentacle since I was eleven. And most of the seamstresses are younger than me." Moishe assumed a heroic stance—or, rather, a stance that would have been heroic if anyone else had assumed it. "The youth is our future!"

"Do you mind if we come in? This might take a while."

"Say," Moishe exclaimed as Sacha followed Wolf into the apartment, "aren't you Bekah's little bro—"

"No!"

"But—"

"I live uptown! Never been here in my life! You must be thinking of someone else!"

"Wha—?" Moishe said, his face frozen into a comical look of surprise. "Oh! Right! Definitely!"

Moishe was a pathetically bad liar. Not that that was a surprise, Sacha thought sourly. He hoped the Pentacle workers weren't depending on Moishe's bargaining skills to end the strike. With that kind of talent on their side, they'd end up paying Morgaunt to let them go back to work.

Luckily, Wolf and Lily were too busy staring at the chaos inside the tenement to notice Moishe's bad acting.

It was a regular Babel. People—girls, mostly—were running around yammering at each other in Yiddish and Italian and English. One gaggle of girls was setting up rickety card tables. Another group was magically unpacking boxes of pamphlets and broadsheets—so enthusiastically that Sacha was sure one of those pieces of paper zinging around the room was going to give someone a nasty paper cut. A third group was huddled around the stove poring over the hot-off-the-presses evening edition of the *Yiddish Daily Magic-Worker*, which one of the girls seemed to be translating into Italian for the others.

"These are your strikers?" Wolf asked Moishe. "Aren't there any grownups working at Pentacle?"

"The grownups are all bourgeois reactionaries," Moishe said with a dismissive shrug. "They have to 'make a living' and 'feed their families.'"

Wolf scrubbed a hand through his hair as if he thought

the friction would help his brain work better. "Is there somewhere we can talk that's a little more private?"

"Sure," Moishe said. And stepped straight out of the open window.

Lily gasped.

"Well?" Moishe said, looking back in at them from the fire escape. "Are you coming or not?"

"Phew!" Lily whispered to Sacha as they stepped out the window behind Wolf. "I didn't know there was a fire escape. I thought he was going to fly or something."

Sacha gave her an incredulous look.

"Well, they *are* the Industrial *Witches* of the World, after all."

"Witches don't fly," Sacha said scathingly. "You've been reading too many penny dreadfuls."

"That's ridiculous! And what do *you* know about witches anyway?"

Sacha decided he'd had it with Lily Astral's know-it-all attitude. "A lot more than some Fifth Avenue debutante who's using her daddy's pull to make Wolf let her play at being an Inquisitor."

Lily spluttered in fury, but Sacha was already stepping through the window onto the fire escape.

Outside, Sacha relished the fresh air and quiet—or rather the relative quiet, since Moishe was already talking Wolf's ear off about how the Pentacle strike was going to blow the lid off Big Magic's corporate conspiracy to keep down the working witch.

But eventually Wolf brought the conversation back around to Morgaunt's accusation.

"You're kidding me!" Moishe cried when he finally figured out what Wolf was getting at. "J. P. Morgaunt is accusing me of trying to assassinate Thomas Edison? That's the dumbest thing I ever heard! What are you going to do now, drag me off to jail and throw away the key until Morgaunt tells you to find it again?"

"Actually, no."

"Why not?" Moishe sounded insulted, as if he actually *wanted* to be arrested.

"Because I don't arrest children."

Moishe put his hands on his hips and glared ferociously at Wolf. Sacha could tell that he was trying to look dangerous enough to be worth arresting. It wasn't working.

Wolf managed to keep a straight face, though he did succumb to a suspicious fit of coughing. When he had recovered, he started explaining about the dybbuk.

"Dybbuk, shmybbuk," Moishe scoffed. "There probably *is* no dybbuk."

"Why would you think that?"

"Isn't it obvious? It's a red herring Morgaunt's throwing out to distract people from the real crime."

"What crime?" Wolf asked hopefully.

"Why, Morgaunt's crime, of course. Running a magical sweatshop!"

"Oh, right." Wolf sighed. "That."

"Everyone knows he pays off the Inquisitors to turn a blind eye to it. And then they go around shutting down mom and pop operations and hounding his competition out of business. And if he gets his way with that Etherograph of his, it's only going to get worse. Magic-workers will become fugitives. They'll have no choice but to take whatever rotten deal he gives them or the Inquisitors will deport them. I'm telling you, someone in this city has to stand up to him or—"

"Right . . . well . . . getting back to the dybbuk . . ." Wolf interrupted.

Moishe shrugged. "What do I know from dybbuks? I'm a dyed-in-the-wool atheist. The only people in the Lower East Side who know from dybbuks are rabbis. And they're all just gutless bourgeois reactionaries who want us to let the Morgaunts of the world stomp all over us so we can reap our reward in heaven or Brooklyn—*neither* of which, allow me to point out, has ever been scientifically proven to exist."

"But—but—" Sacha stammered, "Brooklyn—I mean, come on, Moishe! The subway stops there!"

"Hah! If you believe everything you read on a subway map, I've got a bridge to sell you!"

Sacha was still shaking his head when he followed Wolf and Lily downstairs. Wolf pushed through the front door, muttering something about a cab, and Sacha rolled his eyes. There hadn't been a cab sighted on Hester Street in living memory!

Still, Wolf raised his hand and forged into the crowd like a swimmer wading into rough surf. And, sure enough, an energetic little horse came trotting around the corner just in time for its driver to jump down and usher Wolf inside.

"I'll give you both a ride back to the office," Wolf said while Sacha was still staring. "Otherwise you'll never get home for dinner."

Sacha hesitated. It was late afternoon by now, and it really didn't make any sense for him to ride all the way back to Hell's Kitchen just to take the subway home again. But he couldn't think of any excuse for staying behind. So he climbed in, resigning himself to a long, pointless, expensive round trip.

By the time Sacha finally climbed out of the subway at Astral Place, night was falling.

He hurried nervously down the Bowery. It was that deserted time between rush hour and the after-dinner theater crowd. The only people on the sidewalks were tourists going slumming in Chinatown—and all the petty and not-so-petty criminals who preyed on them. The Elevated roared overhead every few minutes, spitting steam and coal dust. Every time it passed, Sacha looked around warily.

He sped up, trying to look tougher than he felt and telling himself he was only a few short blocks from home.

He had just passed the reassuring lights of the Metropole when he realized someone was following him. Within the space of a few ragged breaths, he went from wondering where that odd echo of his footfalls was coming from to knowing for dead certain that there was someone behind him.

He cursed himself for not having gone into the Metropole. Uncle Mordechai might have been there. Or at least someone he knew well enough to ask them to walk him home. But it was too late now. There was nothing for it but to keep going.

He turned the corner onto Hester Street, hoping to see a friendly face or two smiling at him from the front stoops of the tenements. But there was no one. The shoppers and pushcart peddlers were long gone. The cobblestones were littered with old food and bits of tailors' clippings and sooty drifts of crumpled newspapers. Misshapen piles of crates and boxes loomed outside the shop fronts. Laundry dangled from the fire escapes like hanged men. Sacha had never seen Hester Street so silent and lifeless. Even the mannequins in the shop windows seemed to stare out at him with blank, uncaring expressions.

It was dark too. The Bowery was one of New York's famous White Ways, lit up night and day with Edison's new electric lights. But back in the narrow tenement streets, people still made do with gaslight. And not much of it either. The flickering halos around the occasional lampposts were only faint islands of light in an ocean of shadows.

Now he was a block from his building. Now half a block. Now three storefronts away. And still the footsteps sounded behind him. Not gaining on him, not falling back. Just following. Sacha felt like he was caught in one of those awful dreams where you run and run until you finally realize that the only way to wake up is to stop and let the monster catch you.

Finally, the urge to look back became unbearable. He glanced over his shoulder, trying not to be too obvious about it.

And there it was. A moving shadow just beyond the glow of the nearest streetlight. It was vague and indefinite and yet unmistakably *there*. He couldn't see its face. But there was something unnervingly familiar about the set of its slim shoulders.

Sacha looked away, gauging the distance that still separated him from the front stoop of his own building. His legs trembled. His entire body tensed like a coiled spring. What if he made a mad dash for it? Would he make it? And what would happen if he didn't?

It was only the briefest of glances, a flick of his eyes toward the stoop. No natural creature could have vanished into the shadows that quickly. Nonetheless, when he looked back, the watcher was gone.

Sacha cast his eyes frantically around the silent street, but there was no sign of the shadowy figure. If it weren't for the icy chill still upon him, he could almost have convinced himself he'd imagined it.

As he reached the third floor, he could hear his mother and father bickering affectionately with each other, and Bekah setting the table for dinner, and Uncle Mordechai chuckling over something in the *Daily Magic-Worker*. Sacha was just pausing outside the door for a final moment to enjoy the comfortable sounds of home when a skeletal hand reached out of the shadows to grip his shoulder.

He gasped and spun around, heart pounding—only to see Moishe Schlosky, of all people.

"Shhh!" Moishe whispered. "Stop shrieking like a girl!"

"I was not shrieking like a girl," Sacha protested, torn between anger at Moishe and embarrassment about the admittedly somewhat high-pitched sound that had escaped him when he felt Moishe's bony fingers on his shoulder.

"You were too. Anyway, never mind. I have to talk to you."

"Fine, so talk to me like a normal person! Don't sneak up on me in a dark hallway!"

"Do I look like the landlord?" Moishe asked comically. "Now it's my fault there's no lights in here?"

"Oh, for God's sake, Moishe! What do you want already?"

"A favor, just a favor. You're working for that Inquisitor, right?"

"So?"

"So you know what he's up to and how his investigation is going."

"I guess," Sacha said reluctantly, not liking where this conversation was headed.

"Well, then couldn't you just . . . you know . . . kind of keep me posted on it?"

"I could get fired for that!"

"Class solidarity demands it of you!"

Sacha guffawed. "You've *got* to be kidding me. I dare you to say that again with a straight face."

Inside the apartment the friendly voices were drowned out suddenly by the rapid-fire clatter of Mrs. Lehrer's foot-powered sewing machine. It was probably Mo at the sewing machine, knocking off another dozen shirts while his wife fixed dinner before doing her nightly quota. It seemed a hard life suddenly—miles away from Lily Astral's world of mansions and limousines.

"Is that all you want in life?" Moishe asked, as if reading Sacha's thoughts. "To be an errand boy for the Carbuncles and Vanderbilks and Morgaunts? Don't you believe in anything?"

"I believe in taking care of my family," Sacha said stubbornly.

"Of course you do. We all do. That's what your sister is working for, and a lot of other girls like her. We're just asking you to help."

"Well, ask someone else."

"Look," Moishe said, "couldn't you just think about it?"

"Moishe, I'm not going to do it no matter how long I think about it."

"Oh!" Moishe cried in a voice worthy of the mourners at the Wailing Wall. "Oh, that a nephew of Mordechai Kessler should have come to this!" He was still shaking his head when the door to Sacha's apartment popped open and Bekah stuck her head out.

"Sacha!" she said. "What are you doing lurking in the stairwell! Dinner's already on the ta—"

She caught sight of Moishe and stopped abruptly.

Sacha looked at Bekah. Then he looked at Moishe. Then he looked back at Bekah again. "Are you *blushing?*" he asked her.

"Don't!" Bekah warned. "Don't you dare say one more word!"

"Bekah—" Moishe began.

"And you!" she snapped, sounding uncannily like their

mother. "Haven't you caused enough trouble? Get out of here already!"

Moishe started to protest, but then he took one look at Bekah's furious face, tucked his tail between his legs, and slunk away like a man who knew when he was beaten. Sacha couldn't help grinning at the sight; obviously Bekah already had Moishe's training well in hand.

Bekah held the door to their apartment open, but Sacha wasn't ready to go inside yet.

"No way!" he said, just quietly enough to make sure their mother wouldn't hear him. "Moishe Schlosky?"

"Oh, and I suppose you're dating Mary Pickford? I'd bet good money you've never even kissed a girl!"

"Yeah, but . . . Moishe? He's so . . . so . . . so *skinny!*"

"You are the most shallow, superficial, trivial—"

"Are you two waiting for the Messiah out there?" their mother shouted from inside the apartment. "Come in and sit down already! Dinner's getting cold!"

Sacha was still shaking his head in amazement when he sat down to dinner. Indeed, he was so busy being amazed at the idea of Bekah being sweet on Moishe that he almost forgot Moishe's outrageous idea that he ought to spy on Wolf for the strikers. As if he didn't have enough problems already!

When the rest of his family was settling down for coffee and after-dinner chatter around the kitchen table, Sacha went to the window and cautiously lifted the curtain.

There was nothing there. No watcher in the shadows. No dark figure standing at the edge of the streetlights.

For some unfathomable reason, that made him feel worse instead of better. Who or what had been following him? And could it possibly be a coincidence that this silent watcher had first appeared on the very same night that Edison and Sacha's mother had both been attacked?

He was still wondering about it when he got to work the next morning to find out that the dybbuk had tried to burn down Edison's Luna Park Laboratory.

CHAPTER NINE

The Wizard of Luna Park

NEW YORKERS disagreed about everything else under the sun, but the one thing they all loved was Coney Island. On Coney Island, New Yorkers of every race, religion, and nationality banged elbows with one another in raucous harmony. A Jewish boy from Hester Street couldn't venture into Hell's Kitchen or Little Italy without risking injury to life and limb—not to mention pride. But on Coney Island he could mingle with Irish, Italian, German, and Greek boys, all of them bent on nothing more sinister than riding the rides and ogling the peep shows. Everyday jobs and responsibilities and loyalties were forgotten. Coney Island's philosophy was live and let live. Or rather, play and let play.

Sacha had been there before, of course. Several times a year for as long as he could remember, he and Bekah had piled onto the nickel ferry with their father for the long ride to the famous amusement park. Mrs. Kessler never went; she insisted she had better things to do with her day off than walk up and down the boardwalk wearing out her shoes and gawping like a carp. But Mr. Kessler loved Coney Island. It was the one place in New York where he seemed to be able to forget his worries and just enjoy life. If anyone had asked Sacha, he would have said he loved Coney Island too—but, really, it wasn't the rides he loved, or the boardwalk, or the hucksters and peep shows and shucked peanuts. It was the person his father turned into when they went there.

Going to Coney Island with Inquisitor Wolf, on the other hand, was a somewhat different experience.

Wolf whisked Sacha and Lily into a waiting cab and straight downtown to the Brooklyn Bridge. Then he counted over the unimaginable sum of three dollars at the ticket window and ushered them into the quiet, middle-class luxury of the Prospect Park and Coney Island Railroad Company Special Express: nonstop to Coney Island in a blistering thirty-two minutes.

Wolf settled into one corner, put his long legs up on the seat, and frowned over a copy of the *New York Tribune* that he had bought from a newsboy, in between handing out money to three or four panhandlers. Then he did the crossword puzzle. In ink. In ten minutes flat.

And then they were pulling into the station and Sacha was chasing Wolf's flapping coattails off the train, down the platform, and under the echoing glass domes of the Coney Island Railway Terminal.

The first thing Sacha saw when he followed Inquisitor Wolf outside the station was an elephant—or, rather, *the* Elephant. The Elephant Hotel was the single most famous thing on Coney Island. It was more famous than Luna Park. It was more famous than the Amazing Revolving Wheel of George W. G. Ferris. Indeed, the Elephant so dominated the amusement park's exotic skyline that "seeing the Elephant" had become New York slang for every kind of forbidden pleasure.

The Elephant Hotel looked like the product of a head-on train wreck between the Flatiron Building and a woolly mammoth. Its massive front legs housed a cigar store and diorama. Its back legs enclosed twin spiral staircases (one going up, one going down). Its head contained an astronomical observatory (though critics scoffed that the only "stars" anyone ever saw from it were the electric lights on Luna Park's Loop the Loop). And its four-story-high body housed the World-Famous Starlite Theater, Playground to Celebrities and Royalty.

Between the Elephant Hotel and Luna Park ran Surf Avenue. Surf Avenue was sheer pandemonium. Persian palaces jostled Chinese pagodas. Lapland reindeer rubbed shoulders with camels and snake charmers. Sudanese sheiks mingled with South Sea Island mermaids to the wild strains of fiddling Gypsies and Sioux medicine drummers. And that wasn't even mentioning the rides and the freak shows.

Everywhere Sacha turned, he saw signs advertising Coney Island's famous (or in some cases, infamous) amusements:

ARE YOU MAN ENOUGH
to Ride the
Shoot-the-Chutes?

Do You DARE
Witness the World Debut of the
TASMANIAN DEVIL BOY?

SEE JOLLY TRIXIE!
It Takes Seven Men to HUG HER!
"Holy Smoke! She's fat,
she's awful fat!"

Every sign promised newer, wilder, faster, freakier thrills. And if the signs were blunt, the hucksters calling out from every doorway were even blunter:

"See Little Cairo dance the hootchy-kootchy! Hottest show on earth! If it weren't for Coney Island's cool ocean breezes, she'd burn up in her own fire!"

"Step right up, folks! Don't be shy! See the Mighty Atom in action! Feel his muscles! Hear his story! Watch his mind-boggling feats of strength! *Ev*-er-y ticket comes complete with a free copy of *Bodybuilding for the Millions*!"

"Don't dawdle!" Wolf called out from far up the boardwalk.

Sacha tore his eyes away from *Bodybuilding for the Millions*. "Sorry! Just coming, sir!"

When he caught up, Sacha found Lily happily sampling a very different kind of Coney Island attraction. Somehow she'd found time to buy a huge ring of fried dough.

"Want some?" she asked him through a cloud of powdered sugar.

It smelled awfully good. But he didn't want her to think they didn't feed him at home. And anyway, God only knew what they fried those things in.

"No thanks."

They were at the gates of Luna Park now, and even Lily couldn't help staring in amazement. It looked like the entrance to a Turkish seraglio, complete with crescent moons and minarets. Every square inch of the building was encrusted with twinkling electric lights. Sacha had never seen anything like it, even on the Bowery. It was like looking at a building made of stars. And the inside of Luna Park was even more dazzling than the outside. Rides, amusements, exhibition halls: everything blazed with that clear, sharp, starlike electric light. It was brilliant even in the middle of the day. Sacha couldn't imagine how spectacular it must be after nightfall.

When they finally reached Edison's laboratory, they found the Wizard of Luna Park doing what he did every morning from precisely 8:13 a.m. to 10:09 a.m., excepting Sundays: sitting in his Inventing Chair, inventing.

Before Edison, inventors had been quaint, gentlemanly eccentrics who dabbled in science for the pure pleasure of it. But Edison had done for inventing what Henry Ford had done for motorcars and Cornelius Vanderbilk had done for railroads and J. P. Morgaunt had done for steel mills and shirtwaist factories and practically every other modern American necessity. Edison had turned inventing into big business.

Every minute of Edison's time was scheduled down to the last second. Every experiment, every idea, every stray thought was recorded in his famous notebooks just in case it turned out to contain the seed of a valuable invention. Plus, Edison didn't just wait around for inspiration to strike. He went out and hunted it down.

That was where the Inventing Chair came in. It was a straight-backed wooden chair with paddle-shaped arms. The right-hand arm broadened into a writing desk like the ones children used at school. Two objects rested on it: a sharpened pencil and a black-bound laboratory notebook.

When Wolf and his apprentices arrived, Edison was just sitting there with his hands hanging over the fronts of the chair arms and his head nodding drowsily. In each hand he held a steel ball bearing. Beneath his hands—carefully positioned to catch the ball bearings when they dropped—were two tin pie plates.

"What's he doing?" Lily whispered.

"Inventing."

"If you ask me, it looks more like sleeping."

"Well . . . it is, sort of. He has his best ideas just as he's falling asleep, and he used to forget them overnight. Now he falls asleep under scientifically controlled conditions so he can record his ideas before he forgets them."

"That's ridiculous!" Lily used that word a lot, Sacha had noticed. Usually about people who didn't agree with her.

A moment later, Edison's eyes closed. His head nodded onto his chest. His hands relaxed. The pair of ball bearings dropped from his fingers and clattered into the waiting pie plates . . . and Edison started upright, snatched up his pencil, and began writing furiously.

He scribbled down several pages' worth of notes, and then reread them with a puzzled look on his face. "Hmm. Moving pictures people can watch in their own homes? It's a nice idea, but I don't see how anyone's ever going to make money off it."

Then he shrugged, turned the page, laid the notebook and pencil back on the arm of his chair, and bent down to pick up the ball bearings again.

"Excuse me, Mr. Edison," his assistant interrupted. "Inquisitor Wolf is here to see you."

"Oh—of course!" He hurried over to shake Wolf's hand. "Welcome, Inquisitor! And let me say what an honor it is to meet you. The great Maximillian Wolf, bane of witches, bulwark of freedom, defender of the American way! In short, a real American hero!"

"Er . . . quite," Wolf answered coolly.

Edison didn't appear to notice Wolf's lack of enthusiasm. "I've arranged a little demonstration for you. Nothing formal, you understand. The etherograph is still in its early stages. We've got our work cut out for us before the grand

opening. Oh, yes, we'll certainly be burning the midnight oil—or rather the midnight electricity."

"Actually," Wolf said, "I was hoping to ask you about last night's attack."

"A triviality," Edison said with an airy wave. "Never mind that, the etherograph's the thing!"

He led them over to the back corner of the lab. Sacha realized that this must have been where the fire was: a faint smell of smoke hung in the air, and the floor showed signs of hasty cleaning. Edison pointed to a cluttered lab table. But there was no etherograph on it. There were only advertisements for one.

They came in all shapes and sizes. There were ads for billboards, ads for subway stations, ads for omnibuses and trolley cars and railway sidings. The etherograph in the ads looked a lot like the Edison Portable Home Phonograph Sacha had seen in ads all over the city for the last few months. It had the same fluted speaker horn and the same lunch-box-shaped metal body, the same hinged top that you flipped up to insert a fresh cylinder. But the etherograph's top was emblazoned with a screaming eagle that looked just like the eagle on an Inquisitor's badge, and beneath the eagle was stamped

EDISON ETHEROGRAPHS
Portable Etheric Emanation Detection System

Instead of the two blond girls from the home phonograph ads, the etherograph ads featured a dark-skinned wizard cowering in front of a heroic blond Inquisitor. This Inquisitor was too handsome to look much like Inquisitor Wolf—or, for that matter, any other real person Sacha had ever met. But the artist had made the wizard very realistic in a mean-spirited, nasty kind of way.

That long, pointed nose that arched like an eagle's beak. Those unhealthily thin cheeks with their sharply carved worry lines. The dark eyes, with even darker circles of exhaustion under them. They all looked terribly familiar to Sacha. In fact, the wizard looked like Sacha's father. Or like his father would have looked if he were in the habit of going around with a five-day beard and dressing up in ridiculous penny-opera Kabbalist's robes embroidered with satanic symbols.

It was a brilliant ad. There wasn't a thing that Sacha could have improved upon.

He hated it.

"Thrilling," Wolf said, though he couldn't have sounded less thrilled if he'd actually slipped into a coma right in front of their eyes. "And is there an actual etherograph to go with the advertisements?"

"But you saw it yourself at Morgaunt's libra—"

Wolf silenced Sacha with a flick of his wrist.

"Of course there's an etherograph . . . or rather, that is to say, there will be." Edison gave a nervous little laugh. "Mr. Morgaunt has placed a great deal of operating capital in my hands, and I don't intend to disappoint him!"

Edison turned away from Wolf to fix the two apprentices

with the piercing blue gaze for which he was famous. "What can you tell me about etheric force?" he asked them.

Sacha thought this was a pathetically obvious attempt to change the subject, so he hesitated and glanced at Wolf instead of answering.

Lily, on the other hand, was way too much of a know-it-all to keep her mouth shut. "It's what witches use to do magic. Everyone knows *that*." She pointed at Sacha. "And *he* can see it!"

Suddenly everyone was staring at Sacha.

"I don't do it on purpose," he said, feeling like he had to apologize to Edison for beating his prototype into production. "It just . . . happens."

"Humph!" Edison snorted. "Well, never mind that. I haven't got all day. I'm already three minutes and twelve seconds behind schedule."

He strode into the darkest corner of the lab, where Sacha could just make out a hulking, misshapen *something* crouching in the shadows under an oil-stained dustcloth. Edison whisked the cloth away with a flourish that reminded Sacha of his Uncle Mordechai. Come to think of it, there were a lot of things about Edison that reminded Sacha of Uncle Mordechai. He wondered suddenly how much of Edison's inventing was science and how much was showmanship.

"Behold the Edison Portable Etheric Emanation Detector!" Edison cried.

It was as big as a cookstove. Mismatched gear casings and switch boxes were soldered and bolted onto every visible surface of the machine and connected to one another by a tangled bird's nest of rubber tubes and copper electrical wires. And on the floor beneath the etherograph, a motley collection of pie tins and cracked tea saucers collected the oily fluid that leaked from every joint and valve of the machine.

"Ahem," Edison said with a rather silly look on his face. "The, er, prototype."

Sacha stared at the thing in astonishment. It looked nothing like the etherograph in the ads—or like the machine they'd seen in Morgaunt's library. Had that one simply been for playing the cylinders, not recording them? Or was there more than one etherograph—more than one design, even? Wolf seemed to be wondering the same thing.

"It doesn't look much like the advertisement," he pointed out.

"Yes, well, we have several weeks before the grand opening. And anyway, packaging is ninety-nine percent of the battle when it comes to selling a new product to the public. And this product will sell. Oh, yes! Mark my words, in five years there'll be one in every police station in the country! And after that . . . well, Inquistor, the rest is up to you!"

Wolf just gazed stolidly at Edison. He didn't voice an opinion. He didn't even seem to have an opinion. It was amazing what a chameleon the man was. Sometimes he looked so subtle and clever and humorous that Sacha could imagine him lounging around the Café Metropole with Uncle Mordechai. But back at Morgaunt's house he'd looked like a butler. And now he looked like a dumb Irish cop who didn't have a thought in his head except where the next beer was coming from.

Wolf's dumb-cop look had an amazing effect on Thomas Edison. The inventor seemed to feel that Wolf was accusing him of something, and the silent accusation cut deeper than fine words and flowery speeches ever could. Edison drew himself up to his full height with an outraged look on his face. He was clearly getting ready to put Wolf in his place. But then all the air seemed to go out of him.

Suddenly he wasn't the Wizard of Luna Park anymore. Suddenly he was just plain Tom Edison. It looked as if some tiny puppet master inside of him had packed up his props and gone home, leaving behind only the bare bones of the empty theater.

"You think I like this?" he asked forlornly. "I didn't get into inventing to deport people. If I had my way, I'd be working on moving pictures. Funny ones! Romantic ones! Movies that would make people forget their troubles and have fun for a few hours! That's what I'd rather be doing. But I only invent things. I can't make people go out and buy 'em. And laughter and romance don't sell. Fear sells. Witch hunts sell."

Wolf raised his eyebrows slightly at this—which for Wolf was a big reaction.

"Could we see a demonstration of the etherograph, if it's not too much trouble?" he asked after a moment.

"Is that really necessary? I'm a very busy man, Inquisitor."

"Someone's trying to kill you, Mr. Edison. Don't you want to catch him?"

"Well, of course! It's just that, er, actually, you see—the prototype doesn't exactly work yet."

Wolf blinked. "But we saw the recorded cylinders in Mr. Morgaunt's library. He played one for us."

"Oh! Well, that's different."

"How?"

"It's quite technical. I'm sure you wouldn't understand."

Wolf gazed at Edison for a long, uncomfortable moment. Then he gave a little shrug and changed the subject. "Tell me about the dybbuk. Did it attack you this time? Or just try to set fire to the etherograph?"

"Er . . . both, sort of . . . or, rather, it's hard to say." Edison looked a little embarrassed. "You see, I crawled under the etherograph to get away from it. In the heat of the moment, you understand. And then it tried to drag me out, and then Rosie—ahem—well, that is to say, my laboratory assistant— chased it away."

Wolf frowned. "What did you say this assistant's name was?"

Edison cleared his throat and ran a hand around the inside of his collar as if he'd suddenly developed a rash. "I . . . well . . . Mrs. Edison, you understand. It would be most disruptive of my domestic felicity if word of this, er, *person* got out to the newspapers."

Wolf raised his eyebrows. "And how did your . . . assistant chase the dybbuk away?"

"With a screwdriver. And, er, bubblegum."

Wolf smiled. "That's the first time I've ever heard of anyone fighting off a dybbuk with bubblegum. It sounds like your lab assistant could give the police a lesson or two."

"Oh! Yes! She's a most remarkable girl. But, er, very respectable, you understand. It would be quite improper to involve her in a criminal investigation. I could never forgive myself if . . ."

Wolf gave Edison another of his bland looks, and some silent message seemed to pass between the two men. Sacha smothered a grin. He had a feeling Edison was going to be much more cooperative from now on.

After that, they searched the lab. Sacha had been looking forward to this part. After all, Maximillian Wolf was the best Inquisitor in the NYPD, and searching magical crime scenes was what Inquisitors did best. Sacha figured he'd learn a lot from watching Wolf in action.

He didn't.

As far as he could see, the only evidence Wolf collected from the lab was a dried-up wad of lime green chewing gum and a long, red, curly strand of hair. He seemed to stumble on them largely by accident, since he spent most of his time staring into space as if he were a thousand miles away. And Sacha wasn't even sure Wolf thought they *were* evidence, since all he did was stick them in his pocket. Maybe he was just helping Edison clean up after the fire.

In the end, it was Sacha himself who found the big clue. In the dusty shadows under the etherograph something small and silver glinted. Without thinking, Sacha dropped to his stomach, stretched his arm under the machine, and grabbed for it.

The thing came loose with the little ping of a delicate chain breaking. It was a silver locket. The front was engraved with filigreed leaves and flowers. The back read "To Ruthie from Danny" in Yiddish. And inside the locket were three silken locks of baby hair.

Sacha stared at them, still too bewildered to be afraid.

He barely heard Lily when she came up behind him and said, "Hey, look what Sacha found!"

"Sharp eyes," Wolf said. "Good job there."

Sacha mumbled a reply, but his head was spinning and he barely knew what he was saying. Then Wolf reached for the locket—and before he could even think about what he was doing, Sacha closed his hand around it.

For a moment no one moved. There was a strange, subterranean roar in Sacha's ears, like the rumble of an approaching subway car. He could hear Wolf and Lily speaking to him, but they seemed very far away.

Then something compelled him to look up into Wolf's face. They locked gazes. Wolf's eyes were so pale that they looked almost transparent. Sacha felt like a rabbit cowering between the paws of some arctic predator.

Then the moment passed, and Wolf was his normal self again. "Sacha? I need to look at that. Please?"

Sacha opened his hand and let Wolf take the locket.

Wolf looked at the locket's contents and then turned it over to inspect the inscription. "It's Yiddish. Can you read it?"

"No!" Sacha gasped in a cold sweat of panic.

And that was Sacha's second lie.

CHAPTER TEN

The Handmaid of Science

WHEN THEY LEFT Edison's lab, Sacha was still so frightened that he barely noticed where Wolf was going. They'd loitered around the park entrance for several minutes before he realized that Wolf must be waiting for someone. And just who that someone was became obvious when Thomas Edison hurried past them.

Wolf grinned . . . well, wolfishly. And then he set off in pursuit. Edison led them straight down the boardwalk to Peep Show Row. Sacha figured he was just passing through on his way somewhere else. But to his surprise, Edison ducked into one of the peep shows, right under the marquee sign for the "Dangerously Hot Little Cairo, Star of the Dusky East."

The ticket boy must have known Edison because he let him in without paying. But Wolf was another story.

"I've heard that excuse before," he drawled when Wolf explained they were there on official police business.

Wolf gave him a long-suffering look and flashed his badge—Detective Inquisitor gold and not just beat cop silver.

The ticket boy was less impressed than Sacha expected him to be. "You think I ain't seen one of those before? We pay our protection money nice and regular. We don't need to give out free tickets to the likes of you."

"If I were here to see the show," Wolf asked in rising frustration, "do you think I'd bring two children along?"

The ticket boy's gaze wandered from Wolf's badge to Sacha's worn cloth cap to Lily's white dress and patent-leather shoes. "I've heard that excuse too." He stuck out his hand again. "You stay, you pay."

Wolf sighed and handed over the money, and the three of them stepped through the curtain into the red-velvet-swathed theater.

The show was in full swing—and it was quite astonishing. Little Cairo certainly did have the raven curls and exotic attire of an Eastern houri. And she could also do extremely interesting things with her bellybutton. But as far as Sacha could see, no one else in the all-male audience was there to admire her dancing. Not that it mattered much what they were there for. Little Cairo's virtue was obviously quite safe. It was guarded by a massive woman seated in a folding chair on one side of the stage. She was built like a heavyweight boxer, and her hat was pinned to her head with the longest, sharpest hatpin Sacha had ever seen. The look on her face made it clear that she was willing and able to use the hatpin. And her uncanny resemblance to a much older, much fatter Little Cairo made it clear that she was the dancer's mother.

When the dance finally ended, Little Cairo waltzed off the stage, sweeping up armfuls of flowers and silken veils and feather boas. Mrs. Little Cairo rose ponderously, shot one last threatening glare at the audience, and followed her daughter into the wings.

Wolf cut through the crowd, leaving the two apprentices to elbow their way after him. When they finally caught up with him, he was standing at the door of Little Cairo's dressing room toe to toe with her formidable mother.

"Don't get hoity-toity with me, young man!" Mrs. Little Cairo stuck out her well-padded bosom and brandished a threatening fist in Wolf's face. Underneath her prim lace gloves, her hands were as meaty as a prizefighter's, and they looked just as capable of doing damage. "I already ran off one gentleman caller today, and I can run you off, too!"

"I assure you, madam—"

"Don't madam me! What kind of a girl do you think my daughter is?"

"—that I'm here on official police business."

"Hah! You think I haven't heard that excuse before?"

"Honestly," Lily whispered in Sacha's ear, "between her and the ticket boy, you've got to wonder what the Coney Island police *do* all day!"

Sacha snorted in laughter, earning himself a dirty stare from Mrs. Little Cairo.

"I'll have your badge number!" the dancer's mother bellowed, turning back to Wolf. "Let's see it!"

Wolf shrugged and fished his badge out of his pocket again.

"You'll hear about this," Mrs. Little Cairo huffed. "Let me assure you, Inquisitor Wo—oh!" She stopped cold as she read the name on Wolf's badge, and when she spoke again, it was in a simpering, almost girlish voice. "Inquisitor Wolf? Not *the* Inquisitor Wolf?"

Wolf bowed solemnly. "At your service, Mrs. . . . ."

"Darling. Mrs. Darling. Widowed." She giggled coyly and extended the hand with which she'd been threatening his life moments ago.

Wolf hesitated only for the briefest instant before bending to kiss it.

"Oh, Inquisitor Wolf! I'm sure my daughter will be highly gratified by your appreciation of her art—to which, as you can see, she's simply devoted—though, mind you, she's *quite* unattached in any other sense. A fact which you might just consider mentioning next time you're lunching with one of your Astrals or Vanderbilks or any of your other great Wall Street Wizards or captains of industry—"

At this point the door to the dressing room opened and Little Cairo appeared. She took stock of the situation, pursed her bee-stung lips, and turned to her mother. "Mamma," she announced in an accent straight out of Little Italy, "I need a milk shake."

"Now?"

"*Right* now."

"But, my dear, consider your reputation! To receive a gentleman caller without your dear mother present to—"

"Mamma, I'm sure Inquisitor Wolf wouldn't dream of misbehaving with these two adorable children here." Little Cairo pronounced the word as if it were spelled *adohwable*.

"But really, Rosie—"

"Mamma, I've lost two pounds this week!" Little Cairo plucked at the chest of her skimpy costume. "If I lose any more weight, we're going to have to *take in my clothes!*"

Mrs. Little Cairo gasped. Taking in Rosie's clothes, even by so much as an inch, obviously meant giving up all her motherly dreams of Broadway debuts and high-society weddings. "A milk shake!" she agreed. "And with extra malted powder! Tell me, my pet, do you think you could drink *two*?" She bustled off, muttering about the difficulty of keeping up a growing girl's figure through nightly performances and a doubleheader Sunday matinee.

Little Cairo watched her go with a look of fond exasperation. Then she walked into her dressing room and sat down at a wobbly wicker dressing table in front of a pink-rimmed heart-shaped mirror.

"Take a load off," she told Wolf and the apprentices. "And don't mind me, I gotta get out of this getup. It itches something terrible!"

She turned back to the mirror, primped at her raven black locks—and then lifted them right off her head, veil, spangles, and all. The hair underneath the wig was a deep, rich, glowing auburn: the same color that every fashionable woman in New York coveted. And in Little Cairo's case it was obviously natural—as was the way her curls swept into a ravishing Gibson Girl swirl with only a pat or two from her shapely fingers.

Sacha was still blinking in amazement at this transformation when Little Cairo pushed a pair of coke-bottle glasses onto her lovely nose. Then she peeled a gob of lime green chewing gum off the side of the mirror where she'd been storing it during her dance number, stuck it in her mouth, and started chewing as if her very life depended on beating the gum into submission.

"So," she said between chews, "whaddaya wanna know?"

"Your name and address would be a good start."

"Name's DiMaggio. Rosie DiMaggio."

Wolf had already started fishing through his pockets for the ever-elusive pencil, but now he looked up at her, perplexed. "Your mother said—"

"I know. She thinks Darling has more *social potential*. Mamma's very big on social potential. She says you need more than just talent to become a celebrity. She says you need to build a *persona*."

"I see. And is working for Mr. Edison part of developing your social potential?"

Rosie stuck her hand out like a cop stopping traffic. "Now wait just a minute, mister! Let's get one thing clear from the get-go! If you tell my mother about Mr. Edison, then by gum, I'll . . . I'll . . . I'll . . ."

"You'll what?" Wolf sounded genuinely curious.

She glared at him ferociously. "You don't wanna know!"

"There's no need to threaten me, Miss Darling—er, DiMaggio. I'm investigating a magical crime. I have no interest whatsoever in your romantic entanglements."

"It ain't no 'tanglement," Rosie protested. "I ain't the 'tangling kind of girl! You think I'm just some common chorus-line hoofer? I'm gonna grow up to be an inventor, just like Mr. Edison! After that, maybe I'll have time for romance. But for now"—she pressed a shapely hand to her chest and heaved a romantic sigh—"for now, I am a Handmaid to Science!"

Wolf coughed. "And Mr. Edison is . . . ?"

"He's giving me inventor lessons. You think you can just wake up one morning and start inventing? Not hardly! You gotta practice, practice, practice. It's just like tap-dancing."

"And your mother doesn't know about your inventor lessons."

"She wouldn't understand," Rosie wailed despairingly. "*She* wants me to be a *stawh*."

"Excuse me. A what?"

"A *stawh*. A celebrity. She wants me to be a famous actress and get my picture in the paper and marry a millionaire." Rosie sighed fatalistically. "I know she only wants what's best for me. But a girl can't be practical all her life. A girl's gotta have dreams!"

"And Mr. Edison is helping you pursue your dreams by giving you inventing lessons . . . er . . . free of charge?"

"Not for free! For valuable services rendered! I'm his lab

assistant. Which basically means I take the lab notes and clean up the mess after he explodes stuff, and if someone has to get electrocuted, it's me." Rosie grinned, flashing thirty-two perfect white teeth and one gob of lime green chewing gum. "But like they say on the turf, If you don't risk your money, you can't play the ponies!"

Wolf smothered a grin. "And was Mr. Edison in the process of electrocuting you yesterday when the . . . er . . ."

"When the dybbuk showed up?"

Wolf's pencil paused. "Why is everybody so sure it was a dybbuk, anyway?"

"Because it was."

"How do you know?" Wolf asked curiously.

"Oh, it had all the classic signs. The cold and hungry look. That creepy wailing and gnashing of teeth in the outer darkness kind of aura. Plus, it *looked* like a dybbuk."

"And just what do you imagine a dybbuk looks like?"

"You know!" Rosie waved a hand vaguely in Sacha's direction. "Like . . . like a nice Jewish boy."

"She seems to know an awful lot about dybbuks for an Italian girl," Lily pointed out acidly. "Doesn't anyone else think that's a little odd?"

Sacha jumped at the sound of Lily's voice. He'd been so busy staring at Little Cairo that he'd forgotten all about Lily. But there she was, sitting right next to him with a pinched-up look on her face like she'd just eaten a lemon.

"Oh, I know all about dybbuks," Rosie said, completely oblivious to Lily's hostile tone. "My cousin Maria walks out with a Yeshiva boy. Don't tell my mother, though. She'd tell Maria's mother, and wouldn't they just *scream!*"

"He can't be much of a Yeshiva boy if he's walking out with a Catholic girl," Sacha pointed out.

Rosie blinked in astonishment. Clearly it had never crossed her mind that the boy's parents would be just as upset as her own family. "Well, yeah. I guess *his* mother'd scream too if she found out. Hey, wouldn't it be a hoot if they both found out at the same time? They'd probably break every window in Manhattan!"

Rosie laughed uproariously at this idea, and Sacha couldn't help laughing with her. But he came back down to earth with a thump when Lily kicked him.

"That was a complete waste of a day!" Lily said as they settled into the train for the ride home.

"You think?" Wolf asked.

"Well, wasn't it? We traipse all the way out to Coney Island, and all we have to show for it is a lost piece of jewelry."

"We know the dybbuk is real now," Wolf pointed out.

"Assuming you believe the Star of the Dusky East," Lily scoffed.

"Oh, I don't know," Wolf said. "What do you think, Sacha? You've been awfully quiet today." Wolf had taken the locket out of his pocket and was turning it over and over between his bony fingers.

Sacha stared, mesmerized. He had the oddest feeling that if something didn't stop him, he was about to start talking—and once he got started, he wouldn't stop until he'd told Wolf everything.

It was Lily who saved him.

"What were you saying back at Edison's lab?" she asked him.

Sacha started. "Oh. I just . . . I couldn't understand why Edison was so nervous about his prototype. Or why it looked the way it did. I mean, the one we saw at Morgaunt's library worked just fine. And it wasn't dripping engine oil all over his carpet, either."

"Maybe that one was just for playing souls on," Lily suggested.

"Yeah, but think of all those cylinders Morgaunt showed us. How did they record those if Edison's prototype still doesn't work?"

"You think Edison was lying to us?"

"I don't know. But someone's lying."

"It certainly seems that way," Wolf agreed.

"Well, coming all the way out here just to find out someone's lying to us still seems like a waste of time to me," Lily said. "We didn't learn a thing about the dybbuk. And anyway, who on earth would even *want* to kill Thomas Edison?"

Sacha stared at her in disbelief. What about every Mage, magician, and immigrant in New York? he wanted to ask.

But before he could say anything, Wolf pulled that morning's paper out of his coat pocket and tossed it onto the seat between them.

"HOUDINI ACCUSED OF KABBALISM!" the headline blared in inch-high italics. *"Thomas Edison to Testify!"*

The article explained that Edison had accused Houdini of using magic in his death-defying escapes—and was going to testify about it next week before the Committee on Un-American Sorcery. The article didn't say what was going to happen to Houdini. But it was full of ominous words like *perjury* and *contempt of Congress* and *felony abuse of magic*.

It was outrageous, Sacha thought angrily. Houdini was being tried and condemned in the press without even getting a chance to tell his side of the story. "You'd think someone would at least take the trouble to go talk to the poor guy before they throw him in jail!" he blurted out.

"Actually," Wolf said, still turning the locket in his hands, "we're on our way to talk to him right now."

CHAPTER ELEVEN

The Master of Manacles

SACHA HALF EXPECTED to find Harry Houdini making elephants disappear at the Hippodrome or hanging upside down from the Flatiron in a straitjacket. Instead they found him at home in a discreet brownstone in a comfortable middle-class section of Harlem.

Sacha had seen countless photographs of the famous Illusionist dressed in swimming trunks, his muscles bulging under the weight of chains and padlocks, his eyes starting from his head with the effort of performing some death-defying escape. But the man shaking Wolf's hand and offering them seats in his private study wore a three-piece suit and a polite expression and looked like exactly who he really was: Ehrich Weiss, the rabbi's son from Appleton, Wisconsin.

Sacha waited for Wolf to pull out his chewed pencil stub and start questioning Houdini. But instead Wolf produced

Mrs. Kessler's locket and handed it to Houdini as calmly as if he thought nothing at all of giving key evidence to a suspect capable of making elephants disappear in broad daylight.

"What do you make of that, Harry?"

"Pretty ordinary item," Houdini replied. "Kind of thing you could pick up in any pawnshop. Sorry, Max. If you're trying to hang a case on this, I think it's going to be a slog."

"Me too," Wolf said. "Unfortunately. We found it in Thomas Edison's lab in Luna Park. Someone seems to be trying to assassinate him."

"What, someone finally got ticked off enough at that old windbag to do him in?"

"A lot of people are going to think it was you."

At this news Houdini burst into ringing peals of laughter so genuine that Sacha couldn't help grinning himself. "If I wanted to kill Tom Edison," he said when he finally stopped laughing, "I sure wouldn't pick this week to do it. If he kicks the bucket before the month's up, I'm out ten thousand dollars."

He plucked a sheet of paper off of his desk and handed it to Wolf. "That's to be printed in tomorrow's papers."

Sacha and Lily craned over Wolf's shoulders and read the following:

$10,000 CHALLENGE!

The Great Houdini hereby and herewith agrees to wager the sum of $10,000 against an equal amount, the money to be donated to charity, if Mr. Thomas Alva Edison (a.k.a. the Wizard of Luna Park) can scientifically prove that any of

Houdini's world-famous escapes and illusions are accomplished by means of magic.

The Challenge, should Mr. Edison choose to accept it, shall be held in one month's time in the Starlite Ballroom of the Elephant Hotel, Surf Avenue, Coney Island.

Upon Mr. Edison's request, Houdini shall engage to perform magical feats including but not limited to escapes from straitjackets, handcuffs, and manacles, and the Chinese Water Torture Cell (patent pending), as well as the Disappearing Elephant Trick (elephant to be provided by management).

Signed,

Houdini

"Well, what do you think?" Houdini asked.

"I don't know what to think," Wolf confessed. "Is the whole fight between you and Edison just a publicity stunt?"

"A man would have to want publicity pretty bad to get himself dragged in front of ACCUSE on charges of working illegal magic."

"Don't people in show business say all publicity is good publicity?"

"If they do, they're idiots."

While they talked, Houdini was toying with Mrs. Kessler's locket, spinning it between his nimble fingers and making it disappear and reappear at will. It wasn't real magic. Sacha could see that quite clearly. It was just a stage magician's illusion. But Houdini was so supremely skilled that Sacha couldn't begin to guess how the illusion worked.

"The fact is," Houdini confessed, "this ACCUSE non-sense has put me in a pickle. Whoever gave my name to the Committee on Un-American Sorcery must have known that from the moment I was accused of using real magic in my escapes, I had only three options. One, I can confess that I *have* used magic—and go to jail for defrauding people by magical means. Two, I can claim that I *haven't* used magic—but I can only prove it by giving away all my secrets and ruining the illusion. Or three, I can challenge Edison's etherograph."

"And you don't think it was Edison who gave your name to ACCUSE in the first place?" Wolf asked.

"No. He's a dreadful publicity hound—though some people might think it was the pot calling the kettle black for me to say so. And he doesn't have much use for Jews or magicians—"

"I know. He showed us his etherograph ads."

"Appalling, aren't they?"

"Quite. Have you seen the etherograph in action?"

"I rather had the impression Edison hadn't gotten it to work yet."

"He must have. Morgaunt played us one of the recordings."

"Morgaunt!" Houdini slammed a fist into his palm. "I should have known he'd be at the bottom of this!"

Wolf sighed the same reasonable, put-upon sigh that Sacha's father always sighed when the more volatile members of the Kessler family started ranting about religion or politics. "Keep your hair on," he told Houdini. "I know it's hard to believe, but there *are* a few bad things in New York that aren't Morgaunt's fault."

"Not this one," Houdini snapped.

"Well . . . maybe not."

"The man's a Black Mage, I tell you! A Necromancer! The blackest of the black!"

"He's not a Necromancer."

"Get your head out of the sand, Max! Morgaunt has more power than any Mage can come by honestly. I *feel* him. I feel the ratchets and gears of his spells burrowing under the streets like his damn subway. He's killing New York. He's sucking the magic out of it, and if we don't stop him there'll be nothing left but an empty shell."

"He's not a Necromancer," Wolf repeated patiently. "Not yet, anyway." When Houdini would have protested again, he held up a hand to silence him. "Morgaunt preys on the living, Harry, not the dead. And if he's a Mage at all, then he's a new kind of Mage." He smiled grimly. "One for the age of the machine."

Houdini seemed to shrink in on himself. "You're frightened of him too," he whispered.

"I'd be a fool not to be."

"So what do you want from me?"

Wolf nodded at the locket that Houdini still held in his hands.

Houdini flashed a nervous sideways glance at Sacha. "In front of *him*?" he asked. Then he shrugged. "Sure, why not? Nobody can nail me for working magic on official police business, right? And anyway, I'd like to know what the kid can see. Call it professional curiosity."

Houdini looked straight at Sacha and held up the locket so that it spun in the air between them, winking and flashing like sunlight on water. "So, Sacha Kessler. What do you see now? Spells or illusion? Real magic or stage magic?" As Houdini asked the question, he turned the locket in his hands and made it disappear.

"Illusion," Sacha said. He felt breathless and strangely light-headed. But he was quite sure of his answer. Houdini stood there before him in the clear light of day. No magic flared and flickered around him. No spells flashed from his clever fingers.

"And now?" Houdini reached over and pulled the locket out of Lily's ear.

"Illusion."

"And now?" It vanished again, then reappeared in Houdini's left hand.

"Illusion."

"And now?"

This time, instead of doing another trick, he held the locket up and . . . just looked at it.

"I . . . what are you *doing?*"

"I don't know," Houdini confessed. "But I've been able to do it ever since I turned thirteen. Just like you can see magic. When I hold something in my hand, I see the memories of the other people who've held it before me. Perhaps it's Edison's etheric emanations. Or perhaps it's something else entirely. But people leave a trace of themselves on everything they touch. And if they touch something often, or care deeply about it, then they leave a great deal of themselves."

Sacha watched, breathless with terror, while Houdini weighed the locket in the palm of his hand. Magic pulsed and streaked around him like the aurora borealis. The hand that held the locket was blazing with it.

"I see a woman who has lived through terrors most of us can barely imagine," Houdini murmured. "Fire and death, and people fleeing for their lives with only the clothes upon their backs. She's reached a safe harbor now, and she's not the sort to dwell on past sorrows. But the grief is still there. I can feel it because *she* felt it, every time she touched this locket."

"And the assassin?"

Houdini balanced the locket on his palm for another moment, looking down at it. Then he shuddered and thrust the locket back into Wolf's hands as if it burned him.

Wolf refused to take it. "Try again. Please, Harry!"

Houdini passed a hand over his brow and leaned against his desk. "I can't, Max. I can't bear it. Something touched that locket after her, something not human. All I can sense is cold and hunger and a terrible emptiness."

"A dybbuk?"

Houdini's head snapped up in surprise. "Why would you think that?" he asked in a tone that suggested he was just as unhappy about the idea as Sacha had been.

"One of the eyewitnesses thought it was."

"Oh come on. Don't tell me Edison is hiring Jewish lab assistants!"

"No," Wolf admitted, grinning in spite of himself. "Just an Italian girl who happens to have a cousin who happens to have a Jewish boyfriend."

Houdini snorted. "Only in New York!"

"She seemed to know her stuff, though. *Could* it be a dybbuk?"

"I hate to admit it but . . . it makes sense. More sense than any other explanation I can think of."

"So where does that leave us?"

Houdini rubbed his chin thoughtfully. He and Wolf gazed at each other. Each one seemed to be searching the other's face for a clue to his thoughts, but neither seemed willing to speak first. Looking at them, Sacha couldn't help noticing the contrast between the two men. Houdini short, muscular, and matinee-idol handsome. Wolf long, lanky, and disheveled—and, with his remarkable eyes hidden behind his glasses, completely nondescript. Yet something clearly bound them together.

"If really it is a dybbuk," Houdini said at last, "then there's nothing you *can* do to protect Edison. Sooner or later it will devour him. He'll become a *kelippah*, a mere container for the dybbuk. And once that happens, he'll be the creature of whoever summoned the dybbuk."

"Then the real killer is the man who summoned the dybbuk," Wolf concluded. "And that's who we have to find."

But Houdini still hesitated.

"What are you afraid of, Harry? That it'll be a rabbi?"

"It can't be! No rabbi would do such a thing! And besides, you can't possibly arrest a rabbi for this crime!"

"Can't?" Wolf said in a dangerously quiet voice that Sacha had never heard him use before. It sent a chill down Sacha's spine. It made him remember that Wolf was a cop. A fancy cop who didn't usually have to get his hands dirty the way regular policemen did. But a cop all the same.

"You know what I'm saying," Houdini protested. "If you put a rabbi on trial for assassination by means of magic, this city will go up like a powder keg! The streets will run with blood!"

Houdini was practically shouting by now, but Wolf still answered him in that dead calm policeman's voice. "Keeping the streets clean is someone else's job. My job is catching criminals."

Houdini slammed a fist down on his desk in fury. "Then why don't you go arrest James Goddamn Pierpont Morgaunt? You know he's behind this! You know he's behind every wicked thing that goes on in this city! And yet you wait and wait and wait. You're no better than Roosevelt!"

"At least I'm still here."

"For all the good that does anyone!"

"If you get me enough evidence to bring charges against Morgaunt and make them stick, I *will* arrest him."

"That's what Roosevelt said—and look what happened to *him*."

Wolf shrugged, unimpressed. "I don't have as much to lose as Roosevelt."

"You've got your life, don't you? Even a poor man can lose that."

"You'll be glad to know that Mr. Morgaunt agrees with

you," Wolf said wryly. "He's already warned me about it. I thought it was quite considerate of him."

Wolf got to his feet. Sacha followed him to the door, feeling frightened and bewildered. Judging by the look on her face, Lily felt the same.

Houdini crossed his arms over his chest and heaved a sigh of frustration as he watched them go. "I want to help, Max. I really do."

"I know."

"But you don't make it easy."

That earned a very small smile from Wolf. "I know that too."

"So what can I do?"

"Just keep doing what you're already doing. Send out your challenge to Edison. Give Morgaunt what he wants: a public face-off between you and the etherograph. But, Harry? You be careful too."

"I always am." Houdini flashed his most mischievous grin. "As careful as a man in my line of work can afford to be!"

CHAPTER TWELVE

The Money Coat

ON THE LONG cab ride downtown, Sacha's head spun with questions he couldn't ask. Every question led back to the locket—and he didn't even want to think about that while Wolf could see him.

He glanced at Wolf, slouched in the opposite corner of the cab. Wolf had taken off his glasses and was cleaning them on his tie. He must have felt Sacha staring, because he looked up and smiled at him. In the evening light his eyes were as luminously gray as dawn over the open ocean. Suddenly Sacha couldn't bear the thought of how those eyes would look at him if Wolf found out he'd been lying to him.

How had he gotten himself into this awful mess anyway? He wasn't a liar! There had to be a way to climb back out of this hole he'd dug himself into.

He was just opening his mouth to tell Wolf about the locket when he remembered Edison's awful etherograph ads, and the cold eyes that followed him when he ran the gauntlet through the lobby of the Inquisitors Division every morning. He snapped his mouth shut and turned away to stare out the window. Wolf might believe the Kesslers weren't criminals, but nobody else would. It would be easier for everyone to believe that Rabbi Kessler—a known Kabbalist—had summoned the dybbuk. And once they believed that, nothing Sacha could do or say would ever change their minds.

No, Sacha decided, the only way out of this mess was to keep his mouth shut and help Wolf catch the real killer. And then he'd tell Wolf everything. Even if it meant knowing that he would gaze at him out of those clear gray eyes someday and say, "Sacha? You *lied* to me?"

Telling Wolf now would be crazy.

And telling his own family would be worse. They wouldn't—couldn't—understand the choices he had to make. They'd try to protect him, because parents were supposed to protect their children. But they couldn't see what Sacha had known the first time he went into a shop with his mother and the shopkeeper talked to *him* as if *he* were the grownup because her English wasn't good enough. They couldn't see that Sacha had become an American, while they remained foreigners—and now it was *his* job to take care of *them*.

By the time Sacha finally trudged up the stairs of the Astral Place subway station, it was long past rush hour and even the Bowery saloons had emptied out as the after-work drinkers straggled home to dinner.

He glanced into the Metropole as he passed by, hoping that Uncle Mordechai might be there. But he wasn't. There was nothing for it but to walk home alone again.

It was that hushed twilight hour when most people were safe inside, gathered around the dinner table, and the streets were left to the rats and the cats and the various human scavengers that foraged for scraps in the gutters when everyone who could afford to buy anything had gone home.

Sacha turned down Hester Street and hurried along it, trying not to think about his mother's locket and Houdini's terrifying visions of hunger and darkness. He could see people going about their normal evening routines in the brightly lit windows overhead. He wished he were one of them. This was the time of night when you wanted to be in a warm, noisy, lamp-lit kitchen—not out here where shadows seemed to reach out of every alley.

He was almost home when he thought he heard a step behind him. He spun around, ready to fight, his mind filled with terrifying images of bitter cold and devouring hunger. But there was nothing there—just the dark of the coming night, welling into the narrow streets like the deep Atlantic tide sweeping up the Hudson River.

When he finally got home, Mrs. Lehrer waylaid him before he could make it through the back room. She was holding her money coat—the one she'd been sewing her savings into all these years to get her sisters out of Russia.

"It's finished!" she cried, thrusting the coat toward him. "Go ahead, try it on!"

Sacha didn't want to try it on. It was creepy, and it didn't smell very good. But Mrs. Lehrer was always so nice to him. And his mother was nodding at him from the kitchen, telling him to humor her.

The coat felt amazingly heavy as she settled it on his shoulders. He wondered how many years of savings Mrs. Lehrer had sewn into it. Why was Mrs. Lehrer so crazy, while Sacha's mother was so sane? She'd lived through the pogroms too. She'd even lost a child, which had to be at least as bad as losing your sisters. Was Sacha's mother really so much stronger than Mrs. Lehrer? Or could she crack too if enough new troubles were piled on top of the old ones? But Sacha could never ask these questions. It felt wrong even to think them when all the grownups worked so hard to protect the children from even the faintest memory of Russia and the bad times.

"Raise your arms!" Mrs. Lehrer was saying to him. "See? Do you hear a jingle?"

"No."

"That's craft, not magic, I'll have you know! It takes thirty years of sewing seams to learn to do work like that. Go on, turn around! Dance!"

Over in the Kesslers' kitchen, Sacha's father had realized what was happening in the back room. He was staring through the tenement window at them, looking just as uncomfortable as Sacha felt. But his mother gave him another of her little nods, as if to say, *Go ahead. What's the harm if it makes her happy?*

Reluctantly, awkwardly, Sacha began to dance. Then Mrs. Lehrer laughed. On a sudden whim, Sacha grabbed her up in his arms and waltzed her around the cluttered room, bumping into chairs and ironing boards and piles of unfinished shirtwaists. He waltzed her into the front room, and they whirled back and forth in front of the windows while everyone laughed and clapped and pushed the chairs aside to make space for them.

"Oh!" Mrs. Lehrer cried when she finally collapsed into a chair, flushed and smiling. "I haven't danced like that since Mo and I were young!"

She and Sacha grinned at each other. Then Mrs. Lehrer leaned close to him as if she had a momentous secret to tell him. "This is a great day for me," she confided. "When I said I was finished, I meant it! Just before you came in, I sewed the very last coin into that coat. I have the fares now. Every penny of them. I can walk right down to the steamship office and buy my sisters their tickets tomorrow!"

Sacha felt the smile freeze on his face. Mrs. Lehrer's sisters hadn't written to her in years. No one knew where they were, or even if they were still alive. He looked around for help, but his mother had already turned back to her mending, and his father and Mordechai were talking politics. No one else had heard Mrs. Lehrer's words.

"That's great," he told her, hoping to God that he was saying the right thing. "I'm—I'm really happy for you."

Mrs. Lehrer looked deep into Sacha's eyes. Suddenly she wasn't smiling anymore. And she didn't look even a little bit crazy. It was as if another woman were looking out of her eyes at him—a woman who knew perfectly well that she was never going to see her sisters again.

"You're a nice boy," she told him, reaching up to pat his cheek. "You've always been so kind to me. Just like your father. I know you're going to grow up to be just as good a man as he is."

When Mrs. Lehrer had taken back her money coat, Sacha stood by the window looking out into the night and leaning his forehead against the cool glass—the closest he could get to being alone in the crowded apartment.

By the time he realized that his watcher was down in the street looking up at him, they were already staring into each other's eyes.

Sacha jumped back, chest tight and heart pounding.

The watcher's face looked blurred and vague in the gaslight, like an old photograph. But Sacha could still see that his watcher and Edison's dybbuk were one and the same. And Rosie DiMaggio was right. The dybbuk *did* look like a nice Jewish boy. It looked like half the nice Jewish boys on the Lower East Side.

Sacha shuddered as he thought of what would happen if the dybbuk actually succeeded in killing Edison. The police wouldn't have to look far to find someone to blame. Neither would the mobs. And then the bad times would be back again. Not in Russia, but right here on Hester Street.

CHAPTER THIRTEEN

Rushing the Growler

THE NEXT MORNING Sacha nodded off on the subway and would have missed his stop completely if a large lady in a hat decorated with several pounds of passenger pigeon feathers hadn't tripped over his foot and poked him with her parasol.

He'd been up half the night. When everyone else was asleep, he'd snuck out onto the fire escape with an armload of Grandpa Kessler's Kabbalah books and shivered under the dim light of the street lamps while he read everything he could find about dybbuks.

It wasn't pleasant reading. No one knew how to kill a dybbuk, short of killing its victim along with it. A dybbuk was part of you—like your arm or your leg or your heart. Once someone summoned it here, it was only a matter of time until it stepped into your skin and stole your life—and sent you back to spend all eternity in whatever hell dybbuks came from.

Some men had managed to survive having a dybbuk. But only great and pious rabbis. And even they hadn't defeated their dybbuks. They'd only learned to live with them, like a man sharing his house with a half-tamed lion that would devour him the moment he let down his guard. As he read one terrible story after another, Sacha began to feel honestly sorry for Thomas Edison. If a dybbuk really was after him, he was worse than a dead man. And there wasn't a thing anyone could do to save him.

Which meant that the only way for Sacha to protect his family was to find out who had really summoned the dybbuk.

Sacha was still racking his brain over how to do that when he got to work—which was how he managed to offend Philip Payton yet again.

The trouble started when he reached the Inquisitors Division headquarters just as Maximillian Wolf hopped out of a hansom cab.

"And how are you settling in to the job?" Wolf asked. "Any questions? Anything you need?"

Sacha thought Wolf was probably just being polite, but he supposed he had to say something. "Well . . . I guess a desk would be good. Or at least a chair?"

"That seems reasonable." Wolf waved airily. "Just have a word with Payton. He'll sort you out."

But when they reached his office, Wolf blew through the anteroom without saying anything about it, and Sacha was left to muddle along on his own.

Lily Astral was already there, laughing with Payton as if

the two of them were old friends. Sacha cleared his throat a few times, but no one noticed him.

"Uh . . . excuse me. I need someone to clean up a desk for me to work at?"

Payton turned to face him, one eyebrow raised in polite disbelief. "Do I look like a janitor?"

"Uh. No. But Inquisitor Wolf said—"

"I really think you must have failed to understand him correctly."

"But—"

"Listen, Sandy—"

"Sacha."

"Whatever. Let me explain how things work here. I'll use short, simple words so you can understand me. *I* am the valued employee who keeps this office running like a well-oiled machine so that Inquisitor Wolf can solve crimes and catch criminals. *You* are a useless child whose only function is to gum up the works, get underfoot, and waste time that Inquisitor Wolf and I could be using to get real work done. So if you want a desk, go down to the basement and find one. On your *own* time. And meanwhile, you can make yourself slightly less useless by rushing the growler to the Witch's Brew."

And then Payton fished a dented old tin bucket from under his desk and tossed it casually (but very accurately) at Sacha's head.

Sacha reached up a hand just in time to catch the bucket before it hit him. Then he stared at it in shock and disbelief until Lily snatched it from his hand and marched smartly out the door.

She looked as if she knew where she was going. But of course she couldn't, or she would have been just as shocked as Sacha was.

Sacha had seen plenty of growlers in his day. He'd seen plenty of children rushing the growler, too—carrying it down to the local saloon to buy beer for their parents. It happened every day in every neighborhood of New York, despite all the laws that high-society do-gooders kept passing about selling liquor to minors. But Sacha had certainly never done it. Sacha's father disapproved of anything stronger than seltzer water. And Sacha's mother . . . well, to hear her tell it, rushing the growler was a one-way ticket up the river to Sing Sing prison's fancy new electric chair. First came the childhood trips to fill it up for parents and aunts and uncles. Then came the scrounging of pennies to fill it for yourself. Then you were sliding down the slippery slope of mugging drunks, marrying a gun moll (or worse, a *shiksa*!), and signing on with Magic, Inc., as one of Meyer Minsky's hired thugs.

And it all began with that first fateful trip to rush the growler. A trip Sacha was now being ordered to take as part of his official duties for the NYPD Inquisitors Division. He didn't know whether to laugh or cry.

"Well," Payton snapped, "what are you waiting for?"

Without another word, Sacha turned and dashed out the door after Lily. He found her waiting for him about a third of the way down the long corridor. "So where is this Witch's Brew?" she asked as soon as he caught up with her.

"How should I know? I'm not in the habit of frequenting gin joints."

The door opened and Payton's head emerged into the hallway. "Fifty-second between Eighth and Ninth," he said, and vanished back into the office.

Sacha's stomach sank. Lily might be oblivious to the meaning of that address, but that was only because she'd grown up on Millionaire's Mile. Sacha, on the other hand, came from the real New York. And in his city, neighborhoods were rigidly divided by ethnic group—and each neighborhood was fiercely defended by its own magical street gangs. The Lower East Side was Jewish: you didn't set foot there without Magic, Inc., knowing your business. Chinatown was controlled by Confucian spellbinders and Immortals. Little Italy was the realm of the Italian folk witches called *streganonnas*. And Hell's Kitchen belonged to the toughest Irish gang in town: the Hell's Kitchen Hexers.

"Well, what are we waiting for?" Lily tossed her blond hair and marched off down the stairs without so much as a glance at Sacha. Did she just expect him to trot along behind her like a lapdog? Obviously she did! He muttered something rude under his breath about bossy women. But he didn't really have a choice, so in the end he followed her.

Within a few blocks, however, Sacha's outrage melted into bewildered amusement. Either Lily Astral didn't know the meaning of the word fear or she'd never walked down a New

York City sidewalk before. She'd seemed reasonably normal when they were just following in the wide wake of Inquisitor Wolf's flapping coattails. But on her own she was a public menace.

She marched straight down the middle of the sidewalk like it was her personal property and she expected everyone else to step aside and make way for her. And the weirdest part of it was that most people *did* step aside. As soon as they saw her coming, they just sort of slid out of her way like tugboats clearing the harbor for a luxury ocean liner.

The only catch was that not everyone could see Lily coming. Sacha cringed as she sailed from one near disaster to the next. Bicyclists. Delivery boys. A dry grocer's clerk staggering along under stacked bolts of muslin and cotton. A handcart operator pushing a leaning tower of metal filing cabinets.

Lily was cheerfully oblivious to it all. In fact, the only thing Lily was not oblivious to was food. She kept making lightning-quick detours to investigate edible items in storefronts and on passing pushcarts. Most of them met with her immediate approval, and she seemed to possess an inexhaustible supply of pocket change. This made it really hard to get anywhere. And really frustrating for Sacha, who had to say no again and again because he was pretty sure that half the stuff she was eating wasn't even within spitting distance of being kosher.

"Don't they feed you at home?" he asked after he'd watched her devour a pretzel, a chicken potpie, two oranges, and more candy than he and Bekah saw in a month.

"Sure, but my mother's from New England."

"So?"

"So have you been there?" she asked in a decidedly odd tone of voice.

Sacha hesitated, not sure what she was getting at and not wanting to sound foolish. If it had been anyone but Lily Astral, he would have suspected a joke. "No," he said finally.

"Well, if you ever do go—take food."

He glanced sharply at her. Was that a glint of laughter in the cool blue depths of her eyes? Did Lily Astral actually have a sense of humor? It looked like she did. And now she was even smiling at him.

He'd barely started to smile back when she stepped in front of an omnibus.

Sacha jerked her back from the rails just as the frothing draft horses were about to trample her flat.

"There's no need to panic," she said loftily. "Horses don't step on people. They would have gone around me. I've seen it happen all the time at the polo grounds."

"But they *can't* go around you. The omnibus is on rails!"

"Really?" She peered down at the steel streetcar rails as if she'd never seen such a thing. "How remarkable! When did they put those in?"

Finally he managed to shepherd her safely over to West Fifty-second—only to discover a new danger looming between them and their goal.

"Look!" Lily exclaimed as they turned the corner onto

Fifty-second Street. "There's the Witch's Brew. And finally some peace and quiet too! What a relief!"

Sacha wasn't so sure about that. Peace and quiet might be a good thing on the calm, tree-lined streets where Lily lived. But in the New York Sacha knew, a quiet street was a dangerous one. And this street was far too quiet. Between them and the Witch's Brew stretched a wasteland of blank walls and boarded-up storefronts. Half the block was nothing but a weedy abandoned lot. A huge hand-lettered sign on the jagged fence enclosing the lot read

ALL BOYS CAUT
IN THIS YARD
WILL BE DELT WITH
ACCORDEN TO LAW

Sacha was just about to say that they might want to take the long way around to the Witch's Brew when he heard the unmistakable *crack!* of a bat connecting with a baseball. The ball streaked out of the abandoned lot, bounced off a boarded-up window, and rolled down the sidewalk toward them. An instant later, a dozen raggedly dressed teenagers swarmed after it. The smallest stood a head taller than Sacha, and their bold swaggers and outlandish costumes—one of them even wore a stolen policeman's hat—marked them as Hell's Kitchen Hexers.

"Hey, look!" one of them jeered. "It's Dopey Benny Schleptowitz and his gun moll Irma!"

That set off a chorus among his ragtag little pack of hangers-on:

"Hey, Dopey!"

"Hey, Schleptowitz!"

"Hey, Irma!"

"Coochie coochie coochie coochie!"

"Other way!" Sacha told Lily, grabbing hold of her wrist and giving her a sharp tug backward as the Hexers came toward them.

"Why? They're just a bunch of harmless kids—"

"Just go!" Sacha yelled.

Maybe it was the look of terror on his face, or maybe it was the fact that the "harmless" kids had already started to come after them. But for once Lily didn't try to argue.

Five minutes later they had made it around the block from the other direction and were pushing through the front door of the Witch's Brew.

The first thing Sacha noticed was the smell of beer. It wasn't even ten in the morning, but the rich, yeasty perfume of triple stout already hung in the air like fog. Cigar smoke curled lazily around the cast-iron Corinthian columns and lent an underwater pall to the beveled mirrors and stamped tin ceiling. Electric ceiling fans whined and creaked overhead like propellers churning their way through a beery sea.

One side of the cavernous room housed a forlorn-looking coffee bar where a waiter was reading the newspaper behind a gold-plated coffee boiler. On the other side of the room— the side all the customers were on—was a brass-railed bar stocked with every kind of hard liquor Sacha had ever seen in his life and many he hadn't. Earlier shifts of drinkers had scuffed the bar rail and strewn the floor with broken shot glasses and abandoned lottery tickets. Several of the faces that turned to stare at the two children as the doors swung closed behind them were flushed and bleary-eyed.

The Witch's Brew was clearly a serious drinking establishment—and serious drinking had already been under way for many hours today.

"Well, well!" said the mountainous Irishman behind the bar. "If it isn't Little Miss Muffet and Little Lord Fauntleroy!" He leered alarmingly at the children. His teeth were the size of coat pegs. They looked like coat pegs too: long and widely spaced and oddly rounded. It was quite unsettling.

Before he could lose his nerve, Sacha stepped up to the bar and held up the growler. "I want this filled up," he said, trying to sound like a busy grownup with better things to do than waste time trading insults with bartenders.

"Do you, now? Well, come back in about eight years, and I'll be happy to oblige."

Before Sacha could argue, the man pointed to the hand-lettered sign that hung on the mirror behind him. Judging by the spelling, it must have been penned by the same person who'd painted the sign in the abandoned lot down the street:

WE SURVE NO MINERS!

"I'm sure," said the bartender with elaborate and completely insincere courtesy, "that such fine young ladies and gentlemen as yourselves can read a simple sign without my help. I'm sure you wouldn't want to be getting me in trouble with the police. No, I imagine that'd be the furthest thing from your innocent young minds. I think you'd best be on your way now. Send my kind regards to Commissioner Keegan. And remind him I've already paid this month. Nice and regular, like always. So if he's going to sacrifice some poor bugger to the temperance ladies, it better not be me!"

Sacha turned away, his shoulders slumping in defeat. But Lily grabbed the growler from him and stepped up to the bar as if walking into a Hell's Kitchen whiskey dive were all part of an ordinary day for her.

"But we're not *from* Commissioner Keegan," she said with a winning smile. "We're Inquisitor Wolf's apprentices. And he said you'd fill up his—grumbler—snarler—whatever you call it."

The bartender's face cracked into a grin that displayed both rows of coat pegs right down to their massive roots. "Inquisitor Wolf!" he exclaimed. "Well, and why didn't you say so in the first place? Hey, Sean! Fire up Big Bertha! Wolf's sent down for his morning coffee!"

Across the room, the apron-clad man leaped into action at the massive coffee machine. Minutes later, Lily and Sacha were trudging back toward the Inquisitors headquarters, their growler brimming with the strongest, blackest coffee Sacha had ever seen. Sacha was so busy feeling relieved and embarrassed that he only realized they'd turned the wrong way when a baseball whizzed out of the abandoned lot and hit him smack in the side of the head.

Lily caught the ball in midair as it bounced off his head, but before he had time to be amazed by this, they were surrounded by a jeering circle of boys.

They weren't real Hexers, Sacha realized, just aspiring gangsters. But that didn't mean they couldn't beat up two skinny kids. One of them—a potato-nosed teenager who looked like he was about five pounds short of being able to sign onto the fireman's local ladder company—jabbed Sacha in the chest, sending him stumbling backward. Another one was there to catch him, and for a while the two of them entertained themselves by batting Sacha back and forth like a tetherball. But they soon got bored with that and began casting around for something better to do.

"Let's sell him a raffle ticket!" one of them cried.

"Yeah! A raffle ticket!"

"Who's got a ticket?"

"Who's got a hat fer him to pull it out of?"

"Whew! Your hat stinks, Riley! Don't you never take a bath?"

"Bathin's fer girls!"

Soon the hat was proffered and the tickets—grubby scraps of newspaper—were tipped into it for Sacha to draw. Sacha had been shaken down by street kids many times before, so he sighed in resignation and prepared to do his part. Lily, on the other hand, didn't seem to know the script at all.

"Aren't you going to tell us how much it costs?" she demanded. "And what's the prize? And why should we buy anything from you in the first place?"

" 'Cause we're the Hexers."

"So?"

The boy's eyes narrowed in anger. "Hey, Ratter," he called without taking his eyes off Lily. "Why don't you show her what you can do."

A scrawny boy stepped out from the little cluster of Hexers, grinning nervously. "What d'you want, Joe? Hives or Boils?"

Joe hesitated. But before he could answer, a third boy chimed in. "Aw, can't you do any better'n that, Ratter? It's been nothin' but hives an' boils all month long. We're gonna be the laughingstock of the neighborhood if you don't come up with some new hexes soon!"

"Did I ask for your opinion?" Joe said scathingly. He turned back to the scrawny hex caster. "Give 'er the hives, Ratter!"

"Now, look," Sacha interrupted, putting his hands up. "I'm sure we can work this ou—"

But it was too late. Even as Sacha spoke, angry red welts were spreading across Lily's perfect peaches and cream complexion.

"Oh!" she cried, putting her hands to her face as if she was desperately trying not to scratch at them.

"Now, now, boys," said a voice from over Sacha's shoulder. "Is that any way to treat a lady?"

Their rescuer turned out to be a handsome boy a few

years older than Lily and Sacha, with an open, friendly face and impossibly blue eyes that sparkled with barely contained laughter. He looked like the kind of nice Irish boy even Sacha's mother would approve of.

When Sacha looked back over at Lily, her hives had vanished and she was practically swooning in gratitude. He would never have imagined she could act so silly.

"Thank you!" she fluttered. "Thank you so much, Mr. . . . well, I don't even know your name, do I?"

The young man sketched a humorous bow. "Paddy Doyle at your service, miss."

Sacha frowned. He was sure he'd heard that name before. But he didn't have time to remember where, because the Hexers were exploding into wails of outrage and frustration.

"Paddy!" Joe yelped. "You ain't gonna let 'er off buyin' a ticket just 'cause she's a girl, are you?"

"For sure I'm not." Paddy turned his bright blue gaze on Sacha, and though he was still smiling, he didn't look nearly as friendly as he had just a moment ago. "I believe the tickets are a nickel apiece. Or ten cents, if you'd prefer to pay for the young lady."

"What?" Lily spluttered. "You're not going to stop these—these—*hooligans?*"

"Actually," Paddy explained in his charming Irish brogue, "I'm with the hooligans."

He flashed Sacha and Lily a conspiratorial wink, as if to say they were all good friends and there was nothing to worry about. Sacha didn't have any illusions, though. He shrugged in resignation and reached into his pocket for his subway money. But before he could fish out the coins, Lily opened her mouth again.

"How can you be such a cad?" she demanded, squaring off against Paddy with her hands on her hips.

"That's the way of the wicked world, darlin'."

Lily's eyes narrowed, and for a moment she looked almost as formidable as Paddy Doyle. "Maybe so," she snapped. "But I'm still not buying any stupid lottery ticket."

Paddy's smile broadened into an outright grin. "You got a better idea?"

"Actually, I do."

Lily was still holding the Hexers' baseball, and now she slapped it into the grimy hand of the closest Hexer and grabbed the bat from his slack-jawed neighbor. "One pitch. If I miss, we each owe you a nickel. If I hit a homer, you owe us a nickel. Every one of you." She counted heads. "That makes sixty cents total."

"But—you *can't!*" Sacha said.

"Why not?" Lily asked curiously.

Sacha stared at the shiny blond hair, the immaculate white stockings, the frothy lace petticoats peeping out from under her dress. "Because you're a *girl!*"

"I'll have you know that Smith and Vassar have both fielded baseball teams for at least the last twenty years," she declared as if that settled the matter beyond all question.

"And which professional league do Smith and Vassar play in?" Sacha asked sarcastically.

Lily rolled her eyes. "Oh, for heaven's sake, what hole did you crawl out of? Haven't you ever heard of Lizzie Arlington? Or the Bloomer Girls? Or—oh, never mind!" She broke off in disgust at the depths of his ignorance and stalked off across the vacant lot toward the upturned tin can that served the Hexers for home base.

Meanwhile, the Hexers had clearly accepted Lily's bet. They were running out to take up their fielding positions—or maybe, Sacha thought cynically, just to cut off the escape routes.

Lily limbered up at the plate, spitting on her palms and kicking at the packed dirt of the empty lot like some tobacco-chewing slugger from the heart of the Yankees lineup. Sacha groaned inwardly at the thought of what the Hexers would do to them if Lily actually won. But then he told himself not to worry. She'd just swing and miss. And even if she didn't miss, how hard could a girl really hit the ball?

Pretty hard, it turned out.

In fact, hard enough to send a blistering line drive shrieking across the abandoned lot to shatter a window in the neighboring tenement building.

After the glass shattered, there was a moment of stunned silence that seemed to stretch into eternity. Then three things happened all at once. A woman in curling papers leaned out the window and started screaming at them in language that would have shocked a dockworker. The Hexers scattered across the abandoned lot to hunt for their ball. And Lily rested the bat triumphantly on one toe and crowed, "That'll be sixty cents please!"

Sacha couldn't decide who was being more wildly optimistic: Lily or the Hexers. Sure, most of the time a ball bounced back off a window after cracking it. But Lily had hit that one harder than he'd ever seen a kid hit a ball. And if she thought the Hexers were going to pay up on their bet *after* she'd lost their baseball for them, she was crazy.

"Uh . . . maybe we should go now," he said, tugging on her elbow.

Throughout all this, Paddy Doyle hadn't moved a muscle. But now he laughed and said, "I wouldn't wait around to collect if I were you. In fact, I'd get lost before they realize you put their ball straight through that nice lady's window and they're never gonna get it back again. Nice hit, by the way." He grinned wickedly. "If you field as well as you bat, I might just have to fall in love with you."

Sacha opened his mouth to demand that Doyle apologize for insulting Lily, but then he looked over at Lily and noticed to his annoyance that she didn't look insulted at all. "Let's get out of here," he grumbled. "You're never going to get your sixty cents. They probably don't even *have* sixty cents. And if you stick around to ask for it, they'll just wallop us."

"Are you saying they made a bet they couldn't deliver on?" Lily demanded, her eyes flashing with indignation. "That's . . . why . . . why . . . that's *unsportsmanlike!*"

"I happen to agree with you," Paddy said, flashing his wicked smile again. "But I've a reputation to maintain, and I can't afford to ruin it. Not even for pretty girls who play baseball."

And then it really was too late. The Hexers descended on Sacha, grabbed him by the scruff of his neck, and dragged him behind a broken-down beer wagon. They didn't bother with fancy footwork or pugilist's rules; they just knocked him down and jumped on him. Lily hovered over the writhing pile, brandishing the bat, torn between the desire to help and the fear of seriously hurting someone. Finally she threw the bat away and waded in, armed only with her fists. Not that it did any good. Valiant though Lily might be, she was no taller than Sacha and even skinnier.

Which was why he was so surprised when one of the Hexers was suddenly jerked backward by a strong hand, just as he was about to land a crushing blow on Sacha's nose.

He was even more surprised when he realized that the hand was attached to a crisply ironed shirt cuff and a seersucker suit sleeve.

"Payton!" he gasped. "What—"

"If you don't mind," Payton replied coolly, "I'd rather leave the explanations for later. I'm rather busy at the moment."

The next few seconds went by so fast that Sacha only got a confused impression of flying limbs and scrabbling feet. When the dust cleared, the Hexers were on the run and Payton was calmly brushing off his trousers and inspecting his suit for damage.

Lily sat on the ground a few feet away from Sacha, sucking at a nasty cut on the back of her hand and staring at Payton with an expression that bordered on outright hero worship.

"Wow!" she said. "That was better than a *Boys Weekly* story! What is it, judo?"

"Kung fu."

"Can *I* learn it?"

"You'd better if you plan to go around insulting the Hell's Kitchen Hexers on a regular basis."

Meanwhile the Hexers were busy vanishing down the nearest alley—all except for Paddy Doyle, who was glaring at Payton with open hostility.

"Hello, *Philip*," he said. He made it sound like a girl's name. Or worse.

"Hello, Paddy. You might as well come back to the station with us. You really want the Inquisitors coming 'round to talk to your mother?"

"You leave my mum out of this! She's got enough worries!"

"Shouldn't you have thought of that before you added to them?"

"We can't all be model citizens like you, *Philip*."

"Come on, Paddy! You're smarter than this. How's it going to help your mom if you end up in jail like your brothers did?"

But Paddy wasn't having it. "Wolf knows where to find me," he said with a careless shrug of his shoulders. "Tell him that he can come talk to me at the Witch's Brew anytime he likes. But he'd better leave you behind. Sullivan don't allow no pets on the premises!"

Payton opened his mouth, looking like he was about to let loose some blistering reply to Paddy's insult. But then he turned away and stalked off in stormy silence.

"Is that the same Paddy Doyle whose pig got loose in the Inquisitorial Quotient exam?" Sacha asked when he finally managed to catch up with Payton.

"It wasn't his pig," Payton spat furiously. "He's too piss-poor shanty Irish to afford a pig. Or anything else he hasn't stolen from someone who actually works for a living."

"You *know* him?" Lily asked.

"I used to," Payton said through clenched teeth. "We used to be best friends."

"I suppose this means there's no coffee?" Wolf asked forlornly when he saw their dirty clothes and battered faces.

"What?" Lily snapped. "You send this poor child out into the streets to get beaten up by hooligans, and you have the nerve to ask about your *coffee*?"

"I'm not a child!" Sacha protested. "I'm the same age you are. And why are you all talking about me as if I'm not here?"

Lily brushed Sacha's protests aside. "Look what they did to him! Aren't you going to do anything about it?"

"I'm going to do several things, as a matter of fact. First, I'm going to have Payton find the woman whose window you broke and offer to fix it. I must say, it's a pity you didn't get her name and apartment number. It would have saved a lot of trouble. But never mind. I'm sure we'll get it all sorted out eventually. And meanwhile, I think it's time you two paid a visit to the White Lotus Young Ladies' Dancing and Deportment Academy."

"The *what?*" Sacha protested.

But Wolf wasn't listening. He was already hustling them down to the street and into yet another of the cabs that seemed to pop out of thin air whenever he wanted them. He called an address up to the driver and then turned back to Sacha and Lily with an air of suppressed excitement and a slight flush of color in his normally pale cheeks.

"We're going to Chinatown," he told them. "And when we get there, try to behave yourselves. You're about to meet royalty."

CHAPTER FOURTEEN

The Immortals of Chinatown

NATURALLY, it was Lily who first worked up the nerve to ask Wolf where they were going.

He gave her a long, blank stare instead of answering. Whatever strange mood had come over him at the mention of the White Lotus Young Ladies' Dancing and Deportment Academy, he hadn't recovered from it.

"What do you know about the Immortals of Chinatown?" he asked finally.

"They're the masterminds of magical crime in Chinatown," Lily promptly answered. "They run the tongs—that's Chinese for street gangs—and their word is law, and they brook no opposition and deal harshly with dissenters." She might have been reading straight out of a penny detective novel. "And . . . let's see, what else? Oh, yeah, they have these tunnels that connect everything under Chinatown and have entrances all over the city, kind of like the subway, so they can just sort of pop out anywhere and wreak deadly havoc without warning."

"You forgot to mention the opium smuggling and white slavery," Wolf pointed out. Sacha was pretty sure that even Lily must be able to hear the sardonic edge in his voice. But, amazingly enough, she couldn't. Sacha was starting to suspect that Lily Astral didn't get much of a chance to use her sense of humor at home. It seemed weak and shaky, like a muscle that didn't get enough exercise.

"Right," Lily corrected herself, still oblivious to Wolf's sarcasm. "I knew about that. It just slipped my mind for a minute. Is there anything else I should know?"

"Actually," Wolf said, "I think you'd be better off if you knew less. The Immortals have nothing to do with the tongs. And they have no power over anyone, certainly not the power of fear."

"But they *are* wizards," Lily pestered him.

Or at least Sacha told himself she was pestering. Deep down he was a little jealous, though. He wondered where she got the gumption to talk to Wolf like that, as if she just naturally assumed they were equals. He guessed it came from being richer than God and hobnobbing with Roosevelts and Vanderbilks.

"Yes," Wolf told Lily. "They're just about the most powerful wizards there are."

"So why don't the Inquisitors arrest them?"

"It's not illegal to be a wizard," Wolf replied, "any more than it's illegal to be a Kabbalist or a druid . . . or even a good old-fashioned New England witch."

"So then what *is* illegal?" Lily asked.

Wolf laughed uncomfortably. "That's a gray area. A hundred years ago there were country witches and warlocks all over New England. They put out shingles and even advertised in the newspapers. But then the bankers turned magic into big business. They started squeezing out the little independent witches and warlocks. Then . . . but that's politics." He stopped short, obviously feeling he'd said too much. "And you two are far too young to worry about politics."

But Lily had gotten hold of a bone and she wasn't ready to let go of it. "But that's just . . . just . . ."

"Ridiculous?" Wolf teased.

"Yes, frankly! You talk about Wall Street Wizards as if they were all conjure men. But surely some of them are honest businessmen. My father, for instance—"

"I certainly didn't intend to suggest anything about your father, Miss Astral."

It felt like the temperature inside the cab had just dropped twenty degrees. But Lily was too busy arguing to notice.

"No respectable person uses magic these days!" she said. "When my mother was a girl, all the best New England families used to give their daughters witchcraft lessons, just like they give them drawing lessons and dancing lessons. But nowadays real Americans don't do magic. Isn't that right, Inquisitor Wolf? Or I mean . . . well . . . *is* it?"

Suddenly Sacha forgot to be offended by Lily's crack about real Americans. Something truly strange was going on.

Lily's voice had gone all tight and scratchy during this little speech. And she had the oddest look on her face—like she was trying to trick Wolf into saying something she really didn't want to hear.

Wolf heard it too. Sacha was sure he did. He was looking at Lily as if he felt sorry for her.

"Like I said," he told her, "you're much too young to worry about politics."

By now the cabbie had turned off Broadway and begun to nose his way down Mulberry Street. They were in the heart of Chinatown. And though they were only a few blocks from Grandpa Kessler's synagogue, Sacha barely knew these streets. He stared as they inched past gaudily painted shopfronts full of silks and spices and dusty packets of Chinese medicines. In one store, he even glimpsed a stuffed albino tiger as big as a horse, with its claws unsheathed and its teeth bared menacingly.

The street peddlers here didn't carry their wares in push-carts. Instead, they balanced long bamboo poles across their shoulders with red-lacquered baskets that bobbed on either end like candied apples in a carnival booth. And the smells wafting from those baskets were incredible. Caramel and curry and carp and crispy duck and a thousand other exotic delights tickled Sacha's nose. His head was spinning and his stomach rumbling by the time the cab pulled up in front of a nondescript herbalist's shop.

Wolf whisked them into the shop—and then straight through it and out the back door into a high-walled inner courtyard hung with so many clotheslines that they seemed to be walking under a solid roof of fluttering white sheets and linens. The shopkeeper's entire family seemed to live around the courtyard, along with a flock of unusually lively chickens. As Sacha hurried past, he glanced through an open door and saw them all sitting down to lunch around an ingenious little table with a portable cookstove built into it.

Behind the first courtyard lay another courtyard. This one contained only a very large mulberry tree and a very tiny old man, who was carrying two fat white mice in an ornate wicker birdcage. The old man pantomimed an introduction as they raced by: Children, meet mice; mice, meet children. Wolf paused just long enough to nod politely to the mice. Then he yanked open a narrow metal door that looked like it led to a broom closet, slipped inside—and vanished.

When Sacha stepped through after him, he found himself in a place that was like nowhere he'd ever been before.

It wasn't just the size of the place—though it seemed enormous. It was that, for the first time in his life, Sacha couldn't hear even the faintest sound of traffic. Instead the air was filled with the chirping of crickets and the warbling of sparrows and the sharp smell of the ancient pine trees whose twisted limbs blocked out half the sky. Sacha had the eerie feeling that he was no longer in New York at all, but had stepped through some magical door into the heart of China.

At the far end of a long courtyard stood a massive wooden gate built from age-blackened timbers. It looked as if it had stood there for centuries, as did the tile-roofed building be-

hind it. Above the gate, emblazoned on a fluttering silk banner, stretched four immense golden Chinese characters.

"What does that sign say?" Sacha asked.

Wolf smiled ever so slightly. "It says 'White Lotus Young Ladies' Dancing and Deportment Academy.' But don't worry. There are boys here too. It's an orphanage. And it wasn't a dancing academy even before it was an orphanage. They just call it that to stay out of trouble with the police because it's illegal to teach . . . well, you'll see."

Wolf pulled at the bell rope beside the heavy oak door, and a deep bell tolled somewhere far off inside the building. A moment later they heard the patter of bare feet on stone, and a child opened the door for them. The child was wearing a pigtail and the same white cotton pajamas that Sacha had seen Chinese men wearing. Sacha thought it was a boy, since he was wearing pants, but he wasn't really sure. And after another look, he wasn't even sure if he was Chinese or not. The hair and eyes looked right. But whoever heard of a Chinese person with freckles?

The boy knew Wolf, though. He let them in with a friendly smile before vanishing into the shadows and leaving them to find their own way to wherever they were going.

Wolf led them down a dim hallway and into a cavernous space that smelled pleasantly of wet stones and soapy water. Balconies rose above them on all sides, supported by columns hewn from whole tree trunks and polished smooth by the touch of many hands. Heavy beams supported the high ceiling, and the floor was paved with massive flagstones even larger than the ones that lined New York's sidewalks. The place felt as solemn as a church, yet it was alive with the faint sounds of children's movement and laughter that drifted in from the surrounding rooms.

And it was alive with magic too: a magic as vast as oceans that seemed to belong to a far older city than the New York Sacha knew.

At the moment, the only person in the great room was a thin Chinese woman on her hands and knees next to a bucket of soapy water, scrubbing at the stone floor with a hard-bristled cleaning brush. Wolf glanced briefly at her. Then he walked around the edge of the room, carefully avoiding the freshly scrubbed stones, sat down on a sack of rice, and took out his newspaper as if he knew they were in for a long wait.

Sacha sat down beside Wolf, wishing he had a newspaper too.

Meanwhile the cleaning lady kept scrubbing. This was a woman who took her cleaning seriously, even by Hester Street standards. She scrubbed with intent, like a master baker rolling out his dough or an artist preparing a canvas. Or, Sacha realized, like a *shammes* cleaning the synagogue before a High Holy Day. What *was* this place?

Sacha turned to Wolf, meaning to ask him. But Wolf was watching the woman too. His newspaper had dropped to his lap, forgotten, and he was staring at her with a look of longing that even a thirteen-year-old boy couldn't mistake for anything but unrequited love. Sacha glanced sideways at Lily to see if she'd noticed—and sure enough she had that gushy, dewy-eyed look on her face that girls always got when they smelled romance in the air. Sacha wanted to shake her for mooning around like a silly girl instead of asking the obvious question: How on earth could the most famous Inquisitor in New York possibly have fallen in love with a Chinese cleaning woman?

Finally the cleaning woman gathered up her brush and bucket and slipped out of the room, leaving them alone.

"Is she going to get her master?" Sacha asked, unable to contain himself any longer.

Wolf smiled very faintly. "Not exactly."

She came back a few minutes later—this time bearing a heavy lacquered tray piled high with tea things. She poured tea and handed around warm sweet rolls. Then she sat down opposite Wolf in a way that left Sacha quite certain she was no mere servant, even before Wolf introduced her as Shen Yunying, the proprietress of the White Lotus Young Ladies' Dancing and Deportment Academy.

"So," Shen said when the introductions were over, "the student returns to the master. And he comes bearing . . . children? You don't think I have enough children in my life already, Max?"

Wolf muttered something that sounded like the beginning of an apology, but broke off to run a finger around the inside of his shirt collar as if it had suddenly gotten too tight. "I was hoping you could . . . teach them."

Her dark eyes widened in amazement. "You want me to train a pair of Inquisitor's apprentices? What on earth makes you think I would do that? Unless you think I owe you a favor."

"No!" Wolf lowered his voice, struggling visibly to control himself. But when he spoke again, he still sounded angry. "You don't owe me anything. I just thought . . . well, you taught Payton."

"Payton's different. He's not going to be an Inquisitor."

"He's an Inquisitor in all but name," Wolf said impatiently. "And if it weren't for the color of his skin, you know damn well it would be official."

"You make it sound like the color of a person's skin is just an insignificant detail. Try walking around in *my* skin for a day."

"Come on, Shen!" Wolf protested. "What do you want from me?"

"What do *I* want? You're the one sitting in my house asking me for favors."

"Oh, for God's sake! You're the most infuriating—"

Suddenly Wolf seemed to remember Sacha and Lily. To their bitter disappointment, he clammed up and refused to say anything more. Then the two grownups just sat staring at each other, Wolf with a hangdog look on his face and Shen with an amused smile that seemed to suggest that it would take a lot more than one angry Inquisitor to rattle her.

To Sacha's amazement, however, it was Shen who gave in first.

"All right. I'll teach them. You knew I would."

"Wait a minute!" Lily broke in. "I'm not learning any magic! I won't have anything to do with *that!*"

"Who said I was going to teach you magic?" Shen asked calmly. "Why should I, when I can teach you how to beat a grown man in a fight without using any magic at all?" She shrugged philosophically. "Though if you don't want to learn magic, then you probably don't want to learn kung fu either."

"Oh, don't I?" Lily exclaimed with a dangerous glint in her eye. "Just try me!" But then her face fell. "Except, well . . . I don't have the proper clothes for it."

"I have a number of young lady students. I can lend you a set of clothes that you can leave here and change into when you arrive for your lessons."

"Oh." Lily grinned. "Good idea!"

Throughout this exchange, Sacha had been trying not to stare at Shen too obviously. But he must have been doing a pretty bad job of it because suddenly she looked him square in the eye and smiled. He'd never seen such a smile before. It cut straight through him, sweet and sharp and bracing as the wind off the ocean.

"So tell me," Shen asked, still smiling that astounding smile, "how did you get that beautiful shiner?"

"Uh . . . baseball?"

"Really? The rules must have changed quite a bit since I last played. And it must hurt like the devil. Come along and let's get something on it to take the swelling down. You too, Lily. Let's see what we can do for your scraped knuckles . . .

which I suppose you're also going to claim you got playing baseball?"

She led the two of them around the edge of the stone-floored room to a curtained alcove whose walls were lined from floor to ceiling with the same exotic ingredients Sacha had seen in the cluttered herbalists' windows on their ride through Chinatown. Before they quite knew what was happening, Shen had massaged Sacha's bruises with some sort of pungent concoction, dressed Lily's hand, and talked enough baseball to establish that all three of them were die-hard Yankees fans.

"They should be ready for their first lesson in a week," she told Wolf when she brought them back. She appeared to hesitate, although the hesitation was so brief that Sacha wondered if he'd imagined it. "You needn't bring them. They can come by themselves."

"But how will we find you?" Lily asked.

"Don't worry," Shen told her with a little smile. "People can always find me when they need me. And when they can't, it usually turns out that they didn't really need me in the first place."

Lily didn't look at all satisfied by this explanation, but before she could ask another question, Wolf was herding them back down the long corridor—while he lingered behind to say a frustratingly private goodbye to Shen.

"Wow!" Sacha whispered to Lily while they waited. "She's something, isn't she?"

"I'll say!" Lily's eyes were shining. "I'll bet she's a kung fu master. She's probably even a Shaolin Monk, just like the ones in *Sword for Hire* and *Exotic Adventures*."

Sacha was about to ask Lily if she did anything at all in her spare time but read pulp magazines when Wolf caught up with them.

"That went well," he said. "I think you two made a good impression."

Lily started to ask a question, but Wolf waved it away. "Come on. You two have had a rough day; I'm going to send you home early."

He marched them across the courtyard to the little blue door through which they'd first entered Shen's domain.

But when he opened the door, Sacha and Lily both gasped. Instead of the courtyard with the mulberry tree and the white mice, they were looking at an uptown street—Seventy-second Street, to be precise, just at the corner of Fifth Avenue, next to the Astral mansion.

"But—but—that's *magic!*" Lily protested.

"Inquisitors are law enforcement officers, Lily. Our job is to prevent people with magical abilities from misusing them. Don't you think that would be rather difficult to do if we couldn't use magic ourselves?"

Lily looked horrified. Clearly she had never thought of this before.

"Do you have a problem with magic, Lily? Some kind of phobia? If so, you won't make a very good Inquisitor."

"I—no—I mean—" Lily's face was practically scarlet, though Sacha couldn't tell if it was with embarrassment or anger. "But if Inquisitors are allowed to use magic, then who prevents *them* from abusing magic?"

"That is an excellent question," Wolf replied, "and I wish I knew the answer to it. Now, go home. And apologize to your charming mother for the scraped knuckles or she'll be calling up Commissioner Keegan to complain about me."

Lily opened her mouth to ask another question. Then she gave a little shrug and turned to go. But just as she was about to step through the door, she turned back and walked over to Sacha and held out a hand for him to shake.

He took her hand, feeling silly and awkward. She didn't seem to notice his awkwardness, though; her grip was as firm and no-nonsense as her clear-eyed gaze.

"Good job back there with the Hexers," she told him. "You ought to stand up for yourself more often. You're too quiet. It makes people think they can walk all over you."

"So you think I should go around insulting street gangs instead?"

She grinned. "Life's too short to walk away from a good fight."

Sacha started to grin back, but he stopped when he noticed Wolf watching them. He cleared his throat awkwardly. "Anyway," he said, "sorry about your hand."

"Hah! You should see the other guy!"

Lily strode through the door, and a moment later he saw her dashing up the marble steps of the Astral mansion.

"Your turn, Mr. Kessler," Wolf said cheerfully. "Where to?"

Sacha panicked. "I—uh—that is—"

"Don't tell me you're afraid of a little magic."

"Actually, yes." As much as he hated letting Wolf think he was afraid, Sacha knew this was the perfect excuse. "Can't you just drop me at the nearest subway station? If it wouldn't be too much of a bother."

Wolf gave Sacha a smile that tied his insides in knots. It made Sacha feel as if Wolf actually liked him—and suddenly he felt horribly guilty for lying to him.

"No, Sacha," Wolf said gently. "It's not too much bother. And anyway, grownups like to be bothered. It makes us feel useful. But you're not the sort who bothers grownups with your problems, are you? Pity. You should try it sometime."

Silence stretched between them until Sacha thought he was going to burst into hysterics if someone didn't say something.

"A man solves his own problems!" he blurted out. It sounded like the sort of thing his father would say.

"I see. And are a man's friends allowed to help?"

"I—"

"Never mind. We don't know each other very well. I don't suppose you have much reason to trust me. What subway stop did you have in mind?"

"I—uh—Astral Place?"

"Astral Place it is."

CHAPTER FIFTEEN

A Shande far di Goyim

THAT SATURDAY MORNING Sacha slipped into the Hester Street synagogue late and settled into the last row. You could never hear anything back here, because the old men in the congregation were always wandering in and out and gossiping to each other. But this morning it was the gossiping old men he wanted to see—and most especially his grandfather.

He waited patiently until prayers were finally over and the only people still hanging around were Rabbi Kessler's little gaggle of would-be Kabbalists. Then he tagged along while they meandered over to the storefront *shul* on Canal Street and settled in to do the three things Kabbalists did best—or at least the only three things Sacha had ever seen any Hester Street Kabbalist do. One: shaking their heads over the latest bad news from Russia. Two: complaining about how all the young people were too busy chasing girls and baseballs to remember their religion. And three: discussing the possibility on a purely theoretical level of maybe perhaps coming up with a tentative plan for coaxing an obviously reluctant Messiah into coming back sometime in the next few millennia to do something about the sorry state of the world.

Finally Sacha managed to get his grandfather alone for a minute and ask him about Edison's dybbuk. After a lot of thought, he'd decided to tell a mostly true version of the story, but without mentioning his mother's locket or the alarming fact that the dybbuk had followed him home the other night.

"Isn't that just like the *goyim*?" Grandpa Kessler asked when Sacha finished his story. "Here's Thomas Edison, rich as the czar, with everything a man could want in life, but he runs into a two-week stretch of bad luck and suddenly he's looking around for a Jew to blame. Us Jews, our luck goes down the crapper for two thousand years and we call it being the Chosen People."

"Yeah, well, that's New York for you," Mo Lehrer said, ambling over to join the conversation. "The whole city's coming apart at the seams, and the Inquisitors are running around investigating how some rich *goy* got Yiddish luck."

Sacha laughed at the joke and caught himself thinking he'd like to share it with Lily. But of course he could never do that. He was quite sure that no one in Lily Astral's family ever complained about having Yiddish luck.

"But . . . well . . . do you think a rabbi could have summoned the dybbuk?" he asked tentatively.

"Of course a rabbi *could* have," Grandpa Kessler snapped. "Any rabbi worth his salt can summon a dybbuk—well, except those hoity-toity uptown rabbis who don't study Kabbalah anymore and spend all their time pretending to be Episcopalians. But the point is, no rabbi *would* have."

"Why? Because dybbuks are evil?"

"No, *dummkopf*! Because they're magic!" Rabbi Kessler yanked at his beard in frustration. "Do you have anything between your ears but baseball scores? Don't you remember *anything* you learned for your *bar mitzvah*? The last thing any real Kabbalist would ever do is work magic. As it is written, *They may not save so much as a hair on their heads by magic.*"

Sacha had been hearing that proverb about not saving so much as a hair by magic ever since he could remember—while at the same time watching housewives all up and down Hester Street use magic for just about everything *except* saving a hair on anyone's head. And come to think of it, one of Mrs. Lassky's most popular recipes was her Hair-Be-Here Hamantaschen.

"But *why* can't Kabbalists use magic?" Sacha asked. "Everyone else does."

"Because Kabbalah isn't mere charms and trickery. It's the manipulation of the letters of the names of God! If you use God's name as a spellbook, you've turned Him into a mere device. Is that an occupation worthy of a pious Jew?"

"So the more magic you know, the less you can use it?" Sacha asked disgustedly. "What's the point of that?"

Rabbi Kessler rubbed at his head until his wispy hair stood on end with static electricity. "Mo, help me out!"

"Look at it this way," Mo said in his usual levelheaded, reasonable tone. "Say you've got two friends. One of them spends time with you every week. You know, just hanging out, having a sandwich, taking in a matinee, playing cards . . . being together for the sake of being together. But the other friend only shows up when he needs to borrow money. Pretty soon you'd start to get a feeling about these two guys. Like that one of them's your real friend, and the other one's just a mooch. So that's why Kabbalists don't work magic. We're God's *real* friends."

Sacha shook his head in bewilderment at the image of God playing cards with Mo Lehrer—just two paunchy middle-aged Jewish guys kicking back around the kitchen table with their undershirts untucked and their suspenders hanging around their knees.

"But can't God tell the difference between someone who's just using Him and, well, I don't know, let's say . . . a faithful Jew who happens to need a really big favor for a really good reason?"

"Easy for you to say," Grandpa Kessler pointed out. "But who decides what's a good reason? And how do you know who else God has to stick it to in order grant *your* prayer? Working miracles is like letting out a pair of pants: You can only stretch the fabric of the universe so far before you run out of cloth. After that, you're stuck deciding whether you want cold ankles or a cold tushie."

Mo cleared his throat and nodded toward the other side of the room where the rest of the class was staring curiously at them.

"So!" Grandpa Kessler said in a voice so loud that even

the few students who hadn't been eavesdropping jumped guiltily. "I take it you fellows are masters of Kabbalah now? You've set all the Worlds aright, and defeated the Other Side, and we can expect the Messiah any minute?" He glared sternly at them—or at least sternly for him. "No? Then stop gawping and get back to your books!"

"But I don't get it," Sacha said when the class had bent over their books again. "Kabbalists can't use magic because it interferes with God's plan for the universe, but—"

"Oh, God has a 'plan' now, does He? What do you think He is, a building inspector?"

"But how is evil ever supposed to be defeated if the bad people use magic all the time and the good people aren't even allowed to use it to fight them?"

Rabbi Kessler's only answer was a fatalistic shrug. "What do you want from me? We're in *goles*, exile. Life is *supposed* to stink. If you want to reform the world, go down to the Café Metropole and talk politics with your no-goodnik Uncle Mordechai!"

Sacha still thought this sounded crazy, but he knew it was pointless to argue. "So then what's going to happen to Edison?"

"He's a goner," Grandpa Kessler announced cheerfully. "And, frankly, it sounds like it couldn't happen to a nicer guy."

Mo clarified. "Every time Edison has an impious thought or does an immoral deed, he'll get weaker and his dybbuk will get stronger. Soon the dybbuk will be as solid as you and me.

Then it will start to ooze its way into Edison's life like a fungus. He might come home one night and find the dybbuk sitting down at his dinner table with his family. His friends and family will start mixing them up. Pretty soon they'll start thinking he's the fake and the dybbuk's the real man. Day by day, the dybbuk will suck the life out of him, just like you'd suck an egg cream up through a straw. Soon he'll be nothing but a *kelippah:* a dry scrap of skin with no soul left inside of it. Until one day . . . pfft! Gone!"

Finally Sacha put his finger on what had been bothering him about all of this. "But . . . how can the dybbuk fool everyone into thinking it's Thomas Edison when it doesn't even look like him?"

Mo and Grandpa Kessler were suddenly both very still. And they were both staring hard at Sacha with a look in their eyes he'd never seen before. Sacha remembered what his father had said about how no cheap hexer would mess with a Kessler. Now he could see why.

He cleared his throat and tried to speak in a normal voice. "You're talking about Edison's dybbuk as if it's some kind of twin or double. But it isn't. It doesn't look anything like him."

"Then it's not his dybbuk," Rabbi Kessler said.

"Are you sure about that?"

"What do you mean, am I sure? Your dybbuk is part of you—all your fear and anger and weakness. A dybbuk is the dark half of your soul, ripped out of your body and set against you. So how can your own soul not look like you?"

Sacha's stomach turned over. "But then . . . whose dybbuk is it?"

"How should I know? You're the one who's seen it! Who does it look like?"

"It's hard to tell," Sacha began. "It's all fuzzy. You know, like an old—"

He had been about to say *like an old photograph*. But then he stopped short as he realized which old photograph the dybbuk's face reminded him of: the one of Rabbi Kessler as a beardless young man that hung over the mantlepiece in the Kesslers' kitchen.

"What's wrong, Sachele?"

But Sacha didn't answer. He was too busy staring at his grandfather's familiar face and seeing his features in a new light—the hazy halo of gaslight. And suddenly he realized that who the dybbuk looked like was the last thing on earth he wanted to discuss with his grandfather.

CHAPTER SIXTEEN

Some Old Goat Named Kessler

TO SACHA'S RELIEF, Wolf began his hunt for a Kabbalist not on Hester Street but on the Upper East Side—a neighborhood where Sacha was blessedly certain they wouldn't run into anyone who'd ever heard of Rabbi Kessler.

First they visited a Jungian Kabbalist—a wild-eyed fellow with alarming eyebrows who kept insisting that the dybbuk was an instantiation of Edison's "Shadow Self" and Edison's only hope of salvation was to immerse himself in the "Collective Unconscious" and embrace his "Anima." Then came the Freudian Kabbalist, whose ideas about dybbuks practically set Sacha's ears on fire. And then came the Analytical Kabbalist, who inflicted page after page of alchemical calculus on them. Sacha didn't have to imagine what Rabbi Kessler would say about alchemical calculus, because he'd already heard the speech too many times to count: "God created the Universe in plain Hebrew, and any fool who thinks he knows enough to check God's math deserves whatever he gets."

By the time they staggered up to the last address on Wolf's list, Sacha had sore feet and a splitting headache.

"Wow!" Lily said when they first walked in. "It's like a cathedral!"

She was right. If Sacha hadn't looked closely enough to notice the discreet Stars of David carved into the gothic arches, he would never have known it was a synagogue at all.

The rabbi's office looked like a fancy New York architect's idea of an English country house. Inside, a cheerful fire crackled in the hearth. Outside, red-branched cherry trees swayed in a fall wind that carried the faint promise of snow. The chairs were upholstered in nut-brown leather. The walls were covered with paintings of foxhounds and racehorses. And the books in the oak bookshelves ran more to the collected works of Dickens than to Talmud and Kabbalah.

Rabbi Mendelsohn matched his surroundings perfectly. He was tall and blue-eyed and collegiate-looking, and you knew the minute you laid eyes on him that *his* family hadn't come over from Russia in steerage.

Mendelsohn settled back into his chair and crossed his impeccably trousered legs as he toyed with the letter Wolf had sent him. "Dybbuks," he mused. "Not really my bailiwick, old chap. But I did look through the rabbinical literature to see if I could dig up anything useful for you."

"I appreciate that," Wolf said humbly. He had slipped into his dumb cop act, Sacha noticed.

"Tell me"—Mendelsohn leaned forward confidentially—"is this to do with a *criminal* case? Some poor naïf who committed an act of violence under the delusion that he was attacking a dybbuk?"

"I'm afraid I can't comment on an ongoing investigation."

Mendelsohn hid his disappointment well, except for the irritated tic under his right eye. "Well, I'm certainly delighted to be of assistance in any way possible. I hope you understand you can count on my discretion."

"Very gratifying," Wolf assured him.

"And of course, discretion is paramount in this case. The poorer class of Jew is lamentably superstitious. The faintest rumor that a dybbuk was loose in New York would send them into paroxysms of terror that could threaten public order—"

Sacha must have made some involuntary sound that betrayed his outrage because Mendelsohn trailed off and frowned at him, as if noticing his presence for the first time. He seemed to be taking inventory, registering Sacha's black curls and dark eyes and finely drawn features, and trying to figure out what they added up to. He didn't seem to be able to make the sum come out right—especially in the context of the New York City Police Department.

"You're an interesting-looking young man," he said when he was done staring. "I suppose you're what they call black Irish?"

Sacha had been practicing Wolf's unnervingly bland

smile in front of the mirror at home and he now did his best imitation. The results were, he had to admit, highly satisfactory.

"Ahem," Mendelsohn said. And then he launched into a general history of dybbuks in the rabbinical literature. He seemed to know quite a lot about it. And he was very eloquent. But Sacha got the oddest feeling that he didn't believe a word of it.

In fact, Sacha decided, there was something very odd in the way Rabbi Mendelsohn talked about God. People on Hester Street treated God like a member of the family. You respected Him the way you respected a crotchety and demanding grandparent. You loved Him, but you showed your love the same way parents showed their children love: by nitpicking everything He did and pointing out all His faults and failings so He wouldn't get a big head. And of course by making fun of Him—after all, what else was family for?

But Rabbi Mendelsohn didn't make fun of God at all. Sacha couldn't imagine Rabbi Mendelsohn joking about the Passover plagues or cracking everyone up at Hanukkah by calling out, "But what have You done for us lately?" when Grandpa Kessler recited the line about the miracles God performed of old in the land of Israel. Instead, Mendelsohn seemed to feel that propriety required him to call God "Our Heavenly Father" instead of just plain God and to freeze his face into a strained expression that made him look constipated.

"I know it's hard to credit the fact that people actually believe in such things," Mendelsohn said. "Still, all these tales of demons and dybbuks do perform a necessary social function. It requires a certain degree of, shall we say, cultural development before people can leave behind their Old World ways and begin to think like Americans."

Finally Sacha realized what was so strange about Rabbi Mendelsohn. He talked about God as if he didn't believe in Him. And to his surprise Sacha realized that he didn't much like it. He had no problem with the way Mordechai or Bekah or Moishe talked about God. None of them believed in Him— and one of them didn't even believe in Brooklyn. But they were all perfectly happy to tell you so straight to your face. Rabbi Mendelsohn, on the other hand, believed one thing and said another. And from what Sacha could make out, he only did it because he thought God was a good way to scare poor people into behaving themselves.

"I quite see your point," Wolf told Mendelsohn, "but to be honest, I was hoping you might have some more . . . er . . . practical insights to offer."

It took a while for Mendelsohn to understand what Wolf was getting at. Then he let out an offended laugh. "If you want to talk to a *practical* Kabbalist, you'll have to go down to Hester Street and see the tenement rabbis. There's a whole gaggle of them down there, and they all go to a storefront *shul* run by some raggedy old goat named Kessler. But you won't get any sense out of him," Mendelsohn added scornfully. "He still stinks of the shtetl."

"Now, look here—" Sacha began.

But Wolf interrupted Sacha before he had a chance to

tell Mendelsohn what *he* stank of. "And what about my other question?"

"Oh. Yes. That." Suddenly Mendelsohn sounded halting and unwilling. "I've never come across the idea of building a *machine* that could create a dybbuk. And yet . . ."

Wolf waited, motionless as a cat poised to pounce. He didn't even seem to be breathing.

"I'm sure it's nothing," Mendelsohn said. "It's just that you're not the first person to ask me that question. I had a visit from . . . that is to say, someone asked me about . . ."

Wolf just kept waiting. He really had an amazing talent for creating the sort of awkward silences that people couldn't help babbling into. Was it something you could learn, Sacha wondered, or was Wolf just born knowing how to do it?

"They had blueprints," Mendelsohn blurted. "Someone had filed a patent on the device, and they wanted my opinion as to whether it would actually work or not before they . . . well, I got the impression they were considering investing a rather large sum of money."

"They?"

"I'm afraid I'm not at liberty to tell you the names of the parties involved," Mendelsohn said primly. "A rabbi is like a priest. People repose confidence in him. And they have a certain expectation of—"

"Naturally," Wolf agreed in a pleasant voice. "Your congregation depends upon your discretion. And such a highly respectable congregation as yours must expect their rabbi to be very discreet indeed."

"I appreciate your understanding, Inquisi—"

"But under the present circumstances, I'm sure they'll understand when you explain to them the necessity of cooperating with our investigation. Would Monday be too soon to start questioning people? And do you have a spare office we can use for our . . . well, *interrogation* is a nasty word. Perhaps it would make people less nervous if we just called them interviews."

"You want to drag respectable people down here and question them like criminals?" Mendelsohn yelped, his dignity forgotten. "What on earth could you possibly have to ask them about?"

Wolf smiled beatifically. "I'm sure I'll think of something."

Rabbi Mendelsohn moaned softly and put a hand to his handsome forehead. "If I tell you who it was, will you go away?"

Wolf's smile broadened.

"Fine! It was Thomas Edison. And since you'll probably find out anyway, you might as well know now that it was Mr. Morgaunt's librarian, Miss da Serpa, who made the appointment for him."

"You said someone had filed a patent on the device. Do you remember the name by any chance?"

"No."

Wolf's pale eyes widened. It was such a small movement that you couldn't even really call it an expression. Yet it seemed to have a remarkable effect on Rabbi Mendelsohn.

"That is to say, I didn't really pay attention, but I . . . I think it started with a *W*. And it was an unusual name. Worley, Wormley. Something like that. And I remember what the machine was called. It was called a Soul Catcher."

For a moment Wolf looked like he was about to ask another question. But then he slipped his notebook into his pocket and unfolded his lanky, rumpled frame from the leather armchair. "Thank you, Rabbi Mendelsohn. You've been most helpful."

Suddenly Wolf seemed to be in an unusual hurry. He grabbed the two children by the elbows and practically dragged them back through the synagogue and onto the sidewalk.

"That's ridiculous!" Lily erupted as soon as they were outside. "Morgaunt can't have summoned Edison's dybbuk! Why would he want to kill his own business partner?"

"I don't know," Wolf said shortly. Then, to Sacha's writhing mortification, he asked, "This Rabbi Kessler wouldn't be any relation of yours, would he, Sacha?"

"No! Well . . . maybe."

Wolf raised his eyebrows.

"I have a big family. He's some kind of . . . distant cousin? I'd have to check."

Now Wolf and Lily were both looking at him like he was crazy.

"Well, check, then," Wolf said. "And find out where he lives. I want to talk to him."

CHAPTER SEVENTEEN

Tea with Mrs. Astral

WOLF STOOD OUTSIDE Rabbi Mendelsohn's temple looking up and down the block and blinking in astonishment. "Well, bless my soul!" he murmured. "How extraordinary!"

It took Sacha a moment to see what Wolf was so surprised about. Then he realized this was the first time he could remember that there hadn't been a cab waiting at the curb for them.

Wolf scanned the block again, as if he suspected there might be one hiding behind a tree or under a manhole. "Perhaps on Fifth Avenue?" he hazarded.

But there were no cabs there either, even though they waited anxiously for several minutes.

Wolf produced a battered pocket watch and checked the time. "I really need to get back to Hell's Kitchen and call the Patent Office before closing time. I'd better just leave you two here and walk across the park. Why don't you take the rest of the day off?"

And then he hurried away, leaving Lily and Sacha staring after him.

"Can you get home all right from here?" Sacha asked Lily.

"Of course I can. I live just around the corner."

"Oh," Sacha said, feeling a little silly. "Right."

Lily turned to leave, hesitated, and then turned back to Sacha with a look on her face that suggested she was about to perform an unpleasant but necessary chore. "I guess I should invite you over to my house for tea," she mumbled, as if the words were being squeezed out of her against her will. "If you want. But I'm sure you have better things to do."

Sacha felt a flash of anger. What was the point of giving an invitation she so plainly didn't want him to accept? And how dare she make it so insultingly obvious that she didn't think he was good enough to enter her house? He started to make some polite excuse, then decided to make her squirm a little. "Actually," he said, "tea sounds delightful."

The Astral home was even more spectacularly luxurious than J. P. Morgaunt's mansion. Not that Sacha had much time to look around. Lily hurried him through a side door to a narrow creaking stairway that was obviously only meant to be used by servants. She was plainly terrified that her parents would see him. Sacha felt humiliated. He wished he hadn't come at all. In fact, he decided, there was no reason he shouldn't just turn around and leave right now if this was how Lily was going to act.

Except that when he turned around to stomp back down the stairs, he found himself face-to-face with Mrs. Astral herself.

"You must be Sacha Kessler!" she said with a brilliant smile that made Sacha feel as if he were the only person in the whole world Mrs. Astral cared about. "I can't think why Lily didn't tell me she was bringing you! She knows I've been dying to meet you. I do hope you have time to stay for tea?"

Sacha glanced at Lily. She gave a tiny, stiff shake of her blond head and mouthed a single word at him: *"No!"*

"Thank you," he told Mrs. Astral. "I'd love to."

Sacha took the arm that Mrs. Astral graciously offered him and accompanied her into a vast drawing room filled with palm trees, marble statuary, and overstuffed furniture. Lily trudged behind them like a soldier being ordered into a hopeless battle.

Sacha had read almost as many newspaper stories about Maleficia Astral as he'd read about J. P. Morgaunt. She'd been a famous beauty, the daughter of an old New England family from Salem, Massachusetts. Then she'd married the heir to the Astral family fortune—rumored to be a formidable Wall Street Wizard in his own right. Now she ruled New York high society with absolute authority. No one could be invited into the best houses without her seal of approval. No ball or soiree was a success unless she attended. And any proper New York socialite would rather die a thousand deaths than wear a gown that clashed with whatever Maleficia Astral was wearing.

From what he'd read in the papers, Sacha had assumed

that Mrs. Astral would be haughty and snobbish. But instead, she was bewitching. Her eyes were the brilliant iridescent green of hummingbird wings. Her clothes were impeccably ladylike, yet they flowed over her body like water rippling over rocks, revealing every sinuous curve and graceful movement. And her voice . . . well, when Maleficia Astral spoke to you, it was absolutely impossible to think of anything but Maleficia Astral.

"So you're Lily's little friend," Mrs. Astral cooed at Sacha. "I'm so very pleased to meet you. Lily's told me so much about you."

"No I haven't," Lily said churlishly.

"But, darling, don't be shy! Of course you have! I've heard no end of charming stories about the fun you two have together!"

Sacha doubted that. But he thought it was nice of Mrs. Astral to say so. Unlike her daughter, she apparently *cared* about making people feel welcome and comfortable. Basking in the warmth of Mrs. Astral's smile, he tried to be charitable toward Lily. It must be hard to live up to such a dazzling mother. Not that Lily wasn't pretty enough in her own way. But she couldn't hold a candle to her mother. As for personality, he supposed Lily must take after her father there. And while that sort of personality was no doubt very useful in a captain of industry, it was hardly the thing for a girl!

The tea arrived, and Mrs. Astral made a point of serving Sacha personally. She asked him how much milk and sugar he wanted in his tea as if he were a grown man instead of a boy.

And when she handed him his cup, her hand brushed his in a way that made him feel very grown-up indeed.

"Now, Sacha," she said, fixing him with her brilliant green gaze, "you *must* tell me *all* about your fascinating work with Inquisitor Wolf! He's my hero! I'm simply desperate to meet him!"

"Then why don't you invite him to dinner?" Lily interrupted.

Mrs. Astral cast a cool eye upon her daughter, as if she'd just noticed her presence and wasn't entirely pleased about it. "Darling, what *are* you wearing? If you *must* go out in public like that, can you take some decent clothes in a bag and change before you come home? What if someone saw you?"

Before Lily could answer, Mrs. Astral turned back to Sacha.

"Where has Inquisitor Wolf taken you so far, Sacha? I hope he's not keeping you too much under wraps. I hope he's introducing you to the kind of people who can help your career. Has he taken you to see Teddy Roosevelt yet? They're great friends. Or at least they used to be, back when poor Teddy was still the commissioner of police." Mrs. Astral's lovely face clouded over as if it made her unutterably sad to even think about "poor Teddy" not being police commissioner anymore. "It was so hard on him, being run out of town by that distasteful scandal! Why, he was so mortified that he ran off to Africa on safari and still hasn't come back."

"Yes," Lily said with relish. "And when J. P. Morgaunt heard Teddy was gone, he went straight down to the Union

Club, opened a case of champagne, and made a toast: 'May the first lion Teddy meets do its duty!'"

"Lily!" Mrs. Astral chided. "I'm sure dear Mr. Morgaunt would never say anything so bloodthirsty!"

Actually, Sacha thought this sounded like exactly the kind of thing dear Mr. Morgaunt would say. But it did seem rather coarse of Lily to mention it in polite company. And Mrs. Astral's shock seemed like just another proof of her refined nature and womanly delicacy.

She leaned forward to pour Sacha another cup of tea. "You must be a tremendous help to Inquisitor Wolf. I'm sure he's made use of your extraordinary talents already. Is it really true that you can see witches?"

"Well," Sacha said modestly, "I don't like to brag about it."

"Oh, but you can tell *me*. I wouldn't think it was bragging. I know all sorts of extraordinary people. I cultivate extraordinary people."

"Like mushrooms," Lily muttered. "By keeping them in the dark and burying them in mounds of bull—"

"What's that, darling?" Mrs. Astral interrupted. "You really should learn to stop mumbling. And try not to frown like that. It makes you look even more ill-tempered than you are. I'm sorry, Sacha, you were telling me about how you help Inquisitor Wolf catch witches. How *do* you spot a witch? What is it that gives her away to you?"

On the other end of the sofa, Lily slammed her teacup into its saucer with an outraged rattle, but Sacha ignored her.

"Well, uh . . . I don't see the same thing every time. Some-times it's a kind of aura or halo. And other times it's more like feeling than seeing."

Mrs. Astral rested her chin on one hand and leaned forward as if she couldn't wait to hear more. "And does a witch have to *do* magic for you to see these emanations, or can you see them all the time?"

"They have to do magic in front of me," Sacha said. But this sounded rather unimpressive to him. And he definitely wanted to impress Mrs. Astral. So he added, in what he hoped was a grown-up and mysterious voice, "Most of the time."

Mrs. Astral sat up and seemed almost to catch her breath at this. "*Most* of the time? What about the other times?"

"Well, you know . . . there are different clues."

"Such as?"

"The usual," Sacha said haltingly, trying to stumble out of the lie he'd tangled himself in. "Pointy noses, and warts, and wrinkles—"

"Oh!" She laughed in a way that struck Sacha, just for an instant, as not very nice. But then she smiled at him, and he forgot about it. Her green eyes glittered as she leaned forward to pat his hand. "How very clever of you!"

Mrs. Astral yawned and glanced over Sacha's head at the monumental grandfather clock. "My, how late it's gotten!" she cried. "How time passes when one's in such charming company! Tell me, Sacha, how were you planning to get home? Is your family's car coming to fetch you, or can I offer you a ride in ours?"

"No, thank you!" Sacha practically yelped. He could just imagine the look on the chauffeur's face when he got his first glimpse of Hester Street.

"Really, I insist. In fact, I can't think why I never thought of it before." Lily's mother rang the bell and a uniformed maidservant appeared so fast that Sacha wondered if she'd been listening at the keyhole.

"Biddy," Mrs. Astral ordered, "instruct the chauffeur to drive Mr. Kessler home. And tell him that from today forward I desire him to drive Mr. Kessler home every night when he picks Lily up. That will give you two a little time to relax and chat after work every day. Won't that be fun?" She smiled graciously at the two children and swept out of the room in a fragrant cloud of frangipani and orange blossoms.

As soon as her mother was gone, Lily kicked the coffee table hard enough to send tea sloshing into the saucers. "I don't know why she's being so nice to you!" she snarled. "She must want something, but I can't for the life of me figure out what it is!"

"What's that supposed to mean? You think I have nothing to offer because I'm poor? You think that makes me not worth talking to?"

"Frankly, yes. At least as far as my mother's concerned. She's a dreadful snob."

"It seems to me like you're the snob, not her. She's not the one who could barely bring herself to invite me here!"

She rolled her eyes. "I knew you were rude. But I didn't know you were stupid, too!"

"*I'm* stupid? How stupid is it to take a job where you're too embarrassed to even introduce the people you work with to your mother?"

He expected Lily to fire back a blistering retort, but instead she just stared at him with her mouth hanging open. "Wait a minute. You think I was embarrassed to introduce *you* to *her*?"

Before he could make sense of that question, she half dragged him across the room and pointed to a framed engraving on the wall. "You want to know about my mother? Take a look at *that!*"

The engraving showed two women shaking hands with each other in the middle of a ballroom. Both women were dazzlingly beautiful, and one of them bore a striking resemblance to Maleficia Astral. They smiled at each other as sweetly as if they were the best of friends—but each one held a vicious long-handled ax hidden in the silk folds of her ball gown.

The caption below the picture read "The Reigning Beauty Greets Her Newest Rival."

"*That's* my mother," Lily announced. "And what's more, she's proud of it. Proud enough to hang that picture on the wall and laugh about it. The purpose of her life is running New York society. The only thing she cares about is being rich and beautiful and in control. She doesn't even have time for her own daughter unless it makes her look good in front of her rich friends. So you tell me, Sacha Kessler, why would she waste her time on *you*?"

Sacha opened his mouth to return her insult in kind—

but then he saw something in her face that made him swallow his anger. It wasn't snobbishness that had made Lily sneak him into her house, he realized. It was shame. Lily Astral was ashamed of her own mother. So ashamed that she had been just as desperate to keep Sacha from meeting Mrs. Astral as Sacha was to keep Lily from knowing he lived in the Hester Street tenements.

A tickling little mouse of a thought scampered through his mind. *He* wasn't ashamed of *his* parents, it whispered to him. Now that the beautiful Maleficia wasn't in front of him, he could see that her charming small talk had mostly been mean-spirited gossip. Sacha's hardworking father had a dignity that Mrs. Astral would never match, for all her jewels and money. And as for Sacha's mother, the most embarrassing thing she'd do if she ever met Lily was stuff fattening food down her throat and *shrei* about how skinny she was. So if Lily was brave enough to let Sacha meet the mother she was so ashamed of, then surely he could be brave enough to tell her that he lived in the tenements?

But somehow he couldn't. In fact, knowing how Lily felt about her mother made it even harder. And he knew why, too, though he didn't want to admit it to himself. Lily wouldn't despise his family for being poor. She'd do worse than despise them. She'd feel *sorry* for them. She'd want to *help* them. And the last thing on earth Sacha wanted was Lily Astral's charity.

CHAPTER EIGHTEEN

Up the River

WOLF'S INQUIRIES at the Patent Office must have paid off, because a few days later he received a thick envelope by special courier from Washington, vanished into his office to read it—and then abruptly announced that they were off to see a Mr. Worley in Ossining.

"Ossining?" Lily said with a predatory gleam in her eye. "You mean he's been sent up the river? We're going to visit him in the slammer?"

"Sorry to disappoint you," Wolf said mildly. "But he only lives there. Believe it or not, lots of perfectly innocent people do."

"How vexing of them!"

"Quite." Wolf checked his watch. "We can just make the one-twenty train if we leave now."

As he hurried along behind Wolf, Sacha couldn't help marveling at his new life. Who would have imagined a boy from Hester Street would be climbing onto a real train with a ticket in his hand that cost more than all the clothes he owned put together, in the company of an NYPD Inquisitor and a high-society debutante? He glanced at Lily, but she seemed to think that taking a real honest-to-goodness train was nothing at all out of the ordinary. He imitated her blasé expression and told himself he'd better not stare too much.

But of course that was impossible. From the minute they stepped into the lofty waiting room of Grand Central Station, Sacha was confronted with one wonder after another. Grand Central's magnificent glass-roofed train shed rivaled the Eiffel Tower as one of the engineering marvels of the age. But in New York the pace of progress was so frenetic that it was already considered out of date—and a public safety hazard to boot. It had been slated for demolition for years, in fact, and the only reason it was still standing was that Cornelius Vanderbilt and Tammany Hall were fighting over who would get the lion's share of the bribes that needed to be paid before construction could begin.

Sacha had read that Vanderbilt planned to fund the construction (and the bribes) by burying the train tracks and building an entirely new street on top of them. It was supposed to be called Park Avenue—probably in the hopes that people would forget it was sitting on top of a train yard—and the boosters and speculators were hard at work convincing people to buy, buy, buy. But looking out the window at the blighted wasteland of slaughterhouses and shantytowns that was the Upper East Side, Sacha couldn't believe any decent person would ever want to live here.

Soon there were better things to look at, though. They passed the polo grounds, where the Yankees played. Morning practice had already begun, and Lily glued her nose to the window next to Sacha while they tried to spot their favorite players.

"I guess you go to games all the time," he said wistfully.

"Only stupid, boring polo," she sighed disgustedly. "My mother disapproves of letting young ladies watch baseball."

Then the polo grounds were behind them and the train was launching itself off Manhattan's northern summit and rattling across the soaring trestles to the mainland. Sacha had thought they were going fast before, but now they were fairly flying. They shot along the rails mere feet above the glittering sweep of the Hudson River. They were now farther north than Sacha had ever been. He thought about how the Hester Street housewives called the Bowery "America," even though it was only a few blocks from home. But this really was America. And it seemed to go on forever. Sacha had never seen so much water. Or such cliffs. Or a sky so vast that the flocking seagulls seemed lost in its blue infinity.

Wolf tapped him on the shoulder. "Have a look at this."

He was pulling a thick sheaf of papers out of his pocket. They were freshly pulled blueprints; Sacha could see the cyanotype-blue ink staining Wolf's fingertips as he handled them. Wolf spread the pages out on the train seat so Sacha and Lily could see them.

They were from the Patent Office—stamped repro-
ductions of the technical drawings that Thomas Worley
had originally submitted to obtain the patent on his Soul
Catcher. And the device shown in page after page of detailed
drawings was identical in almost every point to Edison's
etherograph.

"So Edison stole the etherograph from Worley?"
Lily asked.

"Not stole, bought."

"But shouldn't he give him credit, then? And why would
he do that anyway? Just so he could say it was his idea and
people would think he was a great inventor?"

Wolf shrugged. "Maybe. Or maybe there really is some
difference between the two machines that we don't understand yet. That's why I need to talk to Worley."

Wolf put the drawings away, looking thoughtful, and they
passed the rest of the train ride in silence. Wolf had bought a
whole collection of morning papers—in between his usual con-
tributions to New York's panhandling population—and he
was reading them with the occasional raised eyebrow or snort
of amusement. Lily had curled up in one corner of their com-
partment and gone to sleep. And Sacha was free to stare out
the window to his heart's content.

He couldn't get over how green everything was, or the way
the endless forest seemed to roll to the horizon in every direction. People must live here, but he couldn't see any sign of
them beyond the occasional distant road or church steeple.

How could there be so much empty space in the world? And this was just one small corner of New York State, which was just one small corner of the United States! It was hard to understand why people got so upset about immigrants. It looked to Sacha like you could move all of Italy, Ireland, and Russia put together into the Hudson River valley and no one would even notice the difference.

But of course it wasn't lack of space that made so many Americans hate immigrants the way they did. And even the beautiful scenery couldn't keep Sacha from brooding over the dybbuk. What would Inquisitor Wolf do if Sacha told him about it? Would he help? *Could* he help? Or would the Inquisitors just arrest every Kessler in sight and let a jury of "real" Americans sort the guilty from the innocent?

Lily woke up just as they passed Sing Sing Prison and started asking Wolf a bunch of ridiculous questions: Could his Inquisitor's badge get him in there? (It could.) How many criminals had he personally sent there? (Too many.) And had any of them been put to death in Thomas Edison's electric chair? (If they had, he wasn't saying.)

Sacha looked up at the grim gray walls with their jagged crowns of barbed wire and shuddered. If Wolf's investigation took an unlucky turn, it was all too possible that his grandfather could end up in this awful place. A wave of breathless panic swept over him. His chest felt like it was being squeezed by iron bands. He prayed Wolf wouldn't look at him.

Luckily Wolf was too busy answering Lily's endless questions to even notice Sacha. And by the time they passed beyond the prison and chugged into Ossining's regular commuter station, Sacha had more or less recovered.

The three of them climbed off the train, stretching stiff legs and backs, and set off up the steep hill that rose from the river to the town. From what Sacha could see, Ossining was more like a park than a place for people to live. Spreading trees shaded acre after acre of soft green grass. And the gingerbread-swathed houses dotted here and there upon the greensward looked barely substantial enough to keep the weather out.

The Worley house was as elegant and gracious as any of the other homes on its quiet street—or at least it would have been if the lawn hadn't been littered with furniture, books, cooking implements, piles of bedding, and pretty much everything else that ought to have been inside the house.

At first Sacha thought the Worleys must have failed to pay their rent and been kicked to the curb by their landlords. He'd certainly seen that happen enough times on Hester Street to know what it looked like. But he couldn't believe that sort of thing went on in this neighborhood. And even if it had, he would have expected to see the children of the family sitting on top of the piles of furniture to protect them from petty thieves while their parents ran around frantically trying to find a new and cheaper place to rent.

Instead of children, the Worleys' yard was full of hard-eyed men who were all stalking around inspecting the furniture as if they were trying to decide how much to pay for it. And sure enough, Wolf had no sooner set foot on the front walkway than a sweaty little man with piggy eyes thrust a price sheet into his hands and told him to look sharp because the auction was going to start in eight minutes.

"What auction?" Wolf asked.

"The creditors' sale!"

"So Mr. Worley has declared bankruptcy?"

"Mr. Worley hasn't declared anything. He jumped off a bridge last week. It's his widow who's bankrupt."

"And . . . er . . . where is she now?"

"Gone to the devil, for all I care!"

"Did she leave a forwarding address?"

"Nope, and I don't need one either." The man spat in disgust. "This auction won't cover all Worley's standing debts, let alone leave something to send along to the missus."

"Do you happen to know how we could contact her?"

"No," the auctioneer said churlishly. "And I don't have time to find out for you, either." But then he relented—perhaps because he felt bad, or perhaps because he hoped there might be a reward involved. "You could ask Mrs. Worley's maid. She's still hanging around for some reason, though I don't know who she thinks is ever gonna pay her."

They found the maid in the kitchen, blowing her nose into a handkerchief that had already seen plenty of use that day. Wolf sat down across the kitchen table from the girl, smiling far more charmingly than Sacha would ever have thought he could. Within moments, he was drinking a cup of tea and patiently listening to Mary Mulvaney's entire life story (starting in Ballyseede Castle parish, Tralee, County Kerry), followed by Mrs. Worley's entire life story (starting on Rittenhouse Square, Philadelphia), followed by the sad saga of Mr. Worley's bankruptcy and suicide.

As far as Sacha could make out—the maid kept bursting into tears in the middle of sentences, which made it hard to keep track of things—Mr. and Mrs. Worley had enjoyed a nice normal life right up until two weeks after he filed the patent application for his Soul Catcher. But then a smooth-talking lawyer had shown up in a long black motorcar and paid him an unspeakable amount of money for all the rights to his invention. And from the moment he took the money, he was cursed to misery and misfortune.

Every investment he made crashed as soon as he bought into it. Crops failed. Bridges collapsed. Ships sank. Respectable businesses floundered under the weight of unspeakable scandals. Soon he had lost not only the money from Morgaunt but his entire life savings as well.

"It's them Wall Street Wizards what done him in!" Mary Mulvaney wailed. "It oughtn't to be legal, what they do! The stock market's just a cheat and a scandal, and it'll ruin any honest man who puts his faith in it!"

"So why did Mr. Worley put his faith in it?"

"Because of them! Before they got their claws into him, he was as sensible a man as you could ever ask to work for. Well, except for the inventing. But he only did that in his spare time, and he always provided for his family decentlike. And such a loving husband. In the end, I don't think he killed hisself over the money at all. I think he just couldn't live with what he'd done to Mrs. Worley."

"It must have been a terrible shock to her," Wolf sympathized.

"I can hardly stand to think of it. She's always been that nice to me. I would've given anything I had to help her, but what could I do?"

"Well, I'm sure your being here is a great help to her," Wolf said kindly.

The girl sighed. "She couldn't bear to see the auctioneers going through her things, so I stayed behind to close up the house and, and—" Sobs threatened to overcome her again.

"I understand Mrs. Worley isn't here right now?"

"She left for the city last week." More sobs. "She wouldn't let me go with her 'cause she can't afford to pay me no more, but . . . but I can't bear to think of her alone in that awful place!" Mary buried her head in her sodden handkerchief.

Sacha felt a sharp stab of sympathy. It was obvious that she was a nice girl who'd had a hard life, even by Hester Street standards. And it was just as obvious that there had been real affection between her and the Worleys, the kind of attachment that went far beyond doing a job and collecting her wages. They must have been genuinely kind people to have earned such loyalty.

He felt an odd rush of heat that flushed his cheeks and set his heart thumping. It took him a moment to recognize the feeling as anger. He couldn't imagine why he would be so angry about something that had happened to people he didn't even know. But he was. And even though it wouldn't bring back Mrs. Worley's husband, Sacha suddenly wanted very much to punish the men who had driven him to kill himself.

When had he become so vindictive? Was he starting to think like an Inquisitor instead of a normal person? Uncle Mordechai would probably say it was the first step in his transformation into an anti-Wiccanist tool.

"And what are you going to do now?" Wolf was asking when Sacha forced his attention back to the conversation.

"I hadn't even thought yet," Mary sniffled. "Go back and stay with my sister in the tenements while I look for work, I guess."

"I meant what are you going to do about punishing the men who ruined Mr. and Mrs. Worley?"

She shook her head bitterly. "Men like that, they're too rich to be punished."

"Maybe. But if I can't find them, I can't even try. And I can't try to get Mrs. Worley's money back, either."

"You could do that?" she asked, as if he'd just promised a miracle.

"Probably not," Wolf admitted. "But like I said, I can't even try until I find them."

Mary stared down at her handkerchief, biting her lip. Then she went to the breakfront cabinet and flipped through a tin box of recipe cards until she'd found the one she was looking for.

"You understand I wasn't supposed to tell anyone," she

warned Wolf. "She'll be that upset with me, she will! She might not even speak to you."

"Don't worry," Wolf said, flashing that surprisingly charming smile again. "It won't be the first time I've had a door slammed in my face."

She stood in front of him, clutching the recipe card close to her body as if she still hadn't quite made up her mind to give it to him. Then she thrust it into his hands as if it burned her.

Sacha craned his neck to peer at the card over Wolf's shoulder. It was a recipe for Sally Lunn cake, whatever that was. Wolf turned it over to reveal the hastily scribbled address on its back—and looked up in astonishment.

"Mrs. Worley is living on the *Bowery?*"

CHAPTER NINETEEN

Mrs. Worley's Soul Catcher

DUSK WAS DESCENDING on New York by the time they pushed their way off the El and followed the rush-hour crowd down the wrought-iron stairs to the Bowery. The arc lights had just come on, and they blazed so brightly it hurt to look at them. These days Broadway was slowly eclipsing the Bowery as New York's Great White Way. But despite Broadway's high-class theaters and fancy beer gardens, the Bowery was still where ordinary New Yorkers went to have fun when the sun went down and the lights went on.

As they reached the curb, Wolf took Lily and Sacha by the arm to shepherd them safely across the flood of carts and carriages and trolley cars. And then the most extraordinary thing happened.

Wolf dropped their arms and leaped into the middle of the street alone—straight into the path of an oncoming omnibus. Just as it seemed the horses were about to trample him,

Wolf bent down like a baseball player diving for a ground ball, swept something small and dark up off the cobblestones, and flung it into the air with all his might.

There was a swift flash of blue and white and russet feathers. Then, inches in front of the startled horses, the hurtling ball of feathers exploded into full flight. For a moment Sacha was certain the swallow would be dashed lifeless against the hard metal roof of the omnibus. But at the last instant, it swerved up into open air. And then it was gone, its shadow rippling along the cobblestones as it winged away under the blazing lights and vanished.

"A grounded swallow," Wolf explained, rejoining them at the curb. "They're the most perfect flying machines. They live their whole lives on the wing and nest in the cornices of the skyscrapers. But on the ground they're helpless. They can't walk. They can't even take off again unless someone throws them back into the air by sheer force. Landing is practically a death sentence." Wolf suddenly got that sheepish look Sacha had seen him wear when he thought he'd said something too personal—though Sacha couldn't figure out what was so personal about the flying habits of swallows. "Anyway, saving a swallow is supposed to be good luck. And right now we need all the luck we can get."

They didn't have any trouble finding the address Mary had given them. The sign over the door of the building was neither the tallest nor the newest on the Bowery, but it was by far the longest. In fact, it was so notorious that Sacha could have recited it to Lily without even looking at it: MAN-

As they approached the museum, he could hear the practiced patter of the museum's barker promising geeks and egg
cranks and tattooed marvels and waxwork figures. Last but
not least on the list of attractions was Madame Worley and
her mysterious Soul Catcher.

Wolf bought three tickets and handed the change to one
of the beggars who seemed to be drawn to him by some kind
of invisible magnetic force. Then they ran the gauntlet of
freaks and spectacles. And then they were standing at the back
of a half-empty theater whose stage was occupied by a tired-
looking middle-aged woman and a machine just like the one
they'd seen in Morgaunt's library.

The show had just ended. The audience was getting to
their feet, muttering and rubbing their eyes and searching
for hats and gloves. Sacha didn't get the feeling that the performance had been a success. Wolf waited until everyone had
filed out, and then strode down the aisle and stepped onto
the stage.

Mrs. Worley, who had already started to pack away her machine, stopped and shook her head. "The money's all gone."
She sounded like she'd said the words so many times they no
longer meant anything to her. "You'll have to go to Ossining
and put your name on the creditors' list."

"I'm not here about money," Wolf told her. "I'm here
about your husband's murder."

Mrs. Worley stared.

"So," Wolf said, "you *do* believe he was murdered."

"Who are you?" she whispered. But when he showed her his badge, her face twisted with bitterness at the sight of it. "You're wasting your time, Inquisitor. Unless you want to be out of a job tomorrow, I suggest you forget you ever saw me."

"Why don't you just tell me what happened?"

She sighed, and her shoulders slumped a little—but only a little. She was the kind of woman who'd had good posture drilled into her since childhood, and she wasn't about to give it up merely because she was widowed and bankrupt and putting on a glorified magic show in a Bowery dime museum.

"They came with compliments and flattery," she said. "In a big, long, shiny motorcar. They offered my husband more money than he'd ever seen in his life. Far too much to refuse. No matter what conditions they put on it. It was only later that we realized the money was cursed."

"Wall Street Wizardry?"

"Of the subtlest kind, Inquisitor. Nothing you could ever prove even with an army of accountants. They took everything we had. And then they took my husband and replaced him with that . . . that *thing*."

Wolf leaned forward intently.

"Oh, yes. My husband was murdered, all right. He was murdered two days before he committed suicide."

"Are you *sure*?"

"I'm his wife. You think I wouldn't know the difference?" She shuddered. "What was that thing, anyway?"

"A dybbuk. Or something very like one. Is it possible that your husband's machine could have been used to manufacture it?"

Lily gasped. But Mrs. Worley just laughed. "Wherever did you get such a ridiculous idea?"

"Is it so ridiculous?"

"Of course! I've read all the newspaper articles about Edison's etherograph over and over again. It's just my husband's machine dressed up with some new bells and whistles. It's a harmless toy. This idea of theirs about fingerprinting magical criminals is quite distasteful, of course. But manufacturing dybbuks? No, Inquisitor. I know the machine inside and out, and that's quite impossible."

"Perhaps Edison added some other component—"

"There's nothing you could add that could change it into what you're describing. Look, I'll show you how it works if you don't believe me." She smiled at Wolf's apprehensive expression. "I assure you, it's perfectly safe."

Wolf sat down stoically in the chair she offered him, stretching out his long legs as if he expected to be a while. Mrs. Worley flicked a few switches. The machine hummed to life. The spindle turned, and the wax cylinder began to spin. And then . . . nothing. The needle hovered without descending. The fluted trumpet speaker was silent. As far as Worley's machine was concerned, Wolf's chair could have been empty.

"There's a problem," Wolf said.

"Yes. But it's not with the machine. It's with you. I think

it has to do with having magical powers." She bit her tongue, obviously worried she had offended him. "Not that I mean to be impertinent, Mr. Wolf. But you being an Inquisitor, well, one naturally assumes . . ."

"You think I'm resisting the device."

"It's probably something Inquisitors learn to do naturally, dealing with magical criminals the way you do. But if you can just . . . well . . . let it happen?"

Wolf leaned back in his chair. "Mrs. Worley, I surrender myself to you entirely."

She started the machine up again. This time Wolf seemed to be listening intently for some sound no one else could hear. He must have heard it because after a moment he smiled and blinked in surprise. And then he laughed softly to himself and opened his hands in the same quick gesture with which he had freed the grounded swallow.

In that instant the needle sprang to life, and the Soul Catcher began to play the same unearthly music they'd heard in Morgaunt's library.

But where that song had been excruciating, this one was . . . riveting. It was impossible to stop listening, just like it was impossible to stop staring when you rode the Elevated right past people's living room windows. Suddenly Sacha knew things about Wolf that he never would have guessed at . . . things he really didn't have any right to know. He felt embarrassed, like he'd been caught stealing something.

"There," Mrs. Worley said at last, switching the machine off. "Harmless, see?"

"But rather unnerving." Wolf swiped the back of his sleeve across his brow. He looked pale and clammy and even more disheveled than usual.

"That's just because of your being—you know. Ordinary people actually find it rather pleasant. Just as they enjoy admiring themselves in a mirror or looking at old photographs. Vanity, I suppose. But, as I said, quite harmless."

"And that's it?" Wolf asked.

"That's it." Mrs. Worley pulled the little gold and white cylinder out of the machine. "If Edison has made the machine into anything more than a parlor toy, then he's invented something new, and I wouldn't know enough to help you. Would you like your recording, though?" she asked when she noticed that Wolf was still frowning at it. "As a souvenir?"

"Thank you," Wolf said gravely. He took the cylinder and slipped it into his pocket.

Wolf seemed to recover his composure rapidly after that. He decided he wanted to see the machine in action again, and when Lily volunteered to sit for it, he didn't argue. Worley's machine had no trouble recording Lily, though the tune it played back was sweet and wistful and disarmingly un-Lily-like. Sacha gazed at her, searching her face for a hint of this hidden gentleness.

"What are you looking at?" she snapped.

"Nothing!" What on earth had he been thinking? Lily Astral wasn't sweet or sad or gentle. And if Worley's ridiculous machine made her sound that way, then what better proof did you need that it was all a load of hooey?

"And anyway," Lily prodded, "it's your turn now, isn't it?"

"Oh, I don't think I really—" Sacha began.

But then he noticed that Wolf had suddenly gone all vague and bland and absentminded. Wolf wanted him to do this. And resisting would only make Wolf start wondering about the very things Sacha least wanted him to think about.

"Sure," he said, trying to sound nonchalant.

He sat down. The chair seemed to creak unnaturally loudly under his weight. Mrs. Worley turned the machine back on. It whirred and clicked for what seemed like an eternity. The cylinder spun. The needle hovered, and . . .

"That's odd," Mrs. Worley said.

Wolf leaned over her shoulder. "Is he doing the same thing I did?"

"No. And the machine's working perfectly. You saw how well it recorded Miss Astral just now. It's just—well—it's almost as if—"

"Almost as if what?"

"As if there's nothing there to record."

Sacha stared at Mrs. Worley, trying to comprehend her words. He felt numb. He tried to work out what she meant, but all the ideas that occurred to him were so horrifying that he flinched away from them before the thoughts even had a chance to form in his mind.

"Sacha?"

Sacha jumped. How many times had Wolf said his name before he noticed?

"Sacha? Are you all right?"

He looked into Wolf's eyes and saw a depth of sympathy there that he would never have imagined possible if he hadn't just heard the man's soul turned into music.

He had a swift, startlingly vivid image of Wolf snatching him out of danger and throwing him up to safety just as he'd done for the grounded swallow. For one dizzying moment, he thought of confessing everything. Then he thought of Morgaunt's laughing threats and the towering walls of Sing Sing and the sinister Semitic face of the Kabbalist in Edison's etherograph ads. Wolf was a good man, but he was still an Inquisitor. Telling him wouldn't solve Sacha's problems. It would only hurt the people Sacha loved.

"I'm fine," he lied.

Sacha had no idea how he made it back outside without being sick to his stomach. He could see Wolf and Lily staring at him. He could see the questions and doubts and suspicions swirling behind Wolf's eyes. But it felt like he was stuck at the bottom of a well and they were much too far away to reach him.

Wolf ushered the two children into the cab, muttering something about having to apologize to their mothers for keeping them out so late. Sacha looked longingly down the Bowery toward Hester Street, only a few short blocks away. But he was trapped in his lie, and there was nothing he could do about it.

He was cold and weary and footsore by the time he finally turned onto Hester Street. To his relief, everything looked normal. The street was quiet at this time of night, but there were still scattered signs of life on the front stoops and fire escapes. Sacha slowed his pace a little, figuring that now he could take the time to catch his breath before he went inside.

And then he felt it. That same swirling, sinking motion he'd sensed in Morgaunt's library, when he'd felt like all the magic in New York was spiraling down into Morgaunt's golden glass of Scotch. Only now there seemed to be no center to the whirlpool. Just the bleak, aimless, drifting rattle of dead leaves scattering before a storm.

To Sacha's ordinary sight, the street still looked the same as always. But now the men lounging on the front stoops and the women gossiping on the fire escapes seemed to be part of a separate world, as if he were looking up at them through deep water. And in the silent underwater world that Sacha was trapped in, there was another presence—one that was at once mysterious and frighteningly familiar.

He turned to face the shadow that he already knew he would see behind him.

The watcher stopped when he stopped, and they stood staring at each other across the littered cobblestones.

"Who are you?" Sacha called out. "What do you want from me?"

A faint breeze whispered down the street, lifting the hanging laundry only to let it drop back limply the next moment. It seemed to Sacha that the breeze also stirred the watcher's hair and clothes. But the watcher himself never moved.

"Don't you have anything to say for yourself?" Sacha taunted. He took a step forward.

For a moment the watcher seemed to hesitate. Then it stepped forward too. Just one step. Just enough to let the smoky halo of the street lamp light its face.

Its eyes were black pits—dark pools of shadow in a face already cloaked in shadow. But even in the flickering gaslight, Sacha could see that the dybbuk was no longer the disembodied wraith that it had been when it first began following him. He could see it clearly now. He'd racked his memory for weeks trying to put a name to that face, trying to understand why it seemed so hauntingly familiar. He'd compared it to every face in his family, every face in his neighborhood. But there was one face he hadn't thought of . . . one face he knew better than any other . . .

He broke and ran, sprinting for home across the slick cobblestones. But the dybbuk was faster than he was. Or rather—and this thought made his heart stutter in terror—it was exactly as fast as he was.

He stumbled and almost lost his footing. Now the dybbuk was so close that he could hear its breath behind him.

Then, just as he was sure the creature was upon him, Sacha felt a ripple run through the very bricks of the city, as if it were a pond and some unseen hand had cast a stone into it.

An instant later, he heard the most beautiful sound of his life: the silvery jingle of *streganonna* bells on a horse's bridle.

He knew, somehow, that it would be the Rag and Bone Man who rounded the corner. He jumped up onto the broken-down cart and peered anxiously over his shoulder as the Rag and Bone Man flicked the reins and his ancient horse shambled forward.

"Did—did you see that?" he asked.

The Rag and Bone Man gave a single nod of his grizzled head, but he kept just as silent as ever.

Sacha glanced sideways at him. Who was he really? Why was there a file on him in Inquisitor Wolf's office? And what would Sacha see if he ever worked up the nerve to sneak a peek inside it?

The Rag and Bone Man pulled up to Sacha's building, and Sacha scrambled down and took the cast-iron steps two at a time, desperate to get inside before his rescuer left. He raced up the tenement stairs toward the warmth and light and life of home.

He slipped through the Lehrers' room, trying not to wake them. He bolted down the dinner his mother had left out for him, reassured her that he was safe and sound and hadn't caught pneumonia, and got into bed, exhausted.

He was fine, he told himself, hoping to stave off the nightmares. The Rag and Bone Man had saved him. Again.

But he knew that the Rag and Bone Man hadn't really saved him. He had only delayed the inevitable.

CHAPTER TWENTY

The Path of No Action

FOR THE NEXT few weeks, the Edison investigation seemed to go completely cold. If Wolf was still working on the case—and Sacha caught just enough snatches of eavesdropped conversation between Wolf and Payton to be pretty sure that Wolf *was* still working on it—he didn't tell his apprentices about it.

Instead, he let them tag along on his other cases. And he had lots of them. Sacha and Lily watched Wolf solve cases of magical insurance fraud, magical embezzlement, magical blackmail . . . and one unnerving murder where a respectable businessman apparently died of a heart attack but turned out to have been done in by means of a nasty little spell that made its victims' blood boil in their veins.

Gradually Sacha began to see the method behind Wolf's famously eccentric inquisitorial technique. He learned to respect Wolf's silences and to wait for the astonishing leaps of logic that would often follow them. He came to recognize the vague, unfocused gaze that meant Wolf was scouring a crime scene for the one thing that didn't fit, the one loose thread that he could tug on to unravel the most subtly woven conspiracy.

Sacha began to despair of ever becoming the kind of Inquisitor that Wolf was. He just didn't have the talent, he told himself. And the one talent he did have was starting to seem completely useless. After all, what good was being able to see magic when the Inquisitors were never called to the scene of a crime until the magic was played out and the criminals long gone? Even Lily's bulldog tenacity seemed more useful for a real life Inquisitor than Sacha's strange second sight.

Yet Wolf's faith in Sacha never seemed to waver. Wolf would even make odd, disconnected comments from time to time that suggested he assumed Sacha would become a far better Inquisitor than he was. It should have made Sacha proud, but it just made him feel like a fraud. Especially when he knew he was lying to the man.

Even worse, Sacha was no closer to figuring out what to do about the dybbuk. In fact, he could barely bring himself to think about it. Every now and then he would see the hazy halo around a street lamp or smell the dank river air wafting up from the docks—and he would flash back to that terrifying moment when he stood in the dark street face-to-face with the dybbuk and thought . . . almost thought. . . . But whenever he tried to face the memory, a wave of shame, terror, and confusion swept over him.

As if that weren't enough, Hester Street had been struck by a perplexing wave of petty crime. First Mrs. Lassky's cat went missing. It came back a day later, but Mrs. Lassky couldn't stop wondering how it could have gotten out of a locked room when the only key was in her pocket.

Then someone started stealing food: from Lassky's Bakery and the dry goods store next door; from the Lehrers' room; from the IWW headquarters upstairs; even from Mrs. Kessler's own bread box. And the weirdest thing was that whoever was stealing the food wasn't eating it. People kept finding crumbs dribbled down the stairs and scattered in dark corners.

And last—but far from least scary—was the curious case of Sacha's missing socks.

Mrs. Kessler had been knitting a new pair of socks for Sacha. It had taken forever, since Grandpa Kessler always seemed to be around when she had time to work on them, which meant she couldn't use magic and had to do it the slow way. When she finally cast off the last stitch, she rushed them into the wash so Sacha could wear them to work the next morning. Naturally, she washed his old socks too; Mrs. Kessler was not a woman to waste hot water. Then she hung both pairs out to dry on the fire escape.

In the morning the new socks were still there, but the old ones were gone.

"What kind of *meshuggener* steals an old pair of socks when there's a brand-new pair hanging right next to them?" Mrs. Kessler asked.

"Maybe it was a pigeon," Uncle Mordechai hazarded. "Feathering its nest with the stolen fruits of other people's labor like the Wall Street Wizards and Robber Barons!"

"You're thinking of magpies," Sacha's father said from behind the business pages. "And anyway, birds don't wear socks. Their feet are the wrong shape."

"Hah!" Grandpa Kessler cried. "That's where you're both wrong! Sure, you never saw a pigeon in socks. But it's got nothing to do with their feet. I know that for a fact, because demons have bird feet—and there are numerous well-documented cases of socks in the rabbinical literature."

"What about dybbuks?" Sacha asked. It was easier to think about the dybbuk amidst the warmth and laughter of his family— but not much easier. "Do dybbuks have bird feet too?"

For once Grandpa Kessler was stumped. It seemed that no rabbis in all the countless tomes of Haggadah had ever argued about what dybbuks' feet looked like. "Not even the *Hasidim*," Grandpa Kessler admitted. "And those guys really know their dybbuks. Though, come to think of it, I did hear a tale in Breslov about a wonderworking rebbe whose wife realized he'd been possessed because his claws kept wearing holes in his socks."

"That explains a lot!" Sacha's mother said, poking her husband in the ribs.

"What am I supposed to do, walk on my head?" his father asked good-naturedly. "Listen, when Sacha gets rich, I'll stop walking. I'll hire a klezmer band to play wedding marches and carry me around in a chair all day long, and then you'll have to find something else to complain about."

"Really?" Mrs. Kessler said, deadpan, staring her husband in the eye. "A klezmer band? Is that the best you can do?"

Mr. Kessler smiled one of his rare smiles. "Well, I can think of other ways to pass the time without socks on, but I didn't want to mention them in front of the children."

"Dad!" Sacha and Bekah yelped in identical tones of outrage.

"What are you two so embarrassed about?" Mrs. Kessler snapped, which was pretty funny, considering how flushed her cheeks were. "We're old—we're not dead!"

"So was it a dybbuk in that story?" Sacha asked his grandfather, trying to make the question sound casual. "Or was it just a regular demon?"

"Good question!" Rabbi Kessler agreed and shuffled happily off to check his books for the answer.

But try as he might, he couldn't find it. "Oh, well," he admitted. "Maybe I didn't remember it. Maybe I just imagined it. The older I get, the harder it is to tell the difference."

"Don't worry," Sacha said—though he was already frantically searching his memory and trying to think if he'd noticed bird footprints lately in any places they weren't supposed to be.

But Grandpa Kessler *was* worrying. "Your Inquisitor Wolf isn't trying to take on that dybbuk on his own, is he?"

"Uh . . . no," Sacha said. He wasn't exactly lying, he told himself. It just felt like he was.

"Tell him he mustn't! I'm sure he's a very clever young man, but he's really not qualified. He hasn't tried to drag you into anything like *that*, has he, Sachele?"

"Of course not," Sacha said, feeling like a worm.

"If he does, you just walk straight out of that office and come home and tell me about it. Promise?"

Was there anything lower than a worm? If there was, Sacha decided, that must be what he felt like now.

"Of course, Grandpa. Of course I'd tell you."

In fact, between the lies he was telling Wolf and the lies he was telling his family, the only time Sacha really felt like himself was at his kung fu lessons with Shen.

To Lily's disappointment, they didn't take the magical route to Shen's practice hall for their first lesson. Instead, Payton escorted them downtown, grumbling under his breath all the while about wasting his time playing nursemaid. He didn't even walk them through the door once they got there; he just stalked away, leaving them wavering in the tree-lined courtyard wondering whether to go inside or not.

There was a class already in session in the stone-floored practice hall. They could hear the sounds of feet slapping on the scrubbed stones and bodies slamming into woven rush mats.

"What do you think we should do?" Lily whispered.

"I don't know," Sacha whispered back. "Wait, maybe."

Finally curiosity won out over politeness. They slipped through the door and hid in the shadow of the balcony to watch.

They spotted Shen immediately; you couldn't mistake the spotless white cotton pajamas or the shining black braid that flowed down her back like a waterfall. But it was the orphans who really caught their attention. Most of them looked Chinese, at least to Sacha. But he did see a few heads of brown or red hair scattered among the black. And some of the orphans would have looked right at home with Paddy Doyle and his Hexers.

The class was scattered through the great hall, boxing at punching bags stuffed with rice and cotton wadding, tumbling and throwing each other on padded practice mats, stretching like ballet dancers. And half the students were lined up in an almost military formation on the central practice floor, going through the most remarkable set of movements Sacha had ever seen.

They moved in unison, their coordination so perfect that they seemed to be a single body, with a single mind and spirit. Each member of the group remained precisely the same distance from his neighbors throughout every turn and leap and backflip. And they ended the routine with a single thundering *STOMP!*

Now Sacha realized what had worn the divots into the flagstones: the stamping of thousands of bare feet moving in perfect formation hour after hour, day after day, year after year—and for all he knew of this strange and magical building, for century upon century, since long before the rest of New York even existed.

It was unbelievable. Look at that kid doing splits over

there! Or the other one in the corner turning backward handsprings as easily as normal people walked down the side-walk! Not to mention the kids who were sparring with one another on the practice mats—he couldn't even figure out what their lightning-fast feet and hands were doing, much less imagine imitating them. Maybe he should just sneak back out before Shen noticed him, he told himself. After all, it was pretty obvious what the outcome of staying would be: to-tal, absolute humiliation.

He glanced at Lily, who looked like she was having the same second thoughts he was. But before he could open his mouth to suggest that they sneak away, Shen saw them.

"Are you ready?" she asked, sauntering over to them.

"Not to do that!"

"Don't let my orphans intimidate you. They've studied for years, and they enjoy showing off for visitors. Besides, no one expects *dabizi* to be able to do kung fu at all, so they'll be impressed if you manage to survive your first lesson."

"What's a *dabizi*?" Sacha asked.

"It's a rude word for Westerners. It means 'big nose.'"

Sacha blinked. He hadn't thought of Chinese people as having particularly small noses. Lily's nose, for example, was hardly any bigger than Shen's. Or was it? He tried to check out Shen's nose without staring too obviously.

"Yes, I know," she said. "But I'm half *dabizi* myself. My mother was Irish."

"What?" Lily exclaimed. "But you look so—so—"

"So Chinese?" Shen's face took on an ironical cast that

made her look unnervingly like Inquisitor Wolf. "Not to the Chinese, I assure you."

Sacha stared at Shen in frank amazement. He remembered hearing that no Chinese women were allowed into America, and since there were always plenty of children playing in the streets of Chinatown, he guessed he ought to have wondered who their mothers were. But he was still astounded by Shen's revelation. He had grown up in a New York where every aspect of life—from what you wore to where you worked to which streets you could walk down safely—depended on which ethnic group you belonged to. And he had seen enough of the world to know that being half Chinese and half Irish didn't mean you belonged to both groups. It meant you belonged nowhere. He wondered what Shen's life was like and how she managed to protect her orphanage in a city that had no place for people like her.

He was still wondering about it when Shen took them over to one of the woven practice mats and introduced them to a whip-thin boy whom Sacha guessed was about ten years old.

"Joe will get you started," Shen said. "I'll be back in . . . shall we say ten minutes?"

Joe bowed, straightened up, and shook both their hands. Sacha peered curiously at him, trying to decide whether he was half Irish too. But he couldn't tell.

"So," Joe asked them, "are you guys ready to work, or did you just come here to stare?"

Then he stretched, flexing his wiry legs and arms like rubber bands, took a deep breath . . . and demonstrated a move that looked so simple Sacha wasn't even sure it ought to be called kung fu. It began with a smooth flourish of both hands that looked impressively exotic. But it ended in a kind of knees-bent, low-to-the-ground, straddling position that didn't look any different from the squat of a catcher waiting for a pitch behind the plate.

"That's the advanced version, of course," Joe pointed out. "You don't wanna bend your knees that much, trust me." He straightened up and dusted off his hands—though as far as Sacha could see, he hadn't done anything that could get dust on them in the first place. "It's not a contest. Just do as much as you can, all right? And I'll coach your form."

Sacha could have laughed out loud. Ten minutes of doing squats? To a boy who'd grown up on Hester Street pushing foot-powered sewing machines and dragging slopping buckets of water up tenement house stairs, ten minutes of deep knee bends didn't even qualify as effort. His father was right, after all, he decided; Jews were the only people on the planet who knew what real work was.

He shrugged and settled in to practice. But as he straightened his legs to begin his second squat, Joe stopped him. "You call that ten minutes? That's more like ten seconds!"

Several other orphans had drifted over to watch, and now they were laughing and elbowing one another in the ribs.

"The *dabizi* don't get it!" someone laughed. "They think they're doing jumping jacks!"

That was when Sacha realized that they weren't supposed

to be practicing the move over and over again for ten minutes. They were supposed to crouch down once—and stay there.

At first it didn't seem so hard. But after about a minute, it began to seem somewhat uncomfortable. In another minute, Sacha's legs started to burn. Then his knees started to shake. Then his whole leg started to spasm with the sheer effort of staying there.

Then he looked at the clock and realized that he still had seven minutes to go.

His only consolation was that Lily looked at least as bad as he felt. Good thing too, he told himself. At least he could avoid total humiliation as long as he held out longer than she did. The alternative—being beaten by a girl—was unthinkable.

The other students had also realized it was a contest, and they seemed determined to make the most of it. Their laughter began to be sprinkled with bets on who would collapse first. Most wagered on Sacha to win, but Lily had her fans—especially among the girls in the crowd.

As the minutes dragged on, Sacha felt his face redden with exertion. Lily, on the other hand, had turned white as fish bellies. With every breath, Sacha told himself he only had to hold out a second longer because Lily was about to crack. But then the next breath would come and go, and Lily would still be there.

She was in deadly earnest, he realized. She might be a girl, but she wanted to beat him just as badly as any boy would have. He would have shaken his head in admiration of her *chutzpah*—if he hadn't been worried that he'd fall over.

Sacha never got a chance to find out which one of them could hold out longer. Just as he was certain he was about to collapse, Shen reappeared. "That's enough for today," she said, despite the students' boisterous protests that she was ruining their betting. "Well done, both of you!"

Sacha and Lily hit the floor before the words were even out of her mouth. They lay there gasping for breath while Shen herded the others back to their practice mats. Finally Sacha recovered enough to sit up and ask Lily how she felt.

"Sick to my stomach!"

"Me too."

"I guess now you're going to tell me that you would have won if Shen hadn't come along," she said with a challenging toss of her head.

"Actually, I doubt I would have lasted another five seconds."

Lily gave him a surprised look. Then she grinned. "Me neither! That was *awful!*"

Sacha grinned back at her—and then felt his grin fade as he came to an astounding realization. He actually liked Lily. Really liked her. It was too bad she was an Astral. And rich. And blond. And . . . well, he had to admit Paddy Doyle was right; she really was pretty. What a shame. If Lily were any ordinary girl, he really thought they could have been friends.

CHAPTER TWENTY-ONE

Sacha Goes House Hunting

NEXT SUNDAY, in a cold, driving October rain, Sacha went house hunting.

He was looking for a house that was nice but not too nice, a house that he could pretend was his when Lily's chauffeur drove him home every afternoon. He'd been making excuses every day since the fateful tea with Mrs. Astral, but he could tell Lily was starting to get suspicious. And Lily being Lily, he wouldn't put it above her to follow him home out of sheer cussedness.

He started his search near Gramercy Park. But one look at the luxurious row houses and the shady green park cloistered behind its wrought-iron railings convinced him that Lily would never believe he lived in such a place. So he circled around in search of more modest lodgings. The Tenderloin was no good—what respectable people would live there? Lower Fifth Avenue was out too—all those fancy apartment buildings with snooty doormen who would run him off before the Astrals' car was out of sight. In theory at least, Astral Place would work, but no amount of cold and rain would have made Sacha desperate enough to tell Lily he lived on a street named after her own great-grandfather.

As he hurried through the flooding streets, Sacha noticed ads for Edison's etherograph going up all over the city. On building after building, workmen were taking down ads for headache remedies, patent medicines, corsets, and cigarillos, and putting up the now-familiar image of the heroic Inquisitor and cringing Kabbalist. It looked like Morgaunt and Edison were expecting the upcoming Houdini-Edison showdown to spark off a big boom in the witch-detection sector—and Sacha found this prospect even bleaker than the foul weather.

He had just turned onto a sedate block of respectable row houses when he noticed a ghostlike figure slipping along behind him. His blood chilled at the thought that it might be the dybbuk. But no, it was a grownup. A small grownup, true. But that was only because he was Chinese.

Sacha hurried on, pretending not to have seen the man, and trying to play for time while he decided what to do about him. When he reached the end of the block, he had a plan in mind. He looked back toward his pursuer, glaring fiercely as if to demand what the fellow thought he was up to, following him like that. When the man turned away, Sacha bolted around the corner and ran like hell.

Except that instead of running away, he ducked into the

mews behind the comfortable residential block and jumped the gate of the first stable yard he passed in order to cut through the alley and come back around behind the man.

Or at least that's what he'd intended to do. But when he skidded back out onto the street, there was no Chinese man there at all.

There was only Shen, standing with her hands in her trouser pockets and laughing at him.

He could have kicked himself.

"You really didn't know it was me, did you?" she asked when her laughter had finally subsided into intermittent chuckles. "What are you doing, anyway? You've been wandering around all afternoon like a lost dog."

"Just getting some exercise."

"Isn't it a bit wet for that?"

"I, uh, well . . ."

"If I didn't know better, I'd think you were casing out houses to rob."

"Shen!"

"You don't have to take my word for it. Look down at the end of the block."

Sacha peered around Shen—and was alarmed to see a burly patrolman loitering at the corner, making no secret of the fact that he was keeping an eye on the two suspicious characters who had ventured onto his beat.

"Why don't you tell me what's going on," Shen suggested. "After all, wouldn't you rather tell me than him?"

Haltingly, Sacha told her about going to tea at Lily's

house, and Lily's mother, and the situation with the Astral chauffeur. "So," he concluded, "I need a house."

"I don't quite follow. Don't you have a house?"

"Yes, but . . ."

"But you're ashamed of it."

He glared at her, but his angry answer died in his throat when he saw the gentle, understanding way she was looking at him.

"I—yes."

"Of what? I mean, what would be so bad about having him drop you at your actual home?"

From any other adult, the question would have been infuriating, but somehow Shen managed to ask it as if she really wanted to know the answer.

"What would be so bad about it?" He imagined Lily's incredulous face, the chauffeur's haughty stare, the hoots and hollers of the kids on Hester Street, who treated the arrival of any motorcar—let alone a motorcar with someone they knew in it—as if it were Passover, Hanukkah, and the Fourth of July all rolled into one. And then the awful, pitying look on Lily's face when she saw the way the Kesslers lived. "Everything!" he wailed. "I'd rather die!"

For a moment Shen seemed about to ask him something else, but then she shrugged. "Well, we can't have you dying," she said. "Follow me. I've got an idea."

Ten minutes later they were standing on the front stoop of the perfect house. Nice but not too nice. Comfortably middle class, yet still modest enough to be believable. Best of all, it stood in the middle of a long row of identical brick-fronted town houses, so that it would be difficult for even a girl as sharp-eyed as Lily to be quite sure of remembering the right house if she tried to find it again.

When Shen strolled up to the neat red door and rang the bell, Sacha almost jumped out of his skin. "Are we, um—I mean, are we going to get in trouble with the, uh—you know."

"Oh, I don't think so. Most of the people who'd call the police on us aren't likely to be home this time of day."

That wasn't very reassuring. And the haughty stare of the tall housemaid who answered the door was even less reassuring. "What on earth do *you* want?" she huffed, staring down her nose at them.

"I'm here to see James," Shen announced calmly.

The housemaid sniffed. "The *idea* of a respectable house letting the butler receive *personal* callers at the front door! I've half a mind to tell the missus what sort of persons are tromping through her good rooms!"

The maid marched them through an airy hall and down a long corridor toward the back of the house. Here the paintings and wallpaper gave way to glass-fronted cupboards containing towering stacks of dinner plates and sherbet cups and soup tureens and an endless array of china whose names and uses Sacha couldn't begin to imagine. Just as they passed the last of the china cupboards and started to hear the clatter and bustle of a working kitchen, the housemaid stopped short and rapped smartly on a neat little oak-paneled door in the wall.

"Mr. James!" she cried. "*Persons* to see you!"

Behind the door was a neat, comfortable, serviceably furnished sitting room. And in an armchair, reading a book in front of a roaring fire, sat a well-dressed Chinese man.

He put down his book and greeted Shen with obvious affection. "To what do I owe this pleasure?"

Shen cleared her throat and glanced toward the housemaid.

"Thank you, Bessie," Mr. James said. "That will be all."

Bessie beat a reluctant retreat—though Sacha suspected she wasn't going to go farther than the other side of the keyhole. She couldn't have gotten much satisfaction from her eavesdropping, however, since Shen and James immediately broke into rapid-fire Chinese.

At the end of their exchange, James turned to Sacha and gave a dignified little bow. "Very pleased to meet you, Mr. Kessler. Shall I expect you on weekday evenings, then?"

Sacha nodded.

"Very good, sir. I shall look forward to seeing you."

As they walked back out to the street, Shen explained that James had agreed to have Sacha visit him every evening on the pretext that he was looking out for a friend's son who'd come to the city to find work. "Just spend a few minutes talking to him, and then you can be on your way with no one the wiser."

"But won't he get in trouble?" Sacha asked, thinking of the haughty housemaid.

"Not likely. If I know James, he'll probably have the master and mistress of the house inviting you to dinner before the month's up."

"How do you know him?" Sacha asked.

"He used to be one of my orphans."

"But he's . . . so, well, *old!*" Suddenly Sacha felt quite uncomfortable.

"What's wrong?" Shen asked after a moment. "You look like you've got a rock stuck in your shoe."

"How old are you?" Sacha finally blurted out.

Shen grinned broadly. "Don't you know it's rude to ask a woman her age?"

"I didn't—I just—I mean, are you an Immortal?"

"Being an Immortal isn't like having a liquor license, Sacha. You don't just get your piece of paper and stick it in the window and forget about it. You have to live it. And you have to keep living it, every minute of every day."

"But are you . . . you know . . . going to live forever?"

"I really couldn't tell you." Shen flashed her most mischievous grin, the one that made her look both childish and ancient at the same time. "I haven't lived long enough yet to know."

Suddenly Sacha thought of the dybbuk. Shen would know what to do about it. But on the other hand, she might tell Wolf. And then all Sacha's lies would unravel—right back to the incriminating moment when he had hidden the truth about his mother's locket.

"You have a worse problem than just being embarrassed in front of Lily Astral, don't you?"

Sacha nodded, a lump rising in his throat.

"Have you told Inquisitor Wolf about it?"

"No! I can't!"

"And you're not going to tell me either, are you? If I tried to make you tell me, you'd just come up with some lie that would only make things worse."

Sacha felt a flush of shame wash across his face.

They were turning onto lower Broadway now. As they mingled with the Sunday-afternoon crowd, Shen bowed her head, hiding her face beneath her broad-brimmed hat. And she put just enough distance between her and Sacha that passersby wouldn't notice they were together. They walked along like strangers for a block or two, something in her bearing telling him that it would be a bad idea to speak to her.

"Well," she said finally, "I guess I'll have to let you keep your secret. But do take care of yourself, Sacha. You're a boy of unusual talents. And unusual talents attract unusual trouble."

Then she angled off through the crowd without even giving him a chance to say goodbye. Only when he was climbing the stairs to his apartment did it finally occur to Sacha to wonder why Shen had been following him in the first place.

CHAPTER TWENTY-TWO

Gone, All Gone

THE MINUTE SACHA stepped into his apartment, he knew something was terribly wrong.

Mrs. Lehrer was sitting in a chair with her head bowed to her knees. Mrs. Kessler was gently stroking her hair and whispering "shush, shush," as if she were soothing a baby. Everyone else was hovering over the two of them as if Mrs. Lehrer were an unexploded bomb that no one could figure out how to defuse safely.

"Someone stole her coat," Bekah whispered to Sacha.

"*The* coat? What about the money?"

"Gone, all gone."

Sacha stared, horrified. In his mind's eye, he saw himself wearing the money coat, dancing with Mrs. Lehrer in front of the lighted window. Anyone standing in the street looking up at them would have thought it was his coat. And someone *had* been standing in the street watching them. Or some*thing*.

Sacha felt sick. What had he done? How could he ever forgive himself for bringing this trouble on his family? He knew he had to do something . . . but every time he tried to think about it a dull fog of despair and confusion settled over his brain.

"Shush," Mrs. Kessler murmured, still stroking Mrs. Lehrer's hair. "Shush!"

But Mrs. Lehrer pushed her hand away and stood up. "It's all right," she said in a dull, hollow voice that sounded like it was coming from somewhere deep underground. "I never would have been able to spend that money anyway. I've known for years there was no one left to send it to."

Then she walked across the room and sat down at her sewing machine and picked up the next shirtwaist from the towering pile of piecework that was always there waiting for her.

The rest of them stared at one another with stunned, frightened expressions on their faces. Sacha could almost see the unasked questions hanging in the air. What was the woman going to do now that someone had stolen the very purpose of her life? And should they try to make her talk about it? Or was this one of those things in life that just got worse from talking?

Mrs. Lehrer was still at the sewing machine when they all crept miserably off to bed.

Sacha didn't know how long he slept, but he woke up with a terrible fear twisting the pit of his stomach. It was dark. Outside the windows, Hester Street lay so still and silent that he knew it must be three or four in the morning.

What a nightmare he'd had! He'd been lost in a bleak and terrible darkness that stretched out hopelessly for all eternity. What horror to be trapped in such a place, never to laugh or love or feel the warmth of friends and family! The worst thing of all had been the knowledge—though he couldn't say how he knew it—that he hadn't lost his life. It had been stolen from him. And the thief was walking free in the sunlight, wearing Sacha's clothes and body, tricking Sacha's family into loving him.

But it was only a dream, after all! Bekah lay sleeping beside him; he could hear her breathing and make out the shape of her cheek in the faint light from the street lamp. His mother and father lay just beyond her. On his other side Grandpa Kessler was snoring away like a kettle at the boil.

Sacha sighed with relief and nestled into the thick feather bed. He was already half asleep when he saw a flash of movement in the shadows and heard the unmistakable sound of a footfall.

It must be Mordechai coming home late again, he told himself.

But Mordechai was already home. Sacha could hear him snoring over on his mattress by the door, a sprightly tenor accompanying Grandpa Kessler's thundering basso. Besides, this shadow was smaller than Mordechai. And it had come in not through the door, but through the open window from the fire escape.

Sacha watched, paralyzed by fear, as the figure padded around the room. It seemed to be looking for something. It searched among the hooks along the wall that held the family's scant clothing. It seemed to search by smell, not sight; it snuffled among the hanging clothes like a dog hunting for a scent. It pulled something out. A shirt, maybe. Sacha couldn't see clearly and was too terrified to raise his head. Then it started back toward the window.

Halfway there it stopped and wavered in the middle of the room as if it couldn't decide what to do next. Then it turned toward the bed.

It was staring straight at Sacha now. He closed his eyes and tried to slow his breathing so that it matched the rhythm of the rest of the family sleeping on either side of him.

Silence.

Then stealthy, halting footsteps that came toward the bed and paused as the dybbuk leaned over him.

Its breath was cold enough to stop clocks. But its touch was colder still, as cold and soft and heartbreaking as the first winter snow on a newborn's grave. Gently, gently, it ran a finger along his cheek. It touched his hair. It touched the hand that lay outside the blanket.

Then it was gone.

Sacha lay awake, silent and terrified, until the dawn broke through the windows and his mother rose to stoke the cookstove. He washed and dressed with fingers more clumsy from fear than from cold. He watched tensely as the rest of his family got up and dressed and took their hats and coats and mufflers off the hook . . . until he was quite sure that the only missing piece of clothing was his own second-best shirt.

CHAPTER TWENTY-THREE

Bull Moose

"WE'RE GOING *WHERE?*" Lily asked the next morning when Wolf gave the address to the taxicab. "What on earth are we going to investigate on *Long Island?*"

"You don't think there are magical criminals on Long Island?" Wolf asked, sounding amused. "Well, we're not after criminals today, just advice. From the last honest man in New York . . . or at least the last honest man I know about."

By the time they turned off of a quiet country road above Oyster Bay and rolled up a curving drive to a sprawling shingle-clad house shaded by vast oaks and copper beeches, Sacha had a pretty strong suspicion who Wolf's last honest man was.

Any remaining doubt vanished when the cabby reined in his horse to make way for a flock of peacocks, two Irish wolf-hounds, a tame black bear, and a thundering cavalcade of boys, girls, and Shetland ponies playing the wildest game of Cowboys and Indians Sacha had ever seen in his life.

The children, the dogs, and one of the Shetland ponies escorted the visitors up the front steps of the house and onto the gracious porch that shaded the door. Wolf started to ring the bell, only to be stopped by a chorus of protests from the children.

"No, wait!"

"Let Bill do it!"

"Bill's better than a doorbell!"

Bill turned out to be the pony—and with a little nifty trick-riding and a lot of raucous laughter, the kids got Bill maneuvered into place in front of the door and coaxed him into delivering a sharp *rat-a-tat-tat* to the door with one iron-shod forefoot.

The door slammed open to reveal the unmistakable figure of Teddy Roosevelt.

"Good trick!" he cried. Reaching into his trouser pocket, he brought out a handful of sugar cubes and fed them to the delighted pony. "But your mother would never forgive me if I let you bring a horse into the house . . . so don't tell her!"

TR was just about the most famous New Yorker in America and certainly the most popular. He came from an aristocratic family impeccable enough to earn him an automatic place at Maleficia Astral's dinner parties. Worse still, he'd been born so rich that he'd never had to work for a dime. But somehow, in spite of it all, he was a real New Yorker.

People said it went back to his childhood, when he'd had such severe asthma that his father had driven him through the streets of New York all night, night after night, in order to coax enough fresh air into his lungs to keep him from suffocating. Whatever the reason, TR loved New York—and he loved ordinary New Yorkers of every color, creed, and nationality with a feeling so frank and genuine that they couldn't help loving him right back.

When he'd been police commissioner, TR had been famous for his unnerving habit of disguising himself as a regular beat cop and wandering the streets of New York at all hours of the day and night in order to catch corrupt policemen in the act of taking bribes or collecting protection money.

"If you want to take out the garbage," TR had pointed out with his usual bluntness, "you have to be willing to get your hands dirty!"

At the moment his hands were very dirty indeed—but only because he was holding a partially dismantled worm farm.

"Come on in!" he told them after the gang of kids, dogs, and pony had trooped noisily through the hall and out the back door.

He shook Lily's hand first. "The youngest Astral, I believe. Isn't the name Lily?"

Then he gave Wolf a hearty slap on the back. "How'd you know I was back from Africa? It's supposed to be a secret, you rascal."

Wolf smiled. "Let's call it Inquisitor's intuition, shall we?"

Roosevelt harrumphed and then turned to Sacha. "They say you can see magic, young man. What do *you* say? Can you? Have you got a damned clue what you're seeing, or are you just taking everyone else's word for it that it's magic?"

Sacha blinked. In all the excitement over his supposed gift—from the awful moment in Mrs. Lassky's bakery through his hurried induction into the ranks of Inquisitor's apprentices, no one had actually bothered to ask him what *he* thought he was seeing.

"I don't know," he admitted.

"I'll bet you've got some ideas, though." TR grinned. "You look like the kind of chap who's got more things happening inside his skull than he tells the world about. Good thing too, if you ask me. Any boy worth his salt knows grownups aren't big enough to handle the truth. Have you met Morgaunt yet?"

Sacha nodded.

"And? What did you think of him?"

Beside TR, Wolf stirred restlessly. "Perhaps this isn't the time for—"

"Nonsense, Max! I thought the whole point of having apprentices was to avoid rotten apples by going straight to the tree. If you can't trust twelve-year-olds—"

"Thirteen!" Sacha and Lily both objected at once.

"If you can't trust thirteen-year-olds," Roosevelt continued, with a solemn nod to acknowledge the correction, "then who the dickens are you going to trust?"

Wolf shrugged fatalistically as if to say that he was perfectly prepared to face a life of trusting no one. But Roosevelt just took Wolf's silence for agreement and forged ahead. It was the same annoying trick Lily had used on Sacha more than once. And of course the most annoying thing about it was how well it worked. At least when Lily and TR did it. It must have something to do with being rich, Sacha decided.

"You were telling me about Morgaunt," TR prompted, bringing Sacha back to the present with a thump. "Did you see him work magic?"

"I . . . don't know," Sacha confessed. "It didn't look like any magic I ever saw. It didn't feel right."

"What did it feel like?"

He remembered Morgaunt sitting in his dark library, swirling the bright golden tumbler of Scotch. He remembered how it had felt like all the magic in New York was being sucked into that single golden point of light.

"I—I can't describe it exactly. But I've felt it before. Sometimes when I'm on the subway, or just walking down the street . . ."

Sacha struggled for words. He remembered the larger-than-human quality of the magic he had sensed hovering around Morgaunt's library and Shen's orphanage. He thought of the strange ripple that had coursed through the air when the Rag and Bone Man showed up to rescue him from the dybbuk. He remembered all those times when he had passed a construction site or the big pits where they were digging the new subway lines, and felt . . . what? A power far greater than any of Edison's dynamos. A power that was usually buried under the accumulated weight of dirt and mortar and cobblestones, but that could spring up in unexpected places like a volcano erupting from deep underground. Sometimes he felt that the everyday city was just a curtain hung before a darkened stage. Behind it, invisible but ever present, hovered all the lives, all the deaths and loves and sufferings of the millions of souls who had lived in the great city. And they were becoming something. Something that had never existed anywhere under the sun before.

"It's New York," TR told him. "It's the city itself you're feeling. Every city has its own peculiar magic. Its own soul, you might say. And the soul of a city like New York has a power beyond imagining. That's Morgaunt's insanity. He doesn't just want to control the people who work magic. He wants to harness magic itself. He wants to turn New York into a machine that does nothing but make money for him. He's a fool! And he'll destroy us all if we don't put a stop to his foolishness!"

"Teddy," Wolf warned.

"No, Max, they need to know about this!" He turned to the children and went on, speaking with burning intensity.

"Inquisitors don't just protect ordinary people from magicians. They protect magicians from themselves, too. That's the job you two took on when you became Wolf's apprentices. Protecting people like Morgaunt and—"

Wolf cleared his throat and gave TR a warning look.

"Max has a point this time," TR said after a moment. "Why don't you two go play while we talk things over privately?"

Sacha could have screamed with frustration. He and Lily both cast a look of silent protest in Wolf's direction. But Wolf might have been made of stone for all the attention he paid them.

"Run along and play," TR repeated. "You won't, of course.

If you've got an ounce of spirit in you, you'll be listening at the keyhole for all you're worth. But I warn you: I can jerk a door open as fast as the dickens, so you'd better look lively!"

Despite TR's jokes about listening at the keyhole, the heavy oak door turned out to be thick enough to muffle all sounds of conversation except for a vague and tantalizing murmur. When the two men finally reemerged, Sacha and Lily were slumped on a red velvet canapé, looking as discouraged and frustrated as they felt.

"You're hunting big game," Roosevelt told Wolf as he flung the door open. "You'd better be ready to shoot when you catch up to it."

"It's not the catching that worries me," Wolf said. "It's what happens after that."

"So you came all the way out to Long Island to find out if I'd stick by you? I've got a lot of faults, Max, but deserting my friends isn't one of them." TR turned to Sacha and Lily. "What about you two? Will you stick? Can we count on you? What sort of stuff are you made of?"

"I'll do the best I can," Sacha said, torn between admiration for Roosevelt and guilt over the secrets he was keeping.

"That's the spirit!" TR cried. "When people ask you if you can do a job, tell 'em yes! Then get busy and find out how to do it! Each of you, quick, before you have time to think about it: Who's the man you admire most in the world?"

Sacha had never asked himself this question in his life, but he didn't have to think for a heartbeat before answering it: "My father."

"Why?" TR grilled him.

"I guess . . . because he's always put his family first? And he's honest. And he works harder than anyone I've ever met."

TR flashed his infectious grin at Sacha. "Bully for you! Grow up like your father, and you'll be a man I'd be proud to call my friend."

Then he turned to Lily, who was watching this exchange with a curious expression on her face. Suddenly he looked serious and forbidding. "And you, Lily? Do you feel the same way about *your* father?"

The angry flush that flooded Lily's face was all the answer he needed.

"You're a good girl, Lily. And you'll make a good job of your life if you've got the guts to live up to your own ideals. It won't be easy. But I don't pity you. And I guess you wouldn't thank me if I did. You and I are a lot alike." He grinned the big gap-toothed grin that cartoonists loved to caricature. "That wasn't a compliment, by the way, so you don't have to thank me for it!"

"I—I—oh," Lily stammered.

TR turned back to Wolf. "You've got two good ones here," he told him. "Hang on to them."

CHAPTER TWENTY-FOUR

A Long Way Down

"IS THIS WHAT ye call keeping Mr. Morgaunt's name out of the papers?" Commissioner Keegan raged, waving a crumpled copy of the *New York Sun* in Wolf's face.

They were standing in Morgaunt's library again, Lily and Sacha flanking Wolf while the police commissioner stood before them and Morgaunt lounged in his chair. He didn't have a glass of Scotch in his hand this morning—but other than that, Morgaunt looked as if he hadn't moved a muscle since the last time he'd had Wolf dragged onto his astronomically expensive oriental carpet.

"Er . . . may I?" Wolf asked, reaching for the newspaper.

"Is this discretion?" Keegan shook the paper in Wolf's face again. "Is this efficiency? Is this privacy?"

Wolf made another unsuccessful grab for the paper, but Keegan jerked it away.

"Do ye think this is all a bloody game?" he growled.

"Don't ye remember what happened to Roosevelt? Or are ye looking for a rematch? If so, I'll thank ye to warn me. I'll get out of town till the fight's over, and so will every other cop with a brain in his head!"

Finally Wolf managed to coax the newspaper from Keegan's hand. As he uncrumpled it, Sacha glimpsed the headline blazoned across the front page: "J. P. Morgaunt Caught in Love Tryst with Coney Island Cutie!"

"Oh, dear," Wolf said.

"Is that all ye have to say for yourself?"

"Well, I should probably read the article before I say anything else," Wolf pointed out—and proceeded, in a remarkably leisurely fashion, to do just that.

Then he handed it to his apprentices and waited for them to read it. The article was written in the signature *New York Sun* style, full of breezy slang and wink-and-nudge gossip:

A little birdie told us that Inquisitor Wolf of the NYPD Inquisitors Division was sighted on the boardwalk at Coney Island last week questioning eyewitnesses to an unsolved crime.

But was it a crime of magic . . . or a crime of passion? Can it be a coincidence that the main witness the Inquisitor questioned was the luscious Rosalind Darling, a.k.a. Little Cairo? Or that the crack NYPD Inquisitor was also recently seen coming out of J. P. Morgaunt's Fifth Avenue mansion?

When we caught up with Miss Darling at home, her mother had this to say:

"I have no comment at all! I don't wish to speak to you! My daughter lives only for her art, and if Mr. Morgaunt has been paying her some kind attentions, then he is inspired only by his pure appreciation of her artistic accomplishments. Which extend to tap-dancing, singing, photographic modeling, living statue exhibitions, and exotic interpretations. Available for theatrical bookings care of Darling Incorporated, Apartment 3D, 240 Mulberry Street. Did you get the apartment number, dear, or do I need to repeat it for you?"

Your Editors burn to shed the *Sun's* blazing light on this Coney Island mystery! Will Mr. Morgaunt succumb to the delightful Miss Darling? Will she be the next theatrical temptress to join the ranks of high society? Will Mrs. Astral be forced to receive One Who Has Trod the Boardwalk? Only time—and your intrepid *Sun*—will tell!

"Poor Rosie!" Lily whispered to Sacha behind her hand. "And I thought *my* mother was a handful!"

"Well," Inquisitor Wolf said mildly, "Mrs. DiMaggio—er, I mean, Darling—certainly knows how to make the most of her opportunities."

"And what am I supposed to tell Mr. Morgaunt?" Keegan asked, as if Morgaunt weren't sitting right there next to him staring at Wolf with a look of cold amusement on his patrician face.

Keegan was doing all the talking again while Morgaunt sat silent in the background. But this time there was an unnerving quality to his silence that hadn't been there on the first visit. Despite the commissioner's fulminations, Morgaunt seemed pleased about Wolf's slip-up.

Morgaunt's eyes slid sideways, and he caught Sacha watching him. "Hello, Mr. Kessler. Are we still enjoying playing at cops and robbers, or is the fun starting to wear a little thin?"

"Leave him alone," Wolf snapped. "He's not up to your cat and mouse games."

"Ah. So you've taken him under your wing, have you?" Morgaunt chuckled. "You're softhearted, Wolf. That's always been your downfall. Still, he's a bit more interesting than the last stray you brought in off the street. How is your little Chinese friend, by the way? Are you still playing Romeo to her faded Juliet, or have you gotten tired of her yet?"

Wolf and Morgaunt stared at each other. Wolf's face was as bland and expressionless as ever, but a faint flush crept up from his collar and spread over his cheeks.

"Oh, right," Morgaunt said. "*She* got tired of *you*. Or maybe she just decided she'd rather be a prosperous spellbinder's widow than the wife of an insubordinate policeman with uncertain prospects. How poignant." Morgaunt reached across the mahogany wasteland of his desk to thumb through a thick stack of papers that looked suspiciously like official police reports. "Really, Wolf, I ought to pay you. Reading

Keegan's surveillance reports on you is as good as going to the opera."

Wolf flashed Morgaunt a nonplussed look. He recovered quickly, however. "Are we just gossiping now?" he asked. "Or do you have something useful to tell me?"

"I have a job for you," Morgaunt said. "The job you should have done in the first place. Keep Edison alive. And keep my name out of the damn papers. If you do that, then I *might* forget about Shen and her little orphans. If you don't, I'll dig up half of Chinatown and build a subway stop right in the middle of the Ladies' Dancing and Deportment School!"

Whatever Wolf would have said in answer to this threat, Sacha and Lily never heard it. Just as he opened his mouth to reply, a great outcry went up in the courtyard of the Morgaunt mansion. A moment later, the butler appeared at the door, looking harried and disheveled.

"What's happened, man?" Morgaunt snapped. "Out with it!"

"It's the dybbuk! And this time it's killed a man!"

Wolf and Morgaunt sprang toward the door like sprinters bursting forward at the sound of the starter's pistol. Sacha and Lily followed, but Wolf waved them back.

"Wait here," he warned. "No, don't argue! We're not playing games anymore. Stay in the library until I tell you it's safe."

The two children gazed forlornly at the closed door.

"Do you think it *followed* us here?" Lily asked in a small, frightened voice.

"Why would it?" Sacha asked, even though he was afraid he knew the answer.

"Sacha," Lily whispered. "Have you ever wondered if . . . I mean, haven't you noticed that . . ."

But Sacha turned his back on her, not wanting to hear the next words. He put his hand on the door, desperate to know what was happening outside but not daring to disobey Wolf's orders. "I wish we could see what they're doing out there," he fretted.

"Hang on," Lily said. "I've got an idea about that."

And before Sacha could stop her, she was off. She sprinted down the length of the library, climbed the spiral staircase two steps at a time, clattered along the wrought-iron balcony, and leaped onto the rolling ladder so energetically that it whirled down its tracks with a sound like cloth ripping.

By the time Sacha reached the foot of the ladder, Lily was already far above his head.

"Wolf didn't say we couldn't look out the window," she called down to him. "Did he?"

Sacha began to climb. The ladder was steep and narrow, and it quivered alarmingly on its metal wheels with every move he made. Morgaunt probably had some sub-under-butler specifically assigned to oil those wheels every morning. Sacha imagined him arriving tomorrow morning with his rags and oilcan, only to find two nosy children splattered all over the marble floor far below.

"Can you see anything?" he called up to Lily.

"No, it's all stupid stained glass. On the other hand, I guess no one will notice if I just break a little bit."

"Are you sure you should—"

"Cripes, Sacha! Since when did you turn into an old lady? Pass me your handkerchief."

He passed it up to her. A moment later he heard a sharp *crack!* and the bright tinkle of falling glass.

"Darn!" Lily said. "All I can see is more rooftops. Unless the dybbuk's chasing pigeons, we're plumb out of luck."

"Lily! I think I hear someone coming. Maybe we should go back down."

"In a minute." More crackling and tinkling. "I think I might just be able to—"

Before Sacha could protest, Lily had broken several more panes of stained glass and squeezed herself out the window to her waist.

"Wolf told us to stay in the library!"

"I *am* in the library," Lily said. "Or at least most of me is."

Then she gave a sudden gasp of surprise—and her legs and feet vanished as if she'd been pulled out the window by her armpits.

It took less than a second to climb the last few rungs of the ladder, but it felt like the longest second in Sacha's life.

When he looked out, he saw nothing at first but open sky. The library's soaring vaulted roof stuck out above the rest of Morgaunt's mansion like the prow of a clipper ship. From up here you saw just how vast the place was. Acres of slate-tiled roof rolled away on all sides, folding into high tors and steep ridgelines. It was like one of those impassable mountain ranges that travelers in old stories were always getting waylaid in. And, like real mountains, the roof's ridgelines enclosed hidden ravines so narrow that you could walk right past them without ever knowing they existed.

It was one of those ravines that drew Sacha's attention now. Though he couldn't see into it, he could hear Lily Astral's voice coming out of it.

"Do you *live* up here?" she was asking. "I can't tell you how jealous I am! I always dreamed of running away from home and joining a Gypsy band that camped out on the rooftops! You must have some ripping good times!"

Sacha squirmed through the broken window and picked his way down the slope of the roof until he caught sight of her. She looked completely in her element. She was balanced on the slope of the roof like a pirate ready to board an enemy ship. She even had a broken-off broomstick clutched in one hand like a sword.

"What's with the stick?" Sacha asked as he reached her side.

"Oh, when they first pulled me out the window, I thought I might have to thrash 'em. But they're just kids." A wistful tone crept into her voice. "And anyway they're already leaving."

Only then did Sacha notice the little group of children standing at the bottom of the ravine looking up at them.

Lily was right; they were just kids. Most of them were small for their age too, even by Hester Street standards. They were olive-skinned and dark-haired and brown-eyed, and they were dressed like Italians. But not like the prosperous Italians who ran the greengrocers on Prince Street, or even like the poor Italians of Ragpickers' Row. These children were dressed in brightly embroidered peasant costumes like the newly arrived immigrants Sacha had seen coming off the boats from Ellis Island.

And they were definitely leaving. As Sacha and Lily watched, a harried-looking woman in a flowered head scarf popped around the corner, grabbed two of the kids, and dragged them away, scolding furiously.

"Is that Italian?" Lily asked doubtfully.

"I guess so. But it doesn't sound like any Italian I ever heard."

"Come on!" Lily called over her shoulder, already trotting off without waiting to see if Sacha was following. "Let's see where they're going!"

The ravine opened onto an undulating valley that stretched for acres in all directions. And Sacha could barely believe what he saw there: an entire shantytown, set up on the roof of Morgaunt's mansion, where some several dozen women and children seemed to be going about the business of life as naturally and unconcernedly as if they were living at street level instead of hundreds of feet up in the air.

Or rather they *had* lived there. Now they were leaving— and in a hurry.

"Does anyone here speak English?" Lily called out.

A few of the women stared at them, but the rest just kept packing. Then a sturdy-looking boy a little younger than Sacha came forward. His eyes were red, and his face was streaked with tears. "I speak English," he said. "What do you want with us?"

"Who are you?" Sacha asked. "What are you doing up here? And why are you leaving?"

"We're the stonemasons' families. And we live here. Or we used to. But now we have to leave because my father died, and the police are coming."

Lily and Sacha stared at the boy, dumbfounded.

"I—I'm sorry," Sacha said. "Was it the dybbuk?"

The boy shuddered. "If that's what you call that thing."

"Did you see it?" Lily asked.

"My mother did. She said it was a shadow in the shape of a person. She said it was made of smoke, and its eyes were blacker than *Gesù Bambino*."

"She needs to talk to Inquisitor Wolf right now!"

"What are you, crazy? Why do you think we're leaving? The last thing we want to do is talk to any cops!"

"But you have to!" Lily pleaded.

It wasn't going to do any good. Sacha knew that even if Lily didn't. There was no way these people were ever going to talk to the Inquisitors.

"What's your name?" Lily demanded.

"Antonio."

"Antonio what?"

"Why should I tell *you*?"

"You can't just run away!" Lily cried. "The Inquisitors are trying to catch the man who killed your father! Don't you want him caught? Don't you want him *stopped*?"

"The police don't care about my father any more than you do," Antonio scoffed. "And as for stopping his killer, the police don't need to worry. I'll take care of *that* myself."

Suddenly a woman ran up behind Antonio and began tugging him away from Sacha and Lily. She looked like Antonio, and she would have been very pretty if her hair hadn't been so disheveled and her eyes so swollen from crying.

As she pulled Antonio away, she was whispering furiously into his ear. Finally he seemed to grasp what she was saying. His dark eyes flashed toward Sacha, and he tried to struggle free. But two more women had come to help his mother, and finally the three of them managed to drag him away.

As Antonio vanished behind a looming Gothic turret, he looked back one more time at Sacha.

In Sacha's whole life up to that moment, no one had ever looked at him with such naked hatred.

CHAPTER TWENTY-FIVE

The Lone Gunman

WOLF WAS WAITING for them when they got back to the library, and he was furious.

Not that you could tell that easily. It turned out that Wolf got angry just like Sacha's father did: no yelling, just a deafening silence that made you feel like getting boxed on the ear would be a welcome relief.

"Go back to the office," he interrupted when they tried to tell him about Antonio and the stonemasons' children. "Maybe a day of filing papers for Payton will remind you that this is a real job, not a game."

Sacha caught the undercurrent of anger in Wolf's voice immediately and knew they were on seriously thin ice. But Lily just forged right ahead.

"But—"

"Forgive me, Miss Astral," Wolf murmured in a tone that

made the hair on the back of Sacha's neck stand up. "I must have failed to make myself clear—"

"But—"

Wolf leveled a stare at Lily that froze the words on her lips and had her backing toward the door before he even spoke again. "Just go!"

"So," Lily asked as soon as they had passed through Morgaunt's monumental front gate and were out on the sidewalk. "How are we going to find Antonio?"

"We're not. Didn't you hear Wolf? We're going back to file papers for Payton."

"But he didn't give us a chance to tell him about Antonio. He doesn't know there's an eyewitness."

"Lily," Sacha said warningly.

"Look at it this way," she told him in her most reasonable voice. "We're only doing what Wolf would want us to do *if* he knew what we know."

"Lily!"

"Besides." She was warming to her argument. "Wolf's hands are tied. You heard Morgaunt threatening Shen, didn't you?"

"Lily!"

"Listen, Sacha, you ever read *Boys Weekly*?"

"Sometimes," Sacha said grudgingly. He knew that this wasn't a real change of subject and that she was probably going to use the admission to trap him into something.

"So, you know the Westerns?" Her blue eyes flashed with enthusiasm. "They always start out with some poor bunch of bean farmers. You know the type I'm talking about. They're good men. Principled men. But they're *tied down*. They've got wives and children and mortgages. So when the cattle barons try to run them off their land, what can they do? Nothing. But then"—her voice sank to an excited whisper—"then there's always the lone gunman who rides in over the horizon. No name, no woman, no strings attached. Just a hero and his horse and his gun. A hero who can take on the bad guys with no holds barred and no punches pulled." She nodded decisively and tapped Sacha on the chest. "That's us, Sach. The lone gunman on the horizon riding in to save the day."

"But there's two of us," Sacha protested. "Unless you're saying I'm the *horse*. And what does that make Wolf, anyway? A bean farmer?"

Still, even as he said it, his feet were following Lily of their own accord.

"So how are you going to find Antonio?" he asked after half a block. "We don't even know anyone in Little Italy."

"Oh, yes we do! Think carrots!"

"If you're talking about Rosie DiMaggio, then *I* think you're just being jealous. Most people would call her hair auburn. I understand the color is quite fashionable."

He glanced sideways at Lily to gauge her reaction—and almost laughed out loud when he saw how annoyed she looked.

"You're not as funny as you think you are," she snapped. "In the English language *I* speak, the name of that color is plain old orange. And you know what else? I bet I've got just the right stick to make Little Miss Carrot-top help us!"

Rosie DiMaggio's home turned out to be a shabby but surprisingly large wood-frame house. It was in a working-class neighborhood—but still a lot better than anywhere Sacha's family could ever have afforded to live. Obviously the DiMaggios weren't doing too badly for themselves.

"I can't understand why they let the outdoor paint go like that," Lily said with a judgmental shake of her head. "Somebody ought to tell them that keeping up with maintenance is always cheaper in the long run."

"If you say so," Sacha said. "Let's just hope Rosie hasn't left for Coney Island already."

But they were in luck. She was—as Mrs. DiMaggio explained—"between engagements."

"I guess that means they fired her after the newspapers got hold of the Morgaunt story," Lily whispered. If Sacha suspected that there was a hint of satisfaction in her voice, he knew enough not to say anything about it.

"And what do you children want to speak to Rosalind about?" Mrs. DiMaggio asked. She looked back and forth between them as if she couldn't decide whether to chase Sacha away or invite Lily Astral in.

"Oh," Lily answered with an appalling giggle, "I just came over to ask her to my birthday party. Do you think that would be all right?"

Mrs. DiMaggio blinked at Lily. "And what did you say your name was, dear?"

"Lily As—" Sacha jabbed her in the side with his elbow. "Ow! Ah, I mean, Lily Asbury."

Mrs. DiMaggio hesitated. She had taken Sacha's measure in the first glance, but Lily's uptown accent and expensive clothes were clearly puzzling her.

"Oh, *do* let her come," Lily simpered, actually managing to bat her eyelashes at the woman. "It'll be such fun! We're going to have pony rides! And—and tea!"

Sacha thought he was going to throw up. Mrs. DiMaggio, on the other hand, was entranced.

"Oh, you dear, dear child!" the immense woman cooed. Then she waved them up the stairs. "Why don't you just run up and give her the invitation in person?"

"Thank you, Mrs. DiMaggio!" Lily cried, with a sticky-sweet smile pasted on her lips. "Thankyouthankyouthankyou! You're such a darling!"

"You're frighteningly good at that," Sacha teased, as soon as they were safely out of Mrs. DiMaggio's earshot. "I'm starting to think you could pass for a normal girl if you put a little effort into it."

"Perish the thought! Now, how the heck do we find her room without stumbling around until darling Mrs. D. comes up to see if we're stealing her bath towels?"

Now that they were inside the DiMaggios' house, Sacha understood why it was so big: It was a rooming house. One of the doors in the long hallway would lead to Rosie's room, but the rest belonged to lodgers. Not that Lily would balk at barging in on perfect strangers unannounced and uninvited. And if she surprised some poor fellow in his undershirt, she'd probably just give him advice about how to launder his linen better.

Rosie herself rescued them, sticking her head out of a doorway at the end of the hall and greeting them as though they were all the best of friends. She still seemed pretty friendly even when they got inside her room and out of her mother's earshot.

"So how's the Inquisiting going?" she asked around her usual gob of chewing gum. This gob was at least as big as the one she'd been chewing back on Coney Island, but instead of being lime green, it was electric blue.

"Inquisiting is very interesting," Lily answered primly. "But we're here to ask for your assistance in locating some lost persons."

"Some what?"

"Lost persons. People who are—"

"Yeah, I heard you," Rosie interrupted. "I just don't know why you need my help."

"Well, you see," Lily began—and launched into the most convoluted and unconvincing lie Sacha had ever heard anyone try to tell. It featured truancy officers and lost orphans and princely rewards, and it sounded like she'd lifted it straight out of a bad *Boys Weekly* story—which, for all Sacha knew, she had. Uncle Mordechai at his wiliest couldn't have pulled off such a ridiculous story. And Lily was no Uncle Mordechai.

Finally Sacha stepped in to rescue her.

"Okay, so here's the truth," he told Rosie. "The dybbuk killed an Italian stonemason at Morgaunt's mansion this morning, and we met his son—"

"Sacha!"

"Just be quiet, Lily. You should never, ever lie. You're really bad at it. Anyway, like I was saying, we met the dead stonemason's son and a bunch of other kids who were living up on the roof. But they ran away before we could get any information out of them. So we need to find them."

"So where were they from?"

"Who?"

"The stonemasons."

"I told you, Italy."

"Come on! Gimme a little help here!" Rosie held up her hand with her thumb and fingers pressed together and shook it in front of Sacha's nose as if she were trying to shake the information out of thin air. "I mean, tell me he's from Napoli. Or Palermo. Or Abruzzo. Then I could find him for you in half an hour flat. But *Italy*? Do you know how many Italians there are on this island?"

"Oh," Sacha said disappointedly. "But how would we even know where he was from?"

"I dunno. What language were they speaking?"

"Uh . . . Italian?"

Rosie sighed and rolled her eyes. It made her look surprisingly like Bekah. "What *kind* of Italian?"

"Is there more than one?" Lily asked, completely mystified.

"Wait a minute," Sacha said. "He did say something that I thought was really strange. Not that I know anything about . . . well . . ." He flailed around for a minute trying to find a polite word for *goyim*, but then gave up. "Anyway, he said the dybbuk's eyes were blacker than *Gesù Bambino*. I always thought that meant 'Baby Jesus.' But that's definitely the first time I ever heard anyone call Jesus bl—"

Suddenly Rosie was jumping up and down and hugging him. "Sacha," she cried, "you're a genius!"

"Really?"

"They're not just stonemasons—they're Sicilian stonemasons. From Tindari. Betcha dollars to dybbuks! And not just that, but I know exactly where they'd go if they were looking for a safe place to get away from the cops!"

By the time they got to Twelfth Street, Rosie had explained her reasoning—though her whirlwind explanation left Sacha's head spinning.

"It's like this, see. The only person who'd say someone was *nero come il bambino Gesù*, is a person who's seen a Black Madonna. And the only Black Madonna I ever heard of is the Madonna of Tindari. Which I happen to know about because of the Saint's Feast they have every year up on Twelfth Street. Hey, look! They've got fresh pizza at Vesuvio's. Wanna slice?"

"*That's* pizza?" Lily asked. "Wow. Well, if you're getting a slice anyway . . ."

"What about you, Sacha? Don't worry, it's kosher!"

"It *is?*" Sacha asked eagerly.

"Sure," Rosie said with a laugh. "Just like wonton soup."

"*Wonton soup?* Who told you that? Your cousin's boyfriend?" Sacha was starting to have some serious doubts about the fellow.

"It's a joke," Rosie said, laughing. "You know: Why is wonton soup kosher? What, you never heard that one? Come on, ask me!"

"Uh . . . okay . . . why *is* wonton soup kosher?"

"'Cause it's Chinese, stupid!"

"Oh," Sacha said, feeling disappointed. The pizza really had looked good.

"So anyway," Rosie continued when she'd finished her pizza, "they used to have this street fair every year up on Twelfth Street. You know, get out the Madonna, dress her up in fancy clothes, parade her around, play with snakes. All good fun. I used to go every year 'cause they had the best fried squid in town."

"Fried squid?" Lily said in tones of intense interest. "When is this fair again?"

"Yeah, well, unfortunately the health inspectors shut them down for *sanitary reasons*—someone complained about the squid, probably."

"People are so stupid," Lily sighed.

"Tell me about it," Rosie agreed. "That was some really good squid!"

Sacha rolled his eyes. All he needed to do now was get them in a room with his mother, and every city health inspector would be run out of town on a rail.

"So anyway," Rosie went on, "after the street festival was

shut down, the Sicilian Stonemasons Fraternal Association volunteered to build a chapel for the Black Madonna if someone would donate the space for it. So who steps up to the plate? Mr. Rotella of Rotella's Funeral Home on Twelfth Street. He donates his whole basement—well, except for the part where they keep the corpsicles. So the Order of the Santissima Madonna di Tindari builds their chapel there. *Which* my Uncle Louie just happened to be the guy who did the electrical wiring on it. *Which* I just happen to have overheard him telling my mother that those Tindari Sicilians were practically moving into the place, and Mr. Rotella was going to get shut down by the city if he started letting people sleep in his basement. Well, live people, I mean. I guess you don't need a health inspection for dead people. Hey, look, fried dough! Want some, Sacha? No? Well, maybe later."

By the time they reached Twelfth Street, Sacha's stomach was growling—and he was starting to wonder how two reasonably normal-size girls could possibly cram this much food down their gullets without exploding.

"Well, here we are," Rosie said. "Rotella's Funeral Home! Now we just have to figure out how to talk our way into the basement!"

Rotella's Funeral Home presided over a forty-foot stretch of Twelfth Street, transforming an ordinary workaday section of sidewalk into something resembling a wedding cake for giants with very questionable taste in pastries. Its awning was a meringue-like confection of pink and silver satin. Its stained-glass windows twinkled in rainbow colors that would have looked right at home in any Coney Island fun house. Its facade dripped with so many gleaming terra cotta sculptures that it was hard to imagine there was an ordinary brick tenement house somewhere under it all.

Lily gasped. "That's really . . . really . . . uh . . ."

"I know," Rosie breathed, licking fried dough off her fingers. She sighed ecstatically. "Isn't it just *gorgeous?*"

The door to the chapel was no exception to the general wedding cake theme. It might have started out life as a regular basement door, but it had since moved up in the world. When they first spotted it, tucked away neatly at street level in the shadow of the marble-veneered main entrance, Sacha thought it was made of hammered silver.

In fact, it was made of something much stranger. It was entirely covered with shiny little tin plaques, which were nailed onto the wood in a crazy-quilt pattern that reminded Sacha of the way pigeons ruffed their feathers up when they fought over a scrap of food in the gutter. The tin plaques had bumpy hammered-out pictures on them that turned out to be images of legs, feet, hands, elbows, hearts, kidneys, and livers— basically, every body part that Sacha knew the name of and a few whose names he couldn't even guess at.

"People put them up to thank the Madonna for healing them," Rosie explained. "See, this one is from a guy with a heart condition, and this one is thanks for saving a baby from the croup, and this one . . . hey, check it out, she must have healed a bald guy. A whole lotta bald guys, from the look of it. Maybe I oughta look into this place from an inventing perspective. Curing baldness is a real growth industry—did you ever think about that?"

Lily choked on her last bite of fried dough.

"Can we go in now?" Sacha asked.

The first thing he noticed when they stepped through the door was that it was dark—so dark he couldn't see anything at all for a moment. Then he saw the Madonna herself, and that swept every other thought out of his head.

She sat at the far end of the room, in a little alcove whose walls, floor, and ceiling were completely carpeted with more of the silvery talismans. They flickered in the light of the votive candles so that it looked like the Madonna was flying—but flying on human hands and legs and hearts instead of on angel wings.

Still, the thing Sacha really noticed was the statue's face. When Rosie had told them about the Black Madonna, Sacha had expected it to look like black people he had seen around New York. It didn't. It looked like someone had taken an ordinary Italian lady and her baby and painted their skin with black paint from the hardware store. It should have been ridiculous. But it wasn't. In fact, there was something about it that made you want to speak in whispers.

That was how Sacha felt, anyway. But no one else seemed to share his feeling of silent awe. Everyone else in the chapel was screaming. As Sacha's vision adjusted to the darkness, he could see why. Cramming forty people plus all their worldly possesssions into an underground grotto designed to hold maybe twelve at the outside was going to be a noisy proposition no matter how you did it. And when two-thirds of those people were under the age of ten, you might as well try asking crashing freight trains to be quiet.

"Well," Rosie asked, "are these your stonemasons?"

Sacha peered around, searching for Antonio and his mother. He didn't see them. But he did catch sight of a familiar face here, a familiar shawl or skirt or head scarf there. Enough to know that these were indeed the same women and children they'd seen that morning.

"It's them," he whispered. "Can you talk to them for us?"

"Ha! Only if we can find one of them who speaks Italian. Otherwise, good luck."

At first Sacha assumed Rosie was exaggerating. After watching her conduct pantomimed, half-shouted, half-sign-language conversations with several of the children, he realized it was no joke. Finally, however, the children produced a young woman in a plain black dress.

"Great," Rosie said, after speaking to her for a moment. "She used to be the village schoolteacher. *Her* I can talk to."

Unfortunately, she never got to. Because that was when Antonio showed up.

With a gun in his hand.

"This is for killing my father, you black-hearted bastard!" he screamed.

Sacha saw the wicked eye of the muzzle staring him in the face as Antonio pointed the gun at him. "No!" he cried, putting up his hands uselessly. "This is cra—"

Suddenly there was a screaming commotion behind Antonio, and his mother bolted out of the crowd and threw herself on him.

The gun went off with a tearing crash. Sacha heard the ping and whine of the bullet ricocheting off a pipe somewhere overhead.

Antonio had dropped the gun when it went off, and his mother was now hanging on to his knees and screaming at him while he scrabbled on the floor for it. Sacha didn't need to speak Sicilian to guess that she was screaming the same things his own mother would have been screaming at *him* if *he* were about to shoot a total stranger and land himself in jail for the rest of his life.

"Come on!" Lily yelled, grabbing his wrist and dragging him toward the door.

The three of them ran flat out until they were absolutely sure Antonio wasn't chasing them. By the time they stopped, they were somewhere on the wrong side of Houston Street in a neighborhood Sacha barely knew.

"Phew," Rosie gasped. "That was just about the weirdest thing that's ever happened to me!"

"Do you think the police are going to come?" Sacha asked apprehensively.

"I doubt it," Rosie said. "If the police came down to Twelfth Street every time someone heard gunshots, they'd wear out the soles of their shoes in a week. So why do you think that kid thought you killed his father?"

"How can he possibly think *we* killed his father?" Sacha asked.

"Not we, Sacha. *You.*"

"Don't be silly. He meant Lily and me, obviously."

"But *you* were the one he was looking at," Lily argued. "You were the one he was shooting at, too."

"That's crazy!"

"Is it?" She started ticking points off on her fingers. "You show up for your first day of work as an Inquisitor and, presto bango, suddenly there's a dybbuk running around town. Rosie here is the first one to see the dybbuk, and what did she tell Wolf right on that very first day? That she knew it was a dybbuk and not just an ordinary demon because it reminded her of you."

"She said it reminded her of a nice Jewish boy," Sacha protested. "Last time I checked there were a few million of those in New York City."

"Well, actually," Rosie offered, "it did kind of look like—"

"Oh, shut up, Rosie!"

"Well, you don't have to be rude!" she huffed.

But Sacha didn't need to apologize because Lily was already ticking off more points on her fingers. "Then Mrs. Worley can't find your soul—"

"That's ridiculous! She said herself that the Soul Catcher was just a parlor toy!"

"Then Antonio's father was killed when you were at Morgaunt's house—probably because the dybbuk followed you there!"

"I'm leaving!" he shouted. "I'm not going to listen to another word of this!"

"Because you don't believe me?" Lily challenged him. "Or because you don't want to admit it to yourself?"

Sacha stared at her, trembling with anger—anger that he told himself was completely, entirely, one hundred percent justified.

"All right, Little Miss Know-It-All," he snapped, forcing the thought of his mother's stolen locket down into the darkest recesses of his mind, right next to that awful glimpse of the dybbuk's face that he been so resolutely not thinking about for the last few days. "Tell me this. If it's my dybbuk, then why does it keep attacking Thomas Edison?"

Lily's shoulders slumped in defeat. "I don't know. But Mrs. Worley said—"

"She *said* that Morgaunt couldn't have used the etherograph to make a dybbuk. And even if he did, how could it be *my* dybbuk when no one's ever made a recording of me?"

"Are you so sure about that?" Lily asked in a decidedly odd tone of voice.

"Of course I am!" Sacha snapped. But then suddenly he wasn't sure at all. "Wait a minute. Remember all those tests they gave us before they made us apprentices? Remember the one where they had us sit in a dark room and try to do magic? They could have done a recording then." He stopped. "Why are you looking at me like that?"

"Because they didn't give *me* any tests except the normal IQ test everyone always gets." She dropped her eyes and flushed slightly. "Sacha, that cylinder Morgaunt played for us? It was *you*, wasn't it?"

And then she did look at him. A look that slipped through his ribs like a knife blade and cut him to the heart. He hated the very idea of having Lily Astral look at him like that.

Don't think you know me just because you listened to some stupid song, he wanted to tell her. Then he realized that he wouldn't want to tell her that if he didn't secretly suspect she was right. Which made him even more furious.

"You're wrong," he told her between gritted teeth. "You're dead wrong, and I'm going to prove it."

"How?"

It sounded like a challenge. Or maybe Sacha just wanted it to sound that way. A small part of him knew how unreasonable he was being. But it was easier to be angry than to be reasonable. And anything was easier than admitting that Lily might be right.

"By summoning the dybbuk myself!"

CHAPTER TWENTY-SIX

On Horrible Bird Feet

TWILIGHT CAME EARLY on that gray fall evening. And it found Sacha shivering in the shadows across the
street from his grandfather's *shul*.

He'd spent the last two hours hunched in the darkest booth
of the Café Metropole drinking coffee he couldn't afford and
feverishly poring over the armful of practical Kabbalah books
he'd managed to smuggle out of the house under his coat. Rabbi
Kessler disapproved of practical Kabbalah so strongly that he
wouldn't even keep those books at the *shul*. Instead they lurked
on a high shelf at the back of the Kesslers' only closet, safely
hidden from impious eyes and rash young aspiring Kabbalists.

That had been a lucky break for Sacha tonight. Or maybe
not so lucky. Summoning a dybbuk had seemed like a good
idea (sort of) in broad daylight. But as the street lamps flickered on and night settled over the city, it was starting to seem
like a very, very bad one.

He huddled into his coat and tried not to think about what else might be hiding in the shadows with him. It felt odd to be watching Grandpa Kessler's *shul* from across the street instead of sitting inside with the rest of the students. He was seeing it from the outside now, like a stranger would. It looked shabbier than he remembered, and yet somehow more exotic and otherworldly too.

Mostly, though, it looked small. It was just one shop in one street in one neighborhood of a city with a million streets and a thousand neighborhoods. You could walk away from it and turn a corner or two and never find your way back again. And in New York you could do the same thing with everything else in your life, even being a Jew. People did it every day. Now, looking at his grandfather's little *shul* while he waited for Rosie and Lily to join him, Sacha realized for the first time in his life that he could be one of those people. He didn't know whether to be excited by the idea or frightened of it.

Lily arrived first, sneaking up so quietly that he practically jumped out of his skin when she touched his elbow.

"Whose school is this again?" she asked.

"Look—just never mind, okay?"

"Oh, a little nervous, are we?"

"Yes. And you're not helping."

"Are you sure you want to go through with this, Sacha? I mean, don't feel like you have to impress me or anything. Just say the word, and we can go tell Inquisitor Wolf everything."

"I'm fine!" Sacha snapped.

"Okey-dokey. Now where *is* that Rosie! If she's finked out on us—"

But there she was, bustling along the pavement toward them.

"Sorry!" Rosie cried.

"Shhhh!"

"*Sorry!* My mother just *would* not go to sleep. I was at my wits' end trying to figure out how to get out of the house without her hearing me. How'd you two manage it, anyway?"

"My sister's covering for me," Sacha said guiltily. "My parents think I'm at *shul*." Which he was . . . sort of. "I've got a couple of hours until they'll figure out I'm not."

"Two hours?" Lily asked incredulously. "Is that the best you could do?"

"Oh, and pray tell how you managed!"

"Easy. My mother's throwing a fancy dress ball tonight. She always sends me to bed early when she's entertaining."

"But won't she come in to check on you before she goes to sleep?"

Lily made a face. "She's not exactly that kind of mother, Sacha."

Grandpa Kessler's students were filtering out of the *shul* by this time, straggling onto the sidewalk in twos and threes and shuffling down Canal Street with the flatfooted walk of exhausted men who'd been on their feet since before dawn.

When the last student came out and the lights dimmed, Rosie started forward—but Sacha grabbed her by the elbow.

"Wait!" he whispered.

A moment later, Grandpa Kessler joined the last of his students on the way home.

And that left Mo.

It seemed like he'd never be done cleaning up, but at last the *shammes* came out, shut the door behind him, and began to bolt the heavy locks. It took forever. Actually, it took three times forever, because he had to check everything twice after he'd locked it. But at last the wait was over.

"Come on," Sacha whispered, pulling the stolen—no, he corrected himself, just *borrowed*—keys out of his pocket.

Grandpa Kessler probably hadn't unlocked his *shul* himself since the day Mo arrived from Poland, and it showed. The old iron keys stuck in the locks so badly that at first Sacha was convinced he'd taken the wrong ones by mistake. But finally he coaxed open the last lock, and the three of them slipped inside.

He stumbled through the dark room to the cupboard where Mo always kept the candles. He took as many as he could carry, lit them, and set them all around the rickety deal table where his grandfather's students studied. The candlelight flared up and chased the shadows back into the corners. But it didn't help. It just made them look thicker and more sinister and dybbuk-filled than ever.

"So what do we do now?" Lily asked.

Sacha read through the summoning spell one last time. There were a lot of words in it that he didn't understand. In fact, struggling through the archaic Hebrew had reminded him uncomfortably of preparing for his *bar mitzvah*. He was starting to think that he might turn out to be just as bad at summoning dybbuks as he'd been at memorizing Torah lines.

To be honest, he was hoping he would be.

"First we need to draw a circle on the floor," he told the two girls. "Then we need a bedsheet."

"Cripes," Lily complained. "You could have *told* me you needed a bedsheet."

"And chalk," he added. "Did anyone bring chalk?"

"No. Did you?"

"If I'd brought it, would I be asking you?"

"Just because you're scared," Lily observed in her prissiest voice, "is no reason to be rude."

"Shhh!" Rosie hissed. "Someone's coming!"

They all dove to the floor and lay there while footfalls sounded on the street outside and dim lights swept across the room. As the footsteps faded off down the street, Rosie crept to the shopfront window and gave the all clear.

Sacha sat up to find Lily staring at him. The false alarm seemed to have shaken her. She was obviously having second thoughts.

"Sacha?" she asked hesitantly. "Don't you think maybe we really should ask Inquisitor Wolf for help instead of trying to do this ourselves?"

Of course I do, he wanted to tell her, but that would mean admitting why he couldn't ask Wolf for help. So instead he just shrugged.

"He could help you," Lily said stubbornly. "I think—I think he might even be a Mage."

"That's ridiculous," Sacha snapped.

Lily gave him a decidedly odd look. "Are you sure? My mother said—"

"And what does your mother know about magic anyway?" he asked bitterly, wishing his family was as all-American as the Astrals instead of littered with Kabbalists and miracle workers. "But you people are always full of advice, aren't you? It's easy to tell other people what to do when you don't have to live in the real world and you've never wanted a thing in your life that someone didn't hand you on a platter. Just like they handed you this job, when we all know that the only thing you're really going to do with your life is turn into a useless socialite like your *mother!*"

"I'm nothing like my mother!" Lily shouted. Then she stopped and bit her lip as if to keep it from trembling. "Never mind. Forget I said anything. It was a stupid idea anyway."

"Ugh!" Rosie said into the angry silence. "This place is filthy!"

She was right, Sacha realized. Mo Lehrer was a perfectly good *shammes*, of course. But he was, after all, a man. And as Sacha's mother was fond of saying, your average man's idea of housecleaning stopped about where your average woman's notion of slatternly filth started. Mrs. Kessler mopped her floors daily in order to battle the black soot that rose from a million coal fires to blanket every surface in the city. Mo, on the other hand, just swept up occasionally. And it showed.

"Well, at least we won't be needing chalk," Sacha pointed out. "We can draw in the dust. We ought to post a lookout, though. Lily, why don't you stay by the window and watch the street."

"Fine," Lily muttered in a voice that made it clear she was still nursing bruised feelings.

Just like a girl, Sacha told himself. Well, maybe he had been kind of mean. But he could always make it up to her later. And even a girl couldn't expect him to drop everything and apologize now.

"So what do we do next?" Rosie asked. "Shouldn't you put on your phy—phy—you know, those string things."

"I don't know," Sacha said.

"Well," Rosie said with elaborate care, "what do you *think?*"

"I think my grandfather would have a stroke if he knew about this."

"Yeah, but—"

"All right, all right! Enough already, I'm doing it."

Sacha dutifully donned phylacteries and prayer shawl. Suddenly he was dead certain that this was the worst thing he'd ever done in his life. He tried to make himself feel better by thinking about the story of the rabbi who'd said a Yom Kippur service in hell, setting all the demons free to go to heaven and condemning himself to eternal damnation in order to save them. He tried to imagine that he was doing something noble like that, that he was somehow sacrificing his own soul in order to save . . . well . . . someone. Part of him knew it was all hooey. But he was in too deep to back out.

So Sacha drew in the sooty dust. For a bedsheet they used an old furniture cloth Mo had nailed up in the doorway that led into the back room. It took a few curses and torn fingers to pry the rusty tacks loose from the doorframe, but the cloth would do.

"After all," Rosie pointed out, "nothing says it has to be a *clean* bedsheet."

Maybe it was Sacha's bad Hebrew, but Grandpa Kessler's books didn't seem to explain what to do with the bedsheet. It was supposed to go in the circle, that much Sacha got. So first they tried just laying the sheet on the floor in the middle of the circle.

Rosie tucked the corners in so that they weren't smudging any part of the circle—this, at least, the practical Kabbalah books had been quite clear about. Then she backed up and looked at it quizzically.

"What's that supposed to do?" Lily asked from the window.

"The dybbuk's supposed to appear behind it."

"But . . . there *is* no behind it."

"Maybe we should have left the sheet hanging up in the doorway and done the circle over there," Rosie suggested. But none of them liked the idea of having to lift the sheet knowing that the dybbuk could be anywhere in the cluttered back room watching and waiting for them.

In the end they compromised by dragging a couple of chairs into the circle and arranging the sheet over them so it formed a sort of tent. It reminded Sacha of the secret forts he and his sister used to make under the furniture on rainy days. There was still something creepy about that dark cave under the sheet, but at least this way the dybbuk wouldn't have a whole room to run around in.

Sacha neatened up the circle, which had been smudged alarmingly by their rearranging of the sheet. Then he took a final look at the spellbooks just for good measure.

"Oh, no! This book says you have to *feed* the dybbuk." He leafed frantically through the other books. "None of the other ones says anything about food! How was I supposed to know?"

"Not to worry," Rosie said, pulling a newspaper-wrapped package out of her coat.

"What's that?" Sacha asked.

"A cannoli."

"How do you know dybbuks like Italian food?"

"I don't want to knock anyone's national cuisine," Rosie said, "but trust me: even a dybbuk can't prefer dried-up noodle kugel to a cannoli from Ferrara's!"

Over by the door, Lily looked almost as doubtful as Sacha felt. But it turned out that she had a more practical concern than the dybbuk's taste in food. "We don't even know if dybbuks have fingers. Shouldn't you unwrap it?"

"Good point." Rosie undid the strings and paper to reveal what just might have been the most perfect piece of pastry Sacha had ever seen in his life.

"*Where* did you find *that?*" Lily asked in tones of religious awe.

"And what is it again?" Sacha asked.

Rosie gave them the kind of look New Yorkers usually reserved for tourists. "You two need to get out more."

When the perfect cannoli had disappeared under the sheet, Lily sighed deeply and said, "Okay. What do we do now?"

"I'm supposed to make a secret sign and say, 'Spirit of the Invisible World, prisoner of the realm of chaos, I, Sacha, son of so-and-so, summon you. Come. Eat. Eat and be satisfied.'"

Sacha said the words.

Nothing happened.

Lily coughed, and Sacha jumped halfway out of his skin at the sound.

"Sorry. Uh . . . I think you forgot the secret sign."

"Oh. Right."

But when he did the words and made the sign at the same time, nothing happened again.

They waited a minute.

Still nothing.

"Try it with your left hand," Rosie suggested.

Sacha tried it with his left hand.

More nothing.

"Or backwards, maybe?" Lily hazarded. "Do you think you could do it backwards?"

"I'm going home!" Sacha threw up his hands in disgust and walked away from the circle. "This is the dumbest thing I've ever done. I've already ruined a perfectly good pair of pants, and I'm not going to hang around and get arrested by the police on top of it. You two can do whatever you want. I'm leav—"

Then he heard one of the chairs fall over.

He was facing Lily when it happened, and he knew right

then that he would remember the look of terror on her face if he lived to be a hundred and twenty.

"I'm so sorry," she whispered. *"I would never have let you do this if I'd really thought—"*

For one crazy moment, Sacha had the idea that he could just run past her and out the door onto the street and get away. But he knew better. There was no running away now. There was nowhere to run to.

The dybbuk was wearing Sacha's second-best pants and shirt, just as he'd known it would be. The shirt was so clean that Sacha had a bizarre vision of the dybbuk conscientiously washing it at the back lot water pump long after the lights had gone out and everyone in the tenements had drifted off to sleep. It gave him the shudders. However awful it was to think of the dybbuk hurting and killing, it was even worse to think of it trying to be an ordinary boy.

"What do we *do?*" Lily whispered.

Sacha looked at Rosie, who just spread her hands helplessly. "Didn't the book say how to get rid of it?"

"No. Or if it did, I didn't read that far."

"Sacha," Lily whispered urgently behind him.

He ignored her.

"Sacha! The circle!"

Sacha looked down—and saw that somewhere in the process of summoning the dybbuk, he had stepped on the circle. It was barely a smudge, really. A scuff mark at most. But it was enough.

The dybbuk felt its way around the edge of the circle

until it found the smudged spot. Then it wafted out through the gap like cigarette smoke wafting through a keyhole.

There was something about the way it moved that made Sacha queasy. He looked down and felt his stomach heave; the old wives' tales were true, he realized. Or at least partly true. Because even though the dybbuk's feet looked normal enough, the footprints they left behind were very far from normal. It looked like some monstrous bird had scratched its way across the dusty floor of the *shul*.

The dybbuk oozed toward him on its horrible bird feet—and then it oozed past him and over to Lily, who was still frozen by the window in horror.

It raised one filmy hand and touched Lily on the chest, right above her heart. It started to get that sinuous, flowing, cigarette-smoke look again. But this time it wasn't flowing out of the circle. This time it was pulling something out of Lily.

The sight was so strange and awful that for a moment Sacha just stared. Then a sort of electric shock went through him. The dybbuk was sucking the life out of her—and he was standing there watching it happen like some tourist gawking at the Flatiron Building!

He flung himself at the dybbuk. It felt like tearing at a cloud, but finally he grabbed hold of his second-best shirt and dragged the creature back across the room by its collar.

They careened into the circle, and Sacha wrenched one arm free in a desperate motion and somehow managed to redraw it around them.

He had no idea how long the struggle lasted. Later it

seemed that only a few seconds had passed. But while he was grappling with the dybbuk, he felt as if years and decades of his life were sloughing off him.

At first he thought he'd never be able to hold the dybbuk. Every time he tried to lay hands on it, it wafted away, leaving nothing but empty air behind. But as they struggled, the dybbuk took on weight and substance. Soon Sacha wasn't chasing smoke. Now it was more like trying to hold water in his bare hands. He still couldn't get a solid grip, but he could feel it slipping through his fingers, leaving them as numb and painful as if he'd been clutching at ice.

Outside the circle, Lily and Rosie were screaming at him. He could tell they were trying to warn him about something, but their words couldn't seem to reach him.

Meanwhile the dybbuk grew more real and solid with every passing moment.

Its breath smelled like the worst tenement air shaft in the world. It reeked of rancid oil and dead rats and broken razors and deathbed linens and all the other revolting things that people want to get rid of so badly they can't even wait for the Rag and Bone Man to come round for them.

But there was worse, far worse, than the dybbuk's breath. Sacha felt its thoughts and feelings as well. He felt its ravenous hunger for life and warmth and love and family. He felt its fury—so strong that it had become a strange, twisted sort of self-hatred—at the thief who had stolen its life from it.

And now Sacha knew just who the thief was.

The dybbuk didn't know it was a dybbuk. It thought Sacha was the dybbuk and it was the real boy. It thought Sacha had stolen its life from it. And the longer they fought each other, the harder it was to say which of them was right.

It was Rosie who finally ended the fight. She stepped into the circle and flung a book straight at the dybbuk's head as hard as she could.

It passed through the dybbuk like a knife cutting through butter—and it whacked Sacha so hard on the forehead that he fell over in a dead faint.

When he came to, the dybbuk was nowhere in sight and Rosie and Lily were both bending over him.

"Why did you do that?" he asked angrily. "I was winning!"

"No, you weren't." Lily shuddered so violently that her teeth chattered. "You were . . . fading. Every time you touched him, *he* got more solid and *you* got all kind of thin and see-through and dybbuky. If Rosie hadn't done something, you would have . . ." She shuddered again.

"Where did it go?"

"Out through the keyhole," Rosie said. "Like a vampire."

"Do you think it's really gone?" Sacha asked, even though he knew it wasn't.

"No," Lily said bleakly. "And it wasn't anything we did that made it leave."

"What's that supposed to mean?"

"Just what it sounds like. You didn't beat it. And it sure wasn't afraid of Rosie and her book. It just kind of . . . lost interest."

"Yeah," Rosie said unhappily. "Like it suddenly realized it had something more important to do somewhere else."

"That doesn't make any sense. What could be more important to the dybbuk than this?"

Instead of answering him, Lily bent down and picked up the smushed cannoli in its newspaper wrapping.

"Lily!" Sacha cried in exasperation. "Can't you think about anything but food?"

She gave him a put-upon look. "I'm picking up the newspaper so you can read it, you idiot, not so I can lick it. You want to know what your dybbuk has to do tonight that's more important than killing you? How about this?"

He took it from her and read the headline that shrieked up from the page at him: "EDISON-HOUDINI GRAND CHALLENGE TONIGHT. New York High Society Flocks to the Elephant Hotel to Watch Wizard of Luna Park Face Off Against Master of Manacles."

"Oh, my God!" Rosie gasped. "I'm so late. I should have left for Coney Island an hour ago!" She grabbed her coat and dashed for the door. "Sorry, Sacha. I really hope everything works out for you and you don't die or anything, but I have to go *right now!*"

Sacha and Lily looked at each other.

"Uh, hang on a minute, Rosie," Sacha said. "I think we'd better come with you."

CHAPTER TWENTY-SEVEN

No Ticket, No Show

T HE THREE of them tumbled off the train and
sprinted to the Elephant Hotel just in time to see the last
guests arrive.

The cream of New York society filed up the monumental
staircase between the elephant's massive front legs, presented
their engraved, gilt-edged invitations to the doormen, and
vanished into the belly of the beast. But when Sacha, Lily,
and Rosie tried to follow, they found the door guarded by a
phalanx of uniformed New York City police officers.

"I'm Edison's assistant!" Rosie panted to the nearest officer as soon as they were within speaking distance.

He looked her up and down, taking in her disheveled
hair and dust-smudged face. "Sure you are, miss. And I'm
the Statue of Liberty."

"But I have to get in!" Rosie pleaded. "Mr. Edison'll fire
me if I don't show up!"

"I'm sorry, miss." The policeman was younger than Sacha had at first thought. And he really did look sorry. "No one gets in without a ticket, miss, and they're all sold out. Those're my orders. And it's not worth *my* job to break 'em."

"Please!" Rosie flashed her most dazzling smile at him. "I'd be so grateful!"

The patrolman blinked and shook his head slightly. He looked as if he'd just been hit over the head with his own nightstick. But he hadn't completely lost his senses, because he managed to smile back at Rosie and say, "Grateful enough to go out with me next Saturday?"

Lily snorted disgustedly, squared her skinny shoulders, and elbowed Rosie aside. "I assure you, Officer, that we do have tickets," she told him in her most insufferably patrician voice. "Unfortunately we seem to have misplaced them. I'm sure if you'd simply send someone inside to ask—"

"What's going on here?" the patrolman asked Rosie in a wounded tone. "I guess now you're going to try to tell me they work for Mr. Edison too?"

"Look," Sacha interrupted, ignoring Lily's furious glare, "we need to speak to Inquisitor Wolf on a matter of extreme urgency!"

"Do you, now?" the policeman asked with elaborate courtesy. He turned to his colleagues. "You hear that, fellows? They need to speak to Inquisitor Wolf on a matter of extreme urgency. Of course I suppose a big important Police Inquisitor like Maximillian Wolf only deals with matters of extreme urgency. He wouldn't be wearin' out the soles of his shoes walkin' the beat. Or get stuck outside taking tickets." He leaned into Sacha's face, shaking a big finger menacingly at him. "No ticket, no entry. That's the way it is. And dropping names will only earn you a kick in the seat of your pants to send you along your way."

"Well done," Lily muttered as they turned away and trudged back toward the street.

"You're one to talk," Rosie snapped.

"What do we do now?" Sacha asked Rosie.

"Go to the backstage door. It'll be locked by now. But if we're lucky, there won't be a police guard there, and we can bang on it until someone hears us and lets us in. You two! I don't know which one of you is worse. I would have talked my way in for sure if you'd both just kept your mouths shut!"

They picked their way down a blind alley lined with teetering piles of empty packing crates. There was no guard at the door and it was standing ajar—almost, Sacha thought uncomfortably, as if it had been left open for someone. As he slipped through the open door behind Rosie and Lily, Sacha thought of the way the patrolman at the door had reacted to Wolf's mere name and the sycophantic way the police commissioner had laughed at Morgaunt's cruel jokes. He had a sinking feeling that he knew just who—or what—the police had left that door open *for.*

Rosie led them down a long passage and up a spiral staircase that Sacha guessed must be inside one of the elephant's legs. It emptied into a hallway whose walls were lined with untidy piles of stage props and theater equipment. And then they were standing in the wings looking into the vast, opulent, velvet-swathed theater that filled all four stories of the elephant's massive belly.

The show hadn't yet started, but the audience was a show all by itself. It was the kind of scene Sacha could imagine only in New York. Everyone who was anyone was there, and they were rubbing elbows with a whole lot of people who weren't anyone at all. Bankers in formal dress looked down their noses at rough-clad workingmen. Housemaids gawped at society women dripping with rubies and diamonds. And over the whole spectacle, rich and poor alike, hung crystal chandeliers tipped with brilliant electric lights—Edison Everlast Electric Bulbs, naturally.

But it wasn't the lights and diamonds that blazed so brightly in Sacha's eyes. The audience itself was on fire. It burned with the flame that Roosevelt had called the soul of the city. Not the strength of mere spells and charms, but the strength of people who had left everything they knew behind in order to build new lives in a new world where anything could happen. Some of them had failed miserably, and some had succeeded beyond their wildest dreams. They all had dreams, though. And it was the power of those dreams—the magic of ordinary New Yorkers—that Morgaunt sought to bend to his own selfish ends.

Sacha wanted to tell Lily about this revelation. If she found Wolf first, she had to warn him that Morgaunt would use the crowd's magic against him. But just as he opened his mouth to speak, the band began to play.

"They're starting!" Rosie shouted over the strains of "Bewitch Me." "I have to get changed and find Edison!"

"Will you warn him?" Sacha asked.

"If I can get to him in time. But he won't listen. He's stubborn that way."

Rosie raced across the stage, which was still alive with the bustle of stagehands setting up before the curtain rose. It was the strangest set Sacha had ever seen. On one side sprawled the etherograph in a chaotic bird's nest of wires and switches and clamps and insulated footings. On the other side hulked Houdini's Water Torture Cell with its massive padlocks and its threatening glimmer of bulletproof plate glass. The two mechanisms seemed to be facing off across the empty stage like duelists getting ready to aim their pistols at each other.

Sacha and Lily scanned the audience, trying to find Wolf in the crowd. But the only familiar faces they saw were those of Commissioner Keegan and J. P. Morgaunt—both sitting right in the middle of the front row so that there was no way to get into the audience without going past them.

"Houdini's our best chance," Lily said. "At least we know where he is. And even if we can spot Wolf in the crowd, we'd never be able to reach him without Morgaunt seeing us."

Suddenly a ripple of excitement coursed through the audience. The curtain rose and Houdini swept onto the stage, flanked by half a dozen burly bodyguards.

Lily sighed. "So much for that."

While Lily was gazing forlornly after Houdini, Sacha was

squinting into the wings, where he could have sworn he'd seen something moving in the shadows.

Sure enough, he heard a faint noise that he would never have noticed if some part of him hadn't already been listening for it. And off in the gloom he caught a glimpse of the thing he'd been expecting and fearing to see ever since they'd slipped into the theater: a dark, slim, boy-sized shadow.

The dybbuk must have seen Sacha too, because it vanished around a corner as soon as he glanced toward it.

He turned, meaning to call out to Lily. But she had already set off to find Wolf, leaving him alone. If he followed her, he would lose sight of the dybbuk—and lose what might be his last chance to stop it before it got to Edison. If he called out to her, he'd bring every guard and policeman in the building down on top of them. And then the dybbuk would get to Edison anyway.

So Sacha did the only thing he could think of to do.

He followed the dybbuk.

CHAPTER TWENTY-EIGHT

Seeing the Elephant

THE WINGS OF the theater smelled like wet paint and sawdust. Lights swayed overhead, suspended on creaking hemp ropes as thick as Sacha's arm. Canvas backdrops bellied from their riggings like the sails of clipper ships.

Someone whistled overhead. Sacha started in surprise—and then realized it was just a set rigger or spotlight operator whistling out instructions in the sailors' code that stagehands used. When he squinted up into the rafters, he could just see the catwalk where two riggers manned the powerful spotlights that would follow every move Edison and Houdini made onstage.

The dybbuk slipped swiftly through the shadows, as if it knew exactly where it was going. Sacha was hard-pressed to follow without giving himself away. They crossed behind the stage, with only the flimsy backdrop between them and the audience. The band stopped playing. Edison and Rosie stepped onstage, outlined against the backlit canvas like cut paper silhouettes. As he crept along behind the dybbuk, Sacha heard Edison play a sample cylinder on the etherograph and go into his salesman's patter. Sacha barely listened; he was too busy wondering where Wolf was and why he wasn't putting a stop to this madness.

Finally he reached a vantage point where he could look out over the footlights and into the audience. He saw Lily moving down the aisle, looking nervous but determined. She hadn't found Wolf yet, and she couldn't search much more of the crowd without Morgaunt or Keegan catching sight of her. Sacha could have cursed in frustration.

The dybbuk was so close to the stage now that a few steps would reveal it to the audience. As Sacha peered cautiously from behind a pile of stage props, the creature raised its head and the light played along the side of its face. Sacha gasped. This wasn't the vague, smoky shadow he'd grappled with only a few hours ago. Now the dybbuk looked like a real boy—a boy that any witness would swear on his life was Sacha Kessler.

The dybbuk strode over to a spindly wrought-iron ladder and began climbing up into the rigging. Sacha hesitated, but he couldn't risk losing sight of the creature. Whenever it struck, he had to be there to stop it. He steeled his nerve and began climbing.

Balconies branched off the ladder at regular intervals, but the dybbuk never so much as looked at them. It was headed for the catwalk, where it could lurk unseen over Edison's head—in the perfect position to kill him whenever Morgaunt gave the final signal.

When Sacha reached the catwalk, it was all he could do to step out onto it. There were no railings to speak of, and the narrow walkway was littered with coiled ropes, unused winches, and disemboweled floodlights that looked like they'd been abandoned halfway through some complicated repair.

Far below, Sacha could see the top of Edison's head moving around the stage as he demonstrated the workings of the etherograph. Rosie was down there too; the spangles on her costume twinkled like the lights on the Luna Park roller coaster. Down in the orchestra pit Sacha could see the shiny bald spot of the flutist winking up at him as the man nodded and swayed to the beat of the latest show tunes. And on the far side of the stage Houdini now waited, dwarfed by the ominous bulk of the Water Torture Cell.

At last it was Houdini's turn. He stepped forward, his spotlight following him as smoothly as if it were tied to him by an invisible wire.

"Ladies and gentlemen," Houdini cried in a voice that carried clear to the rafters, "there is nothing supernatural about the Chinese Water Torture Cell—or in the methods I shall use to escape from it. The bottom and three of the walls are hewn from solid mahogany. In front, as you can see, is a single sheet of specially tempered plate glass. May I invite a few distinguished members of the audience to step onstage and inspect it? Commissioner Keegan? Mayor Mobbs? And might I be so bold as to ask Mr. James Pierpont Morgaunt to step onstage as well?"

Down in the audience, Sacha saw the mayor, the police commissioner, and Morgaunt rise to their feet, looking like they'd rather be anywhere but onstage with Edison and Houdini.

"Will you gentlemen kindly examine the apparatus and inform the audience of the results of your inspection?"

Sacha could hear only vague embarrassed mutterings from the mayor and the police commissioner. But Morgaunt's voice rang out firm and clear into the hushed theater.

"Solid as a bank vault," the Wall Street Wizard announced. "No trick . . . or no trick that *I* can see, anyway."

Houdini stood before the Water Torture Cell while a crew of mackintosh-clad firemen dragged heavy fire hoses onstage from both sides of the wings and began filling the tank with water.

"As you can see," Houdini announced, "I have dispensed with the silk curtain that usually hides the Water Torture Cell from view during my escape. Every move I make and every breath I take—or rather don't take—once I am lowered into the water, will be in full view of the audience. Mr. Edison has insisted upon this point in order to rule out even the slightest suspicion of a hoax. Of course, it will be absolutely impossible to obtain air once inside the Water Torture Cell. Should anything go wrong, my assistant will be standing by with a fire ax to break the glass and release the water." Houdini smiled. "In which event, I regret to inform you that some of the ladies in the front row may get a little wet."

Another scattering of laughter moved across the audience and faded into nervous silence. They were hooked. They stared at the Water Torture Cell with queasy awe as the water rose behind the plate glass. It was one thing to hear about the trick and wonder how Houdini pulled it off. But it was quite another thing to watch another human being willingly brave what looked like almost certain death.

The dybbuk was all the way out in the center of the catwalk by now, directly over Edison's head. Sacha watched, horror-struck, as the creature laid one hand on a massive spotlight casing. The thing must weigh a hundred pounds. Dropped from this height, it would be as deadly as a bullet.

So what was the dybbuk waiting for?

Then Sacha understood. The dybbuk was waiting for Houdini to perform his escape so Edison could announce the results of the etherograph. Morgaunt wanted every single pair of eyes riveted on Edison when the dybbuk killed him. All the other assassination attempts had just been setting the stage for this one. Tonight every leading citizen and newspaper reporter in New York would see Sacha Kessler, Maximillian Wolf's apprentice and the son and grandson of Kabbalists, kill Thomas Edison right in front of their eyes.

Morgaunt's strategy unfolded in Sacha's mind with all the stark elegance of moves played out on a chessboard. Edison's death would unleash a witch-hunt that would make millions for Pentacle Industries. Sacha would be branded a murderer. It would be pathetically easy to link Harry Houdini to a conspiracy to kill Edison. If Morgaunt played it right, Wolf might even end up in prison alongside Sacha.

It was all going to happen now. And the only person who could stop it was Sacha.

He measured the distance between himself and the dybbuk. He wished he were closer. Yet he knew he couldn't risk creeping forward. If he moved now, he would only put the creature on its guard.

Then the dybbuk turned, as if drawn by some invisible thread, and looked straight into Sacha's eyes. Magic pulsed around them. Sacha knew that it was Morgaunt trying to control the dybbuk from the audience. But he knew something else too, something that he just might be able to use.

Morgaunt couldn't really control the dybbuk. It wasn't a tool. It was a half-tamed animal. No punishment Morgaunt could inflict on the dybbuk was worse than watching the thief walk free under the sun. And no reward Morgaunt could offer was greater than the chance to devour Sacha.

Onstage, Houdini's assistants had bound his ankles with chains and padlocks and were lowering him into the Water Torture Cell. The band struck up the chorus of "Asleep in the Watery Deep" for what seemed like the fortieth time that night, and Sacha wondered why he'd ever liked the song in the first place.

"Come on!" Sacha taunted. "What are you waiting for?"

The dybbuk hesitated. Then it took a single step toward Sacha. It wasn't much. But it was enough to bring him just within reach. Sacha leaped toward the dybbuk, spreading his arms wide to tackle it.

He never got there.

Just as Sacha flung himself toward the dybbuk, a second shadow burst onto the catwalk, caught Sacha in a flying tackle, and brought him crashing down onto the metal grating.

As they grappled with each other, Sacha caught horrifying flashes of the drop below them. It took longer to get a good look at the face of his opponent. When he finally did, he could have screamed in frustration.

"Antonio! What are you *doing?* Can't you see they're about to kill Thomas Edison?"

"I don't care about Edison! You killed my father! You think I'm going to let you live?"

"I didn't kill him!" Sacha gasped. But Antonio wasn't listening.

The fight was over almost before it started. There was no room on the narrow catwalk to use any of the moves Shen had taught Sacha, and Antonio was an experienced street fighter. In one breath, Sacha realized he was completely outclassed. In the next breath, he was lying on his back and Antonio was kneeling on his elbows and throttling him.

Then the dybbuk came up behind Antonio and laid a hand on his head.

It was a gentle, familiar, almost friendly touch. It looked as if the dybbuk were ruffling Antonio's hair. It reminded Sacha eerily of the way his own mother used to wake him when she came home from Pentacle to find that he'd fallen asleep at the kitchen table over his homework.

But then Sacha saw something that made his stomach

turn. When the dybbuk had touched Lily after the summoning, it had looked like it was pulling something out of her. Now, however, the dybbuk was putting something *into* Antonio. Sacha could see it more clearly than he'd ever seen any other magic in his life. Antonio's grief and anger had created an empty place inside him, and the dybbuk was filling it up like a dentist filling a cavity. Except that what the dybbuk was pouring into Antonio was so black and dead and rotten that Sacha knew it would eat away at him from the inside until there was nothing left of him.

"No!" Sacha shouted over the din of the music below. "Leave him alone!"

The dybbuk raised its pale face to stare at Sacha.

"If you're going to take anyone," he said in a shaking voice that sounded like someone else's, "take me."

As if Sacha's words had been an invitation, an oily darkness began to swirl around the dybbuk. It welled up like fetid water flooding from a broken sewer and poured into Sacha, scouring away every memory of joy and warmth and happiness.

He felt the shadow ripple and rise within him. He felt the dybbuk rummage through his thoughts and take possession of the secret places of his heart. He watched with a curious sort of detachment as the final moment approached—the moment when everything human in him would flare and gutter and snuff out like a spent candle.

Then he felt a stabbing pain like nothing he'd ever known in his life—and after that, only darkness.

CHAPTER TWENTY-NINE

Admission to the Burning Ruins 10 Cents

WHEN SACHA opened his eyes, the dybbuk was gone. He looked down at his chest and saw blood. Then he looked up and saw Antonio standing over him, clutching a kitchen knife.

"I didn't mean to cut you that bad," Antonio said. "I only meant to chase out that . . . *thing*."

"By *stabbing* me? And if you had that knife, why didn't you use it when you were actually trying to kill me?"

"I remembered something my mother said about pain driving out evil spirits. And I *was* going to stab you, but it seemed kind of . . . well . . . unfair."

Sacha stared at the other boy, dumbfounded. Then he burst out laughing. "You followed me all the way here in order to kill me, and then you didn't want to use a knife because you thought it wouldn't be *fair*? That's the silliest thing I've ever heard!"

"*I'm* silly?" Antonio asked incredulously. "I'm not the one who just offered to let that *thing* eat me for dinner!" He shuddered. "Do you think it's really gone?"

"I don't know," Sacha admitted. "I hope so."

He lifted his shirt gingerly and tried to see where all the blood was coming from. It wasn't as bad as he'd expected. The knife had skipped along his ribs, and though the cut was long and ugly, it wasn't deep. He obviously wasn't going to die of it. It just felt like he was.

"I don't want to scare you or anything," Antonio said, glancing over Sacha's shoulder. "But I think we should leave."

"We can't!" Sacha struggled to his feet. "Morgaunt won't just give up because you chased the dybbuk off. He'll have a backup plan."

"Uh . . . I think I already know what it is."

Sacha followed Antonio's gaze and saw that the spotlight operators had now left their posts and were moving around behind the painted canvas backdrop.

"What are they doing?"

Antonio gave him a pitying look. "What do people usually do with matches and kerosene?"

The flames began to catch and swell, licking their way up the backdrop. As Sacha watched, he realized that this was just a diversion. Morgaunt was rearranging the chessboard so that Wolf would have to make the moves he'd planned for him. But it didn't matter. The theater was a firetrap, and it was packed to the gills. There was only one decent thing to do— even if it was exactly what Morgaunt wanted them to do.

He raised his head, cupped his hands around his lips, and shouted, "Fire!"

At first no one noticed. The audience was still too focused on Houdini's mortal struggle. Then Sacha saw the white circle of a woman's face staring up at them. Her mouth opened, and her eyes grew wide with terror, and she started screaming.

Onstage, a fireman grabbed the ax next to the Water Torture Cell and smashed the plate glass, freeing Houdini—and several hundred gallons of water, which actually came in pretty handy under the circumstances. Houdini rose to the occasion. And so did Edison, in his own decidedly odd way. In seconds, Houdini had cast off his manacles and begun pushing, dragging, and carrying people toward the exits. Edison, on the other hand, had eyes only for his etherograph. Instead of running for the exit like everyone else, he tried to save his precious prototype.

Meanwhile, Sacha and Antonio were making the slow, painful climb down to safety. Antonio reached the bottom first and helped Sacha down the last few rungs. Finally they were both standing on solid ground. They turned to make their way out through the rising flames—and found themselves face-to-face with a burly fireman in full battle dress.

"This is no place for kids!" he told them. "Let's get you out of here!"

Sacha went limp with relief, half collapsing against Antonio. But then, right before their horrified eyes, the man changed.

There was nothing you could put your finger on, no clear moment when he stopped being himself and became someone else. But Sacha could see the magic flaring and spitting around him. And there was no mistaking that steely blue flame—or the hard-as-steel voice that emerged the next time the fireman opened his mouth.

"Come along, boys!" Morgaunt sounded almost cheerful—and Sacha didn't even want to think about what would make a man like Morgaunt cheerful. "I've got a job for you."

He marched off, and Sacha and Antonio were forced to follow him, though Sacha couldn't have said for his life whether it was magic that compelled them or sheer physical terror.

"Is that the real killer?" Antonio whispered.

Sacha nodded.

"Then I guess it's him I should have been shooting at."

"Where is that gun, anyway?" Sacha couldn't believe he hadn't thought of it before.

Antonio looked shamefaced. "My mother took it. She wanted me to stay home and cry like a girl instead of doing what a proper son should."

"And right she was," Morgaunt interrupted, shocking both of them. "Your father was just in the wrong place at the wrong time. He got caught in the machinery. Only a fool would throw away his future to avenge an accident."

Morgaunt stopped speaking to clear his throat. It was painful to hear his voice coming from the fireman's body. It forced its way out of the man like a grindstone relentlessly pulverizing every obstacle in its path.

"Ah," Morgaunt said as they turned a corner, "there he is."

They had found Thomas Edison, alone and defenseless, desperately trying to drag his etherograph to safety.

"Let me help you," Morgaunt said.

"Careful!" Edison cried. "Grab hold of it here, at the base. And watch out for—"

But Edison never got to say what he wanted them to watch out for. As he bent over the machine, Morgaunt raised the fireman's ax and hammered the flat of it down on the back of Edison's head, knocking him senseless.

"I've been wanting to do that for a long time," Morgaunt said in a satisfied tone. "That man talks enough to kill a horse."

He kicked Edison just hard enough to make sure he was unconscious. Then he hefted the inventor over his shoulder and started walking back into the heart of the fire. Sacha's body followed against its will, and he could see Antonio moving jerkily beside him.

When they got back to the stage, Morgaunt dumped Edison in a heap. With a careless flick of his hand, he forced the two boys down beside the inventor. Then he took Antonio's knife and sat down to wait as comfortably as if he were in his own library.

The fire raged around them. The curtain was a tattered fringe of blackened rags by now, and the backdrop was a translucent web of fire that shed smoldering cinders onto the stage with every puff of overheated air. Sacha's lungs felt like they were on fire too. He wondered how long it would be before the smoke lulled him into a final, helpless sleep.

"What are we waiting for?" he asked, more because he felt compelled to say something than because he expected an answer.

The fireman's mouth twisted into a cruel grimace that looked utterly alien on his honest Irish face. "Inquisitor Wolf, who else?"

"What if he doesn't come?"

"He will. He'll come charging to your rescue just like the little do-gooder he is. And if he doesn't we can just sit here until we burn to death. It's all the same to me. Actually, I think it could be quite interesting. Haven't you always wondered what it feels like to be burned alive? No? But then of course you'll be dead when it's over, so you won't remember it. I imagine that will make the experience a lot less educational."

"But what's the point of killing me if you can't frame me for killing Edison and use that to run Wolf out of the Inquisitors Division?"

For the first time ever, Sacha saw a look of surprise on Morgaunt's face. "But killing you *is* the point. Has Wolf really kept you in the dark that completely?"

Morgaunt paused. He looked down at Antonio's knife, still in his hands, and seemed puzzled to see it there. Then he gave a rueful shrug of the fireman's broad shoulders, set the knife down on the floor beside him, and turned back to Sacha.

"From the moment I heard about the boy who could see witches, I knew you were a danger to me. A Mage-Inquisitor who can actually *see* magic? That would be a disaster worse than ten Maximillian Wolfs! No, Sacha, you were a marked man from that first day in Mrs. Lassky's bakery. Of course, you would have been far more useful to me as an employee than a corpse. That was the point of the dybbuk. But as you've had reason to discover for yourself, the dybbuks of Mages aren't exactly the most biddable of magical beings. I thought yours would be more manageable since you haven't come into your powers yet. My mistake." Morgaunt gave Sacha a peeved look that would have been almost funny under ordinary circumstances. "I should have known what I was in for the minute the wretched creature stole your mother's locket."

What did Morgaunt mean? Sacha couldn't make sense of it, so he focused on the only thing that did make sense to him: his mother's locket.

"The *dybbuk* took it?" Sacha asked. "Then how did it end up in Edison's lab?"

"I took it away from the horrid little beast and had Edison plant it in the lab before you arrived. I was rather proud of that idea. But I paid dearly for it. It only made the dybbuk more suspicious of me. You've got a nasty, sneaky side to your character, Sacha. Has anyone ever told you that?"

Sacha stared at Morgaunt. He felt a rising panic in his

chest. It had begun the moment Morgaunt spoke the word *Mage*. And it had only gotten worse as he realized how completely he had played into Morgaunt's hands.

Morgaunt turned away for an instant to check the doors. Sacha glanced at Antonio—and Antonio nodded toward the knife lying forgotten at Morgaunt's side.

"Keep talking," Antonio mouthed.

He was right, Sacha realized. Even if they couldn't distract Morgaunt enough to get hold of the knife, they could still give Wolf a better chance of taking him by surprise.

"So . . . uh . . . how did you summon the dybbuk?" he asked.

Morgaunt turned back to him with a mocking grin. "Good try, Mr. Kessler, but that's what we Wall Street Wizards call a trade secret."

Sacha cast around desperately for another question to ask. "And what about Edison?"

"You disappoint me," Morgaunt said scathingly. "I knew you had to be a romantic fool to work for Wolf. But I didn't think you were a hypocrite, too. Seriously, Sacha. How much do you *really* care about Thomas Edison? He's a dreadful anti-Semite, you know. For me it's just business, but he actually believes that claptrap."

The smoke was becoming unbearable. Out in the main section of the theater, a heavy rafter groaned and shattered. It hit the floor with a terrifying crash, pulverizing two rows of seats and lighting up the wreckage like a bonfire.

"Well, I don't want him to *die*," Sacha protested weakly.

"Why not?" Morgaunt asked with what sounded like genuine curiosity. "Because you don't want him dead? Or because you just don't want to have to feel guilty about it?"

Sacha didn't have an answer to that.

"Of course, there is another way out," Morgaunt said, quite casually. "You could hand yourself over to the police and confess to having set the fire yourself."

"What?" Sacha yelped.

"It's what the dybbuk would have done if it had succeeded in killing you. Your stubbornness on that front has caused me a great deal of inconvenience. Still, I think the situation is salvageable. And if you examine all your options, you'll see that it's by far the most humane solution. Wolf will be disgraced, of course. But at least he'll be alive. And what's more, I won't be forced to make an example of your unfortunate family."

It was odd how Sacha saw the full force of Morgaunt's personality only now, when he spoke through another man's body. A less honest man would have flattered Sacha. A less honest man would have told him all about the power he would give him and the wonderful things he would do for his family. But Morgaunt didn't stoop to that. He just laid out his plans, logical as clockwork, and made Sacha see that he had no choice but to follow them.

Sacha searched desperately for a way out of the trap. Morgaunt waited for him to think the problem through with the patience of a chess player who has worked out all the moves and knows with mathematical certainty that he will win no matter what his opponent does. When Sacha opened his mouth to give Morgaunt an answer, he still wasn't sure himself what he was going to say.

And he never did find out. Because at that moment Wolf burst into the theater.

Morgaunt was ready for him. He drew down the flames that crackled overhead—just as Sacha had seen him draw magic out of thin air back in his library—and flung them straight at Wolf.

Wolf didn't seem to have a clue what was coming at him. To Sacha's horror, he had even taken off his glasses. Did he think he had time to wipe them on his tie and think things over before protecting himself?

Then, at the last possible instant, as the fireball hurtled toward him, he looked up.

He worked no visible magic. He just stood there with a blank look on his face, watching Morgaunt through eyes as flat and bleak as a winter sky. But Sacha saw—he saw it all, with the second sight that he now understood was a curse as well as a talent.

Morgaunt staggered under Wolf's assault, but he didn't fall. Again he made the gesture he had used to call down the flames. But this time he called on the power of the gathering crowd outside the burning theater. Their fear and panic surged through the air like electrical current. And Morgaunt twisted it, perverted it, made it his.

"Don't," Wolf said, so quietly that Sacha barely heard him above the roar of the fire. "There are powers in this city you don't want me to awaken."

But Morgaunt just laughed.

"I'm so sorry," Wolf said—and he seemed to be speaking more to Sacha than to Morgaunt. And then he began to work a kind of magic Sacha had never seen before.

Space rippled and flowed around Wolf, just as Sacha had seen the streets of New York ripple and flow before the Rag and Bone Man appeared. Suddenly a phalanx of ghostly forms stood beside Wolf. Shen was there: a sort of sunlight-through-clouds echo of her that was the absolute opposite of a shadow. And there were other bright shadows, towering over Wolf like giants, their faces strangely familiar, as if Sacha had known them all his life without ever quite realizing it: the Rag and Bone Man, straddling his ancient horse like a rider of the apocalypse; a tattered, worn-down beggar whose face seemed to change from moment to moment so that he looked like every panhandler Wolf had ever given money to; a pale woman in white whose face was the saddest thing Sacha had ever seen.

But whatever powers Wolf had called upon, they weren't enough. Morgaunt's stolen power was stronger. And it grew stronger still with every person who joined the growing mob outside the theater.

Wolf stumbled. He dropped his glasses, and they shattered with a crack like a gun going off.

Instinctively, Sacha stepped forward to help—and realized that he could move again. He glanced sideways and saw the same realization in Antonio's eyes. They looked at each other for no more than a split second. Then they both lunged for the knife.

Sacha reached it first. He snatched it up and stabbed at Morgaunt. But Morgaunt jerked away at the last second, and the blade cut through empty air. Then Sacha felt Morgaunt's powerful hand close over his, crushing his fingers and threatening to wrench the knife from his grasp.

Antonio tackled Morgaunt, trying to help Sacha, but Morgaunt threw him off with a great heave of his shoulders—and Antonio flew through the air, landed in a heap, and lay still.

Sacha struggled for the knife. His vision tunneled down to the glinting steel blade. His fingers went numb, and he knew he couldn't hang on much longer.

Morgaunt began to twist the knife in Sacha's hands, driving it relentlessly toward his throat. Closer and closer the blade came, until it was only inches from Sacha's face. In desperation, Sacha did the only thing he could think of to do: He clamped his teeth on Morgaunt's hand and bit down as hard as he could.

Morgaunt screamed. He wrenched Sacha into the air and slammed him back down with a bone-jarring thud. Sacha's head swam and his knees buckled . . .

Then Wolf was upon them. He forced Morgaunt's head around so that the man had no choice but to stare into those bleak and colorless eyes, and he unleashed a power colder and more terrible than anything Sacha had ever imagined.

Suddenly Sacha didn't ever want to see magic again. He knew now why ordinary people hated and feared the Inquisitors—and why ordinary Inquisitors hated and feared Wolf. And he knew that after tonight, no matter how long he worked with Wolf or how much he came to trust him, he would always be terrified of the man.

Sacha saw the exact moment when Morgaunt admitted defeat. One instant Morgaunt was in possession of the fireman's body. The next he was gone, and the fireman was crumpling to the floor with a dazed look on his face.

For a moment Wolf stood over the body, blazing with magic like an avenging angel. Then he seemed to fade and shrink right before Sacha's eyes until he was only his everyday self again, as dull and gray as dishwater.

He knelt over Sacha. "I'm sorry," he said. "You shouldn't have seen that yet. I knew you weren't ready, but I didn't have a choice. Are you all right?"

Behind Wolf, other rescuers had arrived to gather up Edison and Antonio. Someone seemed to have placed a protective spell on the theater; there were no more falling rafters, and the flames had a glossy distant look, as if they were burning behind glass.

"Say something, Sacha."

"Morgaunt—he told me—he said I'm—like you." He couldn't even make himself say the word *Mage*.

"Do you believe him?"

"But I can't do magic!" Sacha protested. "I've never done magic!"

"Haven't you?" Wolf's voice was gentle, but it cut through Sacha's words, silencing him. He thought of how Shen had shown up just when he needed her. Of how the Rag and Bone Man had saved him again and again. Of the times he'd felt the city move and ripple around him. Had those things only happened to him? Or had he somehow *done* them?

"Then I'll stop! I can—"

"You can't. You don't have a choice. I learned that the hard way when I was your age. The only choice you have is whether you control the magic or the magic controls you."

"Why didn't you *tell* me?"

"Because you weren't ready to hear it. And I was afraid that being able to see magic would make it even harder for you. I was right, too. Look at you."

"I'll be all right," Sacha muttered.

Wolf looked at him gravely, started to speak, and then stopped himself. "Come on, let's get out of here."

He reached out a hand to help Sacha up—but Sacha flinched away from it and buried his head in his hands. Wolf stood over him for a moment, waiting for Sacha to look up. Then he sighed and walked away.

When Sacha finally raised his head, Lily and Payton were there. They helped him to his feet, and the three of them followed the rescue party through the flames.

Somehow they made it out of the burning building—straight into a street carnival. Sacha had known there was a crowd outside, but he'd had no idea just how big it was. More people were arriving every second. Hucksters were selling hot dogs and roasted peanuts. Some enterprising fellow had even stationed himself by the gate to the hotel grounds with a sign that read ADMISSION TO THE BURNING RUINS 10 CENTS. The fire might have begun as tragedy, but it was rapidly turning into melodrama. The death of the Elephant Hotel had become a genuine Coney Island event.

A squad of Inquisitors led the rescue party down the steps and cleared their way through the crowd. Flashbulbs popped and flared. Reporters shouted questions from every side. The next thing Sacha knew, he and Lily and Antonio were shaking the mayor's hand and being ushered past a gauntlet of newspaper reporters into the terrifying presence of James Pierpont Morgaunt.

"Congratulations," Morgaunt drawled. "You've saved the day."

He reached for Sacha's hand, and flashbulbs sparkled in his diamond cuff links like dying stars. Morgaunt's grip was alarmingly strong. Sacha tried to pull his hand back, but he only managed to flutter his fingers in Morgaunt's grasp like a butterfly caught in a collector's net.

Morgaunt's steely eyes bored into him. "You've played the part of a hero," he said in a voice so level and forthright that only Sacha heard the laughter behind his words. Morgaunt was enjoying himself. He was daring Sacha to accuse him, just as he'd dared Wolf before. He liked knowing that Sacha knew what he was and couldn't do a thing about it.

"I—I just did my job," Sacha stammered.

The faintest hint of a smile glinted behind Morgaunt's eyes. "Inquisitor Wolf is lucky to have such a loyal apprentice. Pentacle Industries could use a fellow like you. Someone who has the guts to take risks and isn't always looking over his shoulder, afraid of his own shadow."

Looking over his shoulder? Afraid of his own shadow? Morgaunt's choice of words couldn't possibly be a coincidence.

"I'm not interested," Sacha whispered.

"I bet I could make you change your mind."

Sacha thought of his family and his mouth went dry with terror.

Morgaunt let go of his hand, releasing it so abruptly that Sacha almost fell over backward.

"Don't look so worried, Mr. Kessler. If you insist on being a policeman, I suppose I'll just have to resign myself to it. For now, anyway."

CHAPTER THIRTY

Beginnings

HANUKKAH was Sacha's favorite holiday, even though according to Grandpa Kessler it wasn't a real holiday at all. Actually, that was probably why Sacha liked it. No one took it too seriously, and the grownups all played along good-humoredly while the kids got to enjoy candy and presents just like their Irish and German and Italian friends.

Even the blessing of the candles—the real part of the holiday—wasn't entirely serious, since Uncle Mordechai always offered a tongue-in-cheek translation into Yiddish for the children's benefit.

"Baruch atah adonai eloheynu melech ha-olam asher kid'shanu b'mitzvohtav vitsivanu l'hadlik ner shel Hanukkah," Rabbi Kessler intoned.

"Blessed are You, Lord our God, King of the Universe, who loved us so much that He gave us twice as many rules to follow as the *goyim*. Enough with the *mitzvahs*! We lit the candles! Can we eat already?"

"*Baruch atah adonai eloheynu melech ha-olam sheh-asah nissim l'avoteynu ba-yamim ha-heym bazman hazeh.*"

"Blessed are You, O Lord, et cetera, et cetera. Okay, so You worked miracles back in Israel a few thousand years ago. But lately . . . not so much. Not that we're complaining! But it is the season for miracles, and we could use a few!"

Everyone laughed at Mordechai's antics. But as Sacha looked around at his family and savored the comfortable warmth of the little kitchen, he honestly couldn't think of a single miracle they needed.

Life was good on Hester Street. Even Mo and Mrs. Lehrer seemed to be doing well. In fact, an amazing change had come over Mrs. Lehrer since she'd lost her money coat. She still staggered up and down Hester Street every morning, bent double under her towering pile of piecework, but the rest of the time she wore the first new dress Sacha had ever seen her in. She'd even bought herself a stylish hat decked out with clusters of fake grapes and flowers.

"That hat's much too young for her," Sacha's mother had told his father the first time she saw it. "But at least she's finally spending some money on herself."

Sacha's father had said nothing, as usual. But later Sacha noticed him speaking quietly to Mrs. Lehrer—and then listening to her for far longer than Sacha could ever remember seeing anyone listen to her. And the next week in synagogue,

Sacha's father stood up with Mo to recite the Mourners' Kaddish for her lost sisters.

The rolling cadence of the ancient prayer sounded through the little *shul* like the tolling of a deep bell, and beneath it Sacha heard something he'd never heard before in all the years he'd lived on Hester Street: Mrs. Lehrer weeping. Sacha didn't understand the point of making her cry, just as he had never really understood the Kaddish. It wasn't even about death, let alone deaths that were wrong and violent. It was only a simple song of praise to the Name of the One beyond all earthly knowing.

But Mrs. Lehrer seemed to understand. She looked more truly content afterward than Sacha had ever seen her. And Rabbi Kessler was content too. "There's a right way and a wrong way to keep the dead alive," he'd told Sacha's father as they locked up the *shul* together. Then he'd given him a shrewd look from under his eyebrows. "Maybe you should have gone into the family business after all."

Sacha didn't know what to make of that—or of the measuring look he'd caught his father and grandfather giving *him* a moment later. Nor did he know what to make of the confusing fact that his dybbuk seemed to have brought some kind of real peace into Mrs. Lehrer's life. When it came right down to it, the only thing he really knew about his dybbuk was that he hadn't seen it since the fire at the Elephant Hotel. He'd worried about it for the first few weeks, but as the months slipped by, he began to think that this might be one of those times when not knowing was better than knowing. If the dybbuk was off living the high life with Mrs. Lehrer's savings, then more power to it. "Live and let live" was Sacha's new motto—as long as the dybbuk didn't plan to live anywhere near him.

Meanwhile, Inquisitor Wolf hadn't fired Sacha after all, which was the miracle of miracles, considering all the lies he'd told. In fact, Wolf had never so much as reprimanded him over the Edison mess. Sacha had come clean about his family too . . . well, mostly. Uncle Mordechai seemed like a bit too much even for Wolf to swallow.

Wolf had taken it all in without so much as a raised eyebrow. And when Sacha asked if he thought the dybbuk was really gone, he just shrugged and said he hoped so.

"So that's it?" Sacha asked. "What about Morgaunt?"

"What about him?"

"Well . . . what do I do now? Just go back to life as usual, knowing that the most powerful man in New York wants to kill me?" He didn't mention Morgaunt's attempt to hire him. Somehow the thought that he could ever end up *working* for Morgaunt was even creepier than the thought of Morgaunt killing him.

"He's not trying to kill *you*, Sacha. He's trying to kill magic. You just happen to be in the way." Wolf grinned. "Welcome to the club."

And that was all Wolf had to say about it—except that a few days later an anonymous package arrived for Sacha's mother containing her locket with the chain carefully repaired.

As for Lily Astral . . . well, she really was a *mensch* once you got to know her a little. If she weren't so ridiculously rich, Sacha could almost imagine being friends with her. In fact, as he looked around the room at his boisterous, laughing family, he caught himself wishing Lily was here right now. But that was crazy! The Kesslers didn't even own a chair that Maleficia Astral's daughter would consider safe to sit in.

And anyway, Lily's parents had spirited her off to their beach house in Newport, Rhode Island, for the Christmas vacation. Sacha had been mystified by this when she first mentioned it, since he couldn't fathom why any sane person would go to the beach in December. But then Lily had let slip that the Astral "beach house" was made of marble and had thirty-two bedrooms. Which sort of said all you needed to know about whether a Sacha Kessler and a Lily Astral could really be friends.

This thought bothered Sacha more than he wanted to admit, and he was just asking himself why he'd want to be friends with a *girl* anyway when Mrs. Lehrer shouted his name from the back room. "Sachele! Someone to see you!"

Sacha started violently. Could Lily somehow have tracked him down at his own home? If she had, he would never forgive her for the humiliation she was about to inflict on him. But then he reminded himself that he was perfectly safe from Lily Astral because she was in Rhode Island.

The next instant, he was at the door and face-to-face with his visitor.

It was Antonio.

Sacha stared at him for a long moment. He wasn't sure what was more shocking, the fact that Antonio had dared to walk alone on streets where no self-respecting local kid would let him pass unscathed, or the fact that he'd come to see Sacha at all.

"Can we talk?" Antonio jerked his head toward the dark hallway behind him to indicate that whatever he had to tell Sacha required privacy.

"Uh . . . sure," Sacha said.

He followed Antonio into the hall and down the two flights to street level. They went outside together and stood awkwardly on the stoop. Sacha sat down on the top step. Antonio stayed on his feet, as if he just wanted to get the whole thing over with.

"I, uh, came to make sure you were okay," he said.

"I am. No dybbuk. And . . . um . . . thanks for saving me."

"You saved me first," Antonio said grudgingly. "Did you really mean it when you told it to take you instead of me?"

"Well . . . yeah. I mean, it's my dybbuk. Was, hopefully. I felt responsible."

This seemed to surprise and disturb Antonio. He turned away abruptly and didn't speak for a moment.

"Are you going to be okay?" Sacha asked.

Antonio turned on him, all the friendliness gone in an instant. "What do you think?" he asked savagely. "My father's still dead, and I didn't even manage to—"

He walked down the steps to the sidewalk.

"I'm so sorry," Sacha said helplessly.

Antonio stared up at him, his dark eyes burning. "I know you are. I know it's not your fault that Morgaunt summoned that thing. And I know it was the dybbuk that killed my father, not you. But that doesn't mean I want to have to look at your face and be reminded of it all over again."

Sacha didn't know what to say to that.

"I guess we could have been friends if things had been different," Antonio offered.

"I guess so," Sacha said. It was true. He was sure they could have been friends. He knew it the way you sometimes do, for no logical reason, the minute you lay eyes on someone.

That wasn't going to happen, though. The memory of Antonio's father would always stand between them, along with the knowledge that if Sacha had done something, anything, differently, he might still be alive.

"I'm sorry," Sacha said helplessly. "I'm so, so sorry."

But Antonio was already walking away, and Sacha couldn't tell if he'd even heard the words.

He sighed and trudged back upstairs. The apartment was just as warm and comfortable as it had been when he left, but suddenly he felt like a stranger in his own home. He went to the window and lifted the curtain to look for Antonio's slim figure in the street. There was nothing to see except lamplight and cobblestones. Sacha peered into the darkness for a moment. Then he dropped the curtain and turned away.

Two stories below, a ragged figure lurked in the shadows. It gazed hungrily at the warm light spilling from the windows.

It listened to the many sounds of the close-packed tenements, straining to hear the tones of a few familiar voices among all the others.

It knew those voices. It knew their names, their faces, their fears and desires and secrets. It knew everything there was to know about them. And it loved them.

But they only loved the thief.

A dead horse lay in the street a few yards away. It had died in the traces that afternoon, and the driver had cut the harness off it and left it for the city cleanup crews. Already, despite the cold of the winter season, the flies were thick upon it.

The dybbuk listened to their buzzing, momentarily distracted from the human voices. It stretched out a pale hand and beckoned them. The flies rose, milling around in a confused swarm. Then they drifted over to the dybbuk and settled on him like a shroud.

If there had been anyone at all there to see him, they would have thought he was a boy made out of coal dust. But the view from inside was different. The wings were all shot through with the light of the street lamps. They flickered and flashed and sparked like stars burning in the blackest sky.

They were beautiful. And they would speak for him.

Once he had lacked the power to summon the flies. Now he had it. Soon he would have the power to summon words and send them forth to work in the world. The thief had his voice now, but he would have it back—along with everything else the thief had stolen from him.

There were no words yet in the flies' buzzing. It wasn't a voice yet. It wasn't even the ghost of a whisper.

But it was a beginning.

A Brief Note on Alternate History

Attentive readers will have noticed a few differences between Sacha's New York and our own.

In our New York, Thomas Edison was the Wizard of Menlo Park, not Luna Park. James Pierpont Morgan never owned a shirtwaist monopoly or an indelible ink monopoly—though he did own a lot of other monopolies. The Yankees were officially called the New York Highlanders until 1913—though their fans had long ago adopted their famous nickname. And the Elephant Hotel, which burned down in 1896, was a lot smaller and seedier than the one Sacha visited.

The reasons for those differences would fill a much longer book than this one. Alternate history is an arcane subject—an inky battlefield where persnickety professors torpedo each other with footnotes, and careers sink on the shoals of unsupported theses and insufficient bibliographical references. So perhaps we'd best leave the arguing to the academics and content ourselves with noting that in the infinite spectrum of parallel worlds, everything that *can* happen *has* happened.

There is a world somewhere out there where Wall Street Wizards deal in magic as well as stocks and bonds, and Mrs. Lassky is selling her Mother-in-Latkes, and Inquisitor Wolf is gazing absentmindedly around a magical crime scene.

And of course some things are the same in every world. Baseball is still baseball. And New York . . . well, New York is magical in any universe.